W9-BQS-021

And Murder for Dessert

MYS DELAN-K
Delaney, Kathleen.
And murder for dessert

WHEELOCK

NO LONGER PROPERTY OF
TACOMA PUBLIC LIBRARY

And Murder for Dessert

Kathleen Delaney

TACOMA PUBLIC LIBRARY
TACOMA, WA. 98402-2098

Poisoned Pen Press

JUL 1 1 2007

Copyright © 2007 by Kathleen Delaney

First Edition 2007

10 9 8 7 6 5 4 3 2 1

Library of Congress Catalog Card Number: 2006940934

ISBN: 978-1-59058-423-1 Trade Paperback

All rights reserved. No part of this publication may be reproduced, stored in, or introduced into a retrieval system, or transmitted in any form, or by any means (electronic, mechanical, photocopying, recording, or otherwise) without the prior written permission of both the copyright owner and the publisher of this book.

The people and events described or depicted in this novel are fictitious and any resemblance to actual incidents or individuals is unintended and coincidental.

Poisoned Pen Press
6962 E. First Ave., Ste. 103
Scottsdale, AZ 85251
www.poisonedpenpress.com
info@poisonedpenpress.com

Printed in the United States of America

To my grandchildren, all eight of you.
You bring joy to my life.

Chapter One

Sundays are supposed to be a day of rest, but it rarely works out that way for real estate agents. Or, for that matter, Chiefs of Police. For some reason, this Sunday I had no appointments, no open houses, and no responsibilities. Evidently neither did Dan. If he did, he was ignoring them.

He sat at my kitchen table, eating pancakes, feeding bites of sausage to Jake, my yellow tom, and muttering under his breath while he turned pages of our local paper. I leaned up against the counter, slowly sipping coffee, watching him. In spite of his old brown bathrobe and his forty-some years, it was a most pleasant sight.

The phone rang. He looked up, frowned and raised one eyebrow at me. I sighed, and reached for it. There went our peaceful morning. Because it was, of course, one of my clients, wanting to see a house, or needing to ask a complicated real estate question that couldn't possibly wait until office hours on Monday, or Dan's office, calling to tell him about some murder that needed his immediate attention. It wasn't a client. And it wasn't a crime.

"Catherine. What a surprise." I hadn't heard from my sister in over a year and couldn't imagine what she wanted. That she wanted something was never in doubt.

"Ellen. I'm surprised you're home. I thought you'd be at work, in which case, I would have left you a message."

"It's Sunday."

"Humn. I thought that was your busiest day." The implication was strong that I was shirking. Typical Catherine. "I got your number from Mother. I knew you'd divorced that good-looking doctor, but when she told me you'd gone back to that dreadful little backwater town, it was obvious you'd lost your senses. She says you're living in our old house. And real estate! Isn't that what bored housewives and retired military men do?"

"Ah." As usual, I had no idea how to respond to Catherine.

"My daughter—you do remember Sabrina, don't you?"

Did she really think I'd forgotten my niece? I hadn't seen much of her. Catherine lived in splendor on the East Coast and couldn't be bothered to bring her to California, but that didn't mean I'd forgotten her.

"Sabrina and her husband are moving to Santa Louisa."

A double bombshell. I had no idea Sabrina had married. No one had told me, or invited me to the wedding. Had there been a wedding? And coming here? Why? I didn't have long to wait for that answer.

"Sabrina's husband makes wine. It's supposed to be a good job, but I'm not convinced. Anyway, they, well, it seems that their last job ended a bit abruptly, some kind of conflict over winemaking or something, and they got jobs with a place in Santa Louisa called Silver Springs."

"Silver Springs? That's the most prestigious winery on the central coast. He's their new winemaker? That's a wonderful job."

I could almost hear a sniff. "Maybe. Anyway, they'll be there tomorrow. I told them they could stay with you while they house hunt. After all, you have all that space and it is the house where we grew up. You can find them a rental. Sabrina will call you."

The line went dead.

I stood for a moment, looking down at the phone, then carefully placed it back in the cradle. Dan put down his paper and grinned at me.

"I take it that wasn't for me."

"It was Catherine." I filled my coffee cup before turning around to look at him. "Why would it be for you? Did you give the station this number?"

"Of course. Do you think there's anyone in town who doesn't know I spend half my nights here?"

He grinned at me. I sighed.

"From the scarcity of conversation on your end, I take it Catherine wants something and was giving you instructions."

"Sabrina, my niece, and her husband are coming to stay with me. Tomorrow."

The newspaper was pushed away and he sat up straighter. "Why?"

"Sabrina's husband, whose name I never got, is the new winemaker at Silver Springs and it sounds as if Sabrina is going to work there as well. They took the job rather suddenly and need a place to stay."

"And Catherine immediately thought of you. How nice." There was a pause. "What's Sabrina like?"

"I really don't know. The last time I saw her, she was fourteen. Pretty, shy, a few years older than Susannah, but completely intimidated by her."

Dan laughed. "Vivacious, confident, beautiful Susannah? I can't believe it." Dan and my daughter had taken an instant liking to each other. He admired her irrepressible vitality and she liked the way he treated me. So did I.

"You may think that's funny. I didn't then. It was the only time we went back east to visit and—well, it wasn't a success."

Dan's expression changed. The grin faded. "Is that why you didn't tell her about our wedding?"

"She didn't give me a chance." I turned away to top off my cup. "Besides, you only asked me last night. We've got plans to finalize before we start announcing the date and—"

Dan didn't say anything, but he kept watching me. I wondered if he knew about the butterflies, make that starlings, fluttering around in my stomach.

It had been close to midnight. We'd had dinner on the coast, had taken in a romantic movie, and finished the evening with a very satisfactory episode of our own. I was in bed, more than half asleep, cuddled close to Dan, my face buried in his shoulder, when he murmured, "I think we should get married. December would be good. That's only four months, but that's plenty of time, isn't it?"

"Sure," I agreed, and fell asleep, full of contentment, completely at peace.

This morning the sun had streamed through the bedroom window, promising a beautiful fall day. I was instantly awake, wondering what I'd done. I crept out of bed and into the bathroom, staring at my face in the mirror. My marriage to Brian McKenzie had been a slow, disintegrating disaster. Could I face that possibility again? Dan wasn't Brian, but still...I washed my face, brushed my teeth and hair and resolutely returned to the bedroom, prepared to tell Dan I liked our relationship just the way it was, him spending several nights a week, lunches, dinners, no commitments. He lay there, smiling at me, the gray in his hair bleached to gold by the sun. Damn the man. He looked like he belonged in my bed.

"Where've you been? I missed you." He pulled the cover back and looked at me expectantly.

Oh well, I thought. Oh well.

Only now we were in my kitchen, doing ordinary things, like eating pancakes, and the doubts were back.

Time to change the subject. "More sausage? There's one left."

"Give it to Jake. He's begging for it."

"Dogs beg. Cats expect the best as their God-given right." I cut up the sausage and put it in Jake's dish. "Dan, there was something funny about my conversation with Catherine."

"Other than the fact that she bothered to call you at all?"

I smiled somewhat ruefully. Dan had grown up next door to us. His parents and mine had been best friends. He was in and out of our kitchen as much as his own. Catherine and her supreme indifference to anyone's needs but her own was no surprise to him. "That, of course. And, since I've lowered my standards by returning to this backwater town and becoming a lowly real estate agent, I can make myself useful and find them a rental."

"You don't do rentals."

"I know." Evidently I did now.

"She called Santa Louisa a backwater town?" He sounded torn between amusement and irritation. "Guess she doesn't know about the new housing tracts, all the new restaurants the wine industry has brought here, the new shopping center…"

I had to laugh. "I'm sure Catherine still thinks we have one stoplight in town and that going out to eat means the bowling alley. But that's not what's bothering me. She told me Sabrina and her husband had left their last job in a hurry. Some kind of conflict."

"So? People do change jobs, sometimes because it's a move up their own personal ladder. Getting a job at Silver Springs is hardly a move down it."

"I know, but Catherine said there was some kind of problem. At least, I think she did. It all sounds so rushed. I wonder what happened."

Dan pushed aside his paper and got up. He came around the table to where I was leaning up against the counter. He took my coffee cup and put it on the countertop behind me. His hands slid down my shoulders to my waist and he pulled me close. His mustache scratched my ear, then my neck. It felt wonderful.

"They got a better job, Ellie. That's it. A better job. Quit worrying about them and start worrying about wedding plans. We're—"

The phone rang.

I squirmed out from under Dan and reached for it. "It's for you."

I could tell by the look on his face our peaceful Sunday was gone.

"Four-car pileup on 46E, just inside our city limits," he told me, already on his way towards the stairs and his clothes. "Sounds like I'll be a while."

He pushed open the swinging door that led to the dining room, paused, and turned back. "How long are Sabrina and her husband planning on staying here?"

I had no idea. "Just a few days, I'm sure."

"Yeah? I'll bet you a hot fudge sundae it's more like a couple of weeks."

The door swung shut. I picked my coffee cup back up, wondering if Dan was right.

He got his hot fudge sundae. A month came and went and they were still with me.

Chapter Two

"Sign here." I pushed the contract in front of Mark Tortelli, Sabrina's husband. He looked down at it dubiously.

"Are you sure this is the best we can get?" he asked for the fifteenth time.

"Yes," I answered, trying hard not to grit my teeth. I didn't do rentals, my office didn't do rentals, and finding them this little house had cost me several still-to-be-paid back favors. "We've been over this, Mark; there are very few rentals, and practically none who will take dogs. Especially standard poodles. He's big. Landlords worry. And this rent is fair. Sign."

He scowled at the paper, but he signed. "You're sure this is a month to month?"

"Yes." We'd been over that point just as many times. Why it was so important to Mark, I didn't know. I thought he and Sabrina were both thrilled with their jobs and planned to stay around for some time, so a lease would have been better, but Mark had been adamant.

"Sabrina," he finally said, "here, sign right under me."

Sabrina obediently signed, and I picked up the rental agreement. A month of Mark's mood swings and Sabrina's nervous attacks was about to end. I should have been relieved, and part of me was. Another part, a much smaller part, was going to miss them. Mark wasn't easy. He was charming one minute and ready to bite someone's head off the next. Anyone's but Sabrina's. He treated her with a tenderness that astounded me. She was simply a nervous wreck. She was startled at the ring of the phone or knock at the door, and she clung to Mark like a drowning sailor does to a life preserver. But not all the time. Sometimes she was fun, laughing, joking, helping Mark in the kitchen, where he delighted in showing off his not inconsiderable cooking skills. That part I'd miss. The rest of it…

"Okay," I said, "I'll drop this off on my way to the office and we'll all be back here for the big dinner. Oh, I need the deposit check as well."

Mark opened his desk drawer, pulled out his checkbook and started to write. "How do I make this out?"

I told him and turned to go, stepping over Paris, who was stretched out in the middle of Mark's office floor. Snowy white coat, coal black eyes, and the personality of a born clown, he was the main reason it had been so hard to find Mark and Sabrina Tortelli a rental. Dogs, especially dogs the size of a standard poodle, were not universally welcomed by landlords or by cats. My yellow tom, Jake, would be ecstatic on moving day.

"Ellen." Sabrina's soft voice stopped me.

I turned, prepared to wait. It sometimes took a minute or so for Sabrina to get out what she wanted to say and this time was no exception.

"I wondered," she started, "ah, if you, ah, had to get back to the office right now. You know, if you had an appointment or anything."

As it happened, I didn't. I was planning on using the afternoon to do my nails, wash my hair, and make sure the zipper on the dress I had planned to wear tonight still was willing to go to the top. And I made the mistake of saying so.

"Well, if you have a little time, I was wondering if, you know, if you wouldn't mind, I thought…"

I found Sabrina's insecurities irritating, but anyone who had spent a lifetime with my sister was bound to have some. I tried not to let my impatience show. "What do you need, Sabrina?" I tried to make my voice reassuring.

"Well, Melanie is home sick. She thinks it's a cold, but it might be the flu, and we certainly don't want her around if she's sick…"

I broke in. "You need help? Is that it?"

"If you don't mind. The tables take so much time, and I really want them to be, you know."

Light brown hair pulled tightly into a ponytail, huge brown doe eyes filled with anxiety, faded jeans threatening to fall off of skinny hips, she looked like an abandoned waif. I've never been good at saying no to waifs, abandoned or not, and this time was no different. Tonight's Harvest Festival Dinner at Silver Springs winery had been a constant source of nervous conversation since Mark and Sabrina had arrived. It seemed to be some kind of milestone for them, so table setting was obviously in my immediate future.

"Of course, I don't mind," I replied, pushing thoughts of a leisurely tub bath out of my mind. "What do we do?"

She immediately brightened. "Oh, thank you. We'll start with the glasses. I'll get them down from the attic and…" She broke off and looked around. "Let's get going."

Mark pushed himself back from his desk and came around to gather Sabrina in his arms. He dropped a quick kiss on her forehead. Still holding her, he reached out and, a little awkwardly, patted me on the arm. "Thanks, Ellen. Tonight needs to, we told you, after tonight everything's going to be fine." He squeezed Sabrina again. "Gotta go find Hector." He hurried out of the office.

"Mark's not very good at handling stress," Sabrina said with a little sigh. "It's just got to be perfect. I don't think I could handle starting over again."

Mark wasn't good with stress? He wasn't the one I would have picked. And starting over? Again? Did their jobs really depend on this dinner? I found that hard to believe, but it would account for Sabrina's bad case of nerves and Mark's hair trigger temper. I'd wondered why they had left Napa so abruptly, but my gentle probing had gotten me nothing but evasions. Had something gone wrong with the job up there? They obviously didn't want to talk about it, and it was none of my business anyway. But I had become fond of both of them in the month they had stayed with me, in spite of all the mystery and mood swings, and I wanted them to be happy. However, I was more than glad they were going to be happy in their own kitchen and not mine.

"Okay," I repeated. "I don't have much time. First, point me to the fax machine so I can get this contract over to the owner of your house. We don't want someone else to get in before us. I'll drop the check off on my way back into town. Second, where are those glasses?"

I watched Sabrina straighten up, smile, and grab a clipboard off of Mark's desk. "First, go find Hector and have him bring up the wines for tonight. Here's the list." Her tone was almost brisk. "You'll find him on the cellar floor. The stairs are that way. Then come into the tasting room. I'll be there."

I faxed my contract, wondering a little at Sabrina's abrupt switch to competent manager, a side I hadn't seen much of until today. Odd, I thought as I walked down the corridor between the offices and the kitchen on my way to the back stairs that led to the cellar floor. I could hear agitated voices behind the closed door that led to the kitchen, one high-pitched voice in particular, and thought Mark and Sabrina weren't the only ones on edge about tonight's dinner. The corridor ended, and steep stairs led down to the cellar floor. The odor of fermenting wine filled my nostrils, and the chill in the air made me shiver. It was ninety degrees outside on this early fall day, but wine isn't fond of heat so the storage room and fermenting tanks were never allowed to bask in it. I wondered how I was supposed to locate Hector in this stainless steel maze, but Sabrina had made it clear that she needed the wines on that list. Some were to be served with dinner but most were for sale. Evidently wine sales after a successful dinner could be substantial. I'd looked at the menu and the different wines that she planned to pour that evening, and had no trouble believing that, for a number of people, budget concerns would be poured away with the wine.

I had no idea what Hector did down on this cold cement floor. Huge stainless steel tanks surrounded me, each with a nozzle at the bottom that looked like a fitting for a fire hose. There was a wheel on each one but I didn't know what it opened, and a glass valve ran up the side. I guessed it must tell how much juice was in the tanks. They all sat on the concrete floor, and running around the huge room, in front of the tanks, was a small open drain. The floor was damp with what looked like water, but there was red liquid in some of the drains. Tasting? Testing? I must remember to ask someone, but first I had to find Hector.

"Looking for us?"

I recognized Mark's voice, but I couldn't see him anywhere. I turned around and peered into the cavernous room adjoining the cellar floor that held stack after stack of wine barrels on one side and pallets of boxed wine bearing the famous Silver Springs label on another.

"Up here."

Amusement was evident in Mark's voice. I looked up toward the high ceiling, and there he was, standing on a catwalk with a black-haired young man, both grinning down at me. I hadn't noticed the catwalk before, probably because it ran high along the wall and was partly obscured by the tanks.

"What are you doing up there?" I shouted.

"Pumping over the juice."

"What?" I shouted up, convinced I'd heard wrong. Pumping over?

"I'll explain later. Are you looking for Hector?"

"Yes. Sabrina wants the wines on this list up in the tasting room."

"Be right down." Hector started along the catwalk, much too quickly in my opinion, and ran down a steep staircase located next to huge roll-up doors at the end of the building. Mark stayed where he was. "Want to come up and see the tanks, Ellen?" he hollered down.

I waved at him and shook my head. No way was I going to scramble around up in the air on that treacherous-looking narrow board. Hector took my note, grinned at me and headed for a forklift. I headed back the way I'd come. There was a wide, well lit staircase close to the roll-up doors that led up to the tasting room and I looked at it longingly, but I had left my fax to run through by itself and wanted to make sure it had been received before I joined Sabrina, so up the back stairs I went.

The door to Mark's office was closed, but the door to the room used by the office staff was wide open. Only the person intently staring at the computer monitor shouldn't have been there.

"Carlton Carpenter, what are you doing here?" I walked into the office and stood in the middle of the room, hands on my hips. Carlton always had that effect on me.

He didn't even have the decency to jump. "Hello, Ellen," he said, swinging around in the office chair. "I didn't know you worked here." He managed to work a little sneer into that statement.

"You know I don't." I tried not to let impatience show. "I'm helping Sabrina set up for the Harvest Festival dinner tonight."

"That's right," he said thoughtfully. "She's your niece, isn't she? Catherine's daughter. Yes. Sweet girl. Not a bit like her mother. Not too efficient, though. And her husband. What do you know about Mark Tortelli? Does he seem like an honest man to you? They're living with you, aren't they? Have you noticed anything suspicious about him?"

"What?" Surprise caught me short, and it took a moment to respond. "What are you talking about? It's none of your business who's living with me or anything else, and, I repeat, what are you doing here?"

I wasn't very polite to Carlton, but then, I never was. We'd grown up together, gone to Bible study, grade school and high school, and during all that time, he'd never given me a reason to change how I thought about him. He was pond scum. Handsome, admittedly, but still, pond scum. Carlton really didn't care what he did as long as it benefited him and he didn't get caught. For years he had managed to stay out of trouble by flashing that perfect white-toothed smile and using his leading-man good looks and his smarmy charm. He'd been in a number of "businesses" and seemed to have a sixth sense about when to get out before a hole opened up and he fell in it. If someone else fell in, oh well. Currently, he ran a one-man real estate office. Every old-time agent in town avoided him, but there were plenty of new people in town to prey on. I couldn't imagine what he was doing here. "Carlton," I said, trying to sound threatening. If he didn't answer soon, I'd start tapping my foot.

"I have a perfect right to be here. I'm a partner in the winery." I got the white-tooth flash, but was too stunned to respond.

"What?" Originality had fled, at least for the moment. "You? How did you?" I was about to ask where he got the money but stopped myself in time. Carlton was always either rolling in it or dead broke. Depended on how big he'd dug the current hole. Unfortunately, I couldn't ask whom he'd fleeced lately, so I changed my sentence in mid-structure and asked instead, "How did you do it? I mean, how does anyone become a partner?"

He gave me a patronizing look, the one that always made me want to hit him with a shovel, and said "Mildred Banks."

That cleared things up nicely. "Mildred Banks?"

"Yes. Remember her husband, Henry, died a little over a year ago?"

I'd never heard of the Banks. However, I wanted to hear what they had to do with Carlton's partnership, so I nodded, and Carlton went on.

"Henry had bought a few shares in this winery, and Mildred needed money. I went over to talk to her about maybe selling her house." (I inwardly groaned at this. I didn't know Mildred but sure hoped she hadn't trusted her sale to Carlton.) "I ended up buying her shares instead."

"Did Mildred list her house?"

Carlton frowned. "No. She managed to keep the house. Why? You aren't thinking of going out to see if you can get a listing, are you? Keep away from her. She's my client."

I wanted to tell him that I had plenty of clients of my own and that I didn't need to arm-wrestle poor old widows to get listings, but I had something more pressing to ask Carlton. "Okay, you're a partner. Do all of the partners mess around with the computers?"

"I'm doing some investigating," he said, using his most pompous voice. "And it's about your nephew, Mark Tortelli."

"What?" I asked, surprised again. Damn. I had to find another word. "What are you talking about?"

"I'm monitoring the inventory. Mark left his last job because he was caught trying to steal some of the wine. I'm making sure it doesn't happen here."

This time I couldn't even say "what?" I simply stood there with my mouth open. "That is the most ridiculous thing I've ever heard. Does Mark know you're in here doing—whatever you're doing?"

Carlton's eyes shifted. "He knows I'm in here."

I'd had enough. "Mark Tortelli is not a thief," I stated as firmly as I could, "and I would strongly suggest you don't go around telling people you think he is." I turned on my heel and stomped out.

"You'll see," I heard Carlton mutter as I left, but I ignored him and hurried down the hall toward the tasting room. Mark a thief. Not a chance. But a thought, unbidden, snuck through my indignation. Mark and Sabrina had been more than on edge since they'd arrived, and they'd avoided any mention of their life before Santa Louisa. What had happened on Mark's last job? No time to wonder. I walked into the tasting room to find an angry Mark, a tearful Sabrina, and an irate round little man in striped pants, an immaculate white jacket, and a tall chef's hat, yelling at both of them in the high-pitched voice I'd heard behind the kitchen door.

"You lied to me," he screamed. "Frank Tortelli's son, and you didn't tell me."

"For God's sake, Otto, you're here as the guest chef for tonight's dinner," Sabrina said between sniffs. "What does Mark's father have to do with that?"

"Everything." The venom in the little man's voice would do credit to a rattler. "Ask him. He'll tell you." He pointed at Mark. Sabrina looked at Mark. So did I. So did the tall, somewhat good-looking man standing directly behind the little chef. He, too, was dressed in striped pants, but his white jacket was smudged. He kept nodding his head slightly, as though he was agreeing with everything Otto said. His hat swayed with each nod.

"Otto and my father were partners," Mark said, his eyes fastened tightly on Otto, "but that was years ago, when I was a little boy. They had a falling out; you'd never guess that, would you, and haven't spoken since."

"Why?" Sabrina asked.

"They fought over a recipe," Mark answered.

"Not 'a' recipe," Otto stated. "*The* recipe. The one your larcenous father stole from me, the one he based Tortelli's on. It was mine, and I will never forgive him. I will never forgive any member of his family."

"Come on, Otto," Mark said. I could see the muscles in his jaw tighten and knew he was struggling to keep his temper. "I was a baby when all that happened; it has nothing to do with me, and tonight is important. Very important. Can't we just forget the past and have a great evening? Think of all the people who are coming tonight, important people, just because you're the chef."

I thought Mark was laying it on a bit thick but evidently Otto didn't think so. He turned and looked at the man standing behind him, who was now staring at me and turned back around to face Mark. "Oh, we will have a spectacular dinner tonight, but not because of you. Because of me. Because of my new bed and breakfast. These people are indeed coming to taste my food. Some will write about the fabulous dinner they had and tell the world to come to Otto's new bed and breakfast and single seating dinner restaurant. Others will tell their friends. Either way, I will once again be famous. But I, Otto, do not forget. You lied to me, and you will pay."

On that cheerful note, he swung around again, faced his companion, and shouted, "Why do you stand there? Do you not have a job? Must you listen in on my private conversations? Go! Go! We have work to do."

If the poor man had a tail, he would have tucked it under himself as he turned and scurried back toward the kitchen, followed by Otto, hurling invectives at him all the way down the hall.

"Oh, Mark," Sabrina sobbed, "I'm so sorry. I've ruined everything. The dinner will be a disaster. Otto will do something horrible, I know he will, and…"

"Hey," Mark said, pulling her toward him, drying her eyes with a filthy bandana he produced from his pocket. "It's not your fault. There was no way you could have known. It'll be fine."

"You think so?" Sabrina looked up at him, hope flickering across her face.

"It's going to be great," I said, wondering if I should butt in, wondering even more if I was telling the truth. "You heard Otto. Making this dinner a success is something he wants for himself. People rarely go against their own self-interest."

Mark grinned at me. "Only too true. So, let's cling to that hope."

"I don't know." She dried her eyes once more, then looked, really looked, at Mark's bandana. She handed it back to him, holding it carefully between her thumb and forefinger, and used the back of her hand to brush away the last few tears. "I hope you're both right. But so far, this day has been a disaster."

"Ah, so far," Mark told her, shoving his bandana back in his pocket. "But now we've used up all our bad luck. What more could go wrong?"

"Frank could show up," Sabrina said in tones of direst doom.

Mark laughed. "Even we couldn't be that unlucky." Then he dropped a kiss on her nose and left.

Chapter Three

"For heaven's sake, Dan, slow down." Aunt Mary's voice, coming from the backseat, was part irritation and part pain. "Thanks to that last turn, my seat belt is practically strangling me."

"I thought you wanted to get there early," Dan said. But he slowed down. Growing up, he'd always done what Aunt Mary said. Evidently, the habit had stuck.

"Early, yes," she replied, unsnapping her seat belt, "but alive would be nice also."

I smothered a laugh. Dan had been in an increasingly foul mood for the last couple of weeks, and when we told him he had to go to the first event Mark and Sabrina were hosting at the winery, the Harvest Festival Dinner, and he would have to wear a tux, he'd rebelled.

"Not a chance. Eighty bucks a plate and tux rental on top of that? Do you know how many steaks we could barbeque for that kind of money?"

I'd used every argument I could think of. "We have to support Mark and Sabrina. After all, they're family."

"Not my family," he'd replied.

"You owe it to the community. You being an important public servant and all that."

"I keep this community safe from crooks," he'd said through tight lips. "And that's all I owe it."

It was Aunt Mary who persuaded him. How, I didn't know and wasn't about to ask. But here we were, on our way to the winery, dressed in rarely worn evening clothes, and looking dashing. At least, Dan looked dashing. I looked expensive in my prettiest designer dress left over from my previous life. I'd always loved this dress, if not the circumstances in which I used to wear it. Even Aunt Mary looked good. A firm believer in supporting the many charity rummage sales she runs, her clothes sometimes left viewers a little breathless. The dress she had planned to wear tonight was awful. Black, with red fringe in all the wrong places, and sort of hiked up on one hip. I'd cringed when I saw it but was afraid to say anything in the face of Aunt Mary's supreme indifference. My friend, Pat Bennington, didn't share my qualms. "Oh no," she'd said when she saw it, "not to Sabrina's shindig." She'd somehow turned the dress into a simple, figure-flattering, elegant gown. I would be forever in her debt.

"Have you had any more of those phone calls?" Aunt Mary asked from the backseat, breaking the silence.

"What phone calls?" Dan wanted to know.

I looked out the car window, watching the sun linger a few minutes before it sank behind the hills that separate our town from the Pacific Ocean. The sky changed from blue to pink to orange to fiery red, following its descent. A lot like the pattern of Dan's temper this past month. I hadn't planned on telling him about the phone calls.

"What phone calls?" Dan repeated.

"Somebody from high school," I said.

"Who? I knew everybody you ever knew. I dated most of your girl friends. Who is she?"

"Why didn't you ever date me?" I asked, turning back toward him.

"I lived next door to you. No one dates the girl next door. Besides, you wore braces. Who is your mysterious caller?"

"Larry Whittaker."

"Who?" Dan's face looked as blank as his tone.

"I dated him our sophomore year. Sort of. We went to the movies once."

"I don't remember any Larry Whittaker." Dan looked puzzled, as well he might. In a school the size of ours, everyone knew everyone.

"He didn't stay long," I said. "One day he was gone. He sent me a postcard from Paris. I thought that was pretty romantic."

"Paris?" Dan asked, taking his eyes off the road for a moment to stare at me. "What was he doing in Paris?"

"Going to school," Aunt Mary said from the backseat. "I remember his grandmother telling me how his father whisked him off to boarding school after his mother died."

"Paris. So what brings him back here and what does he want with you?"

"No idea," I said. "I haven't talked to him, just picked up the messages he's left on my machine. He says he's back in town, heard I was back also and divorced, and thought maybe we could get together."

"That's pretty nervy." Dan frowned.

"No it's not," I told him, a little amused.

"Have you tried to call him back?"

"No. He hasn't left a number."

Dan looked stormy again. Great. Our relationship this past month had been difficult enough. I didn't need some man I barely remembered ruining an already shaky evening.

"I hope he doesn't call again," I said, as dismissively as I could. "If it weren't for the postcard, I probably wouldn't remember him at all."

"Humph." Dan swung the car a little too hard into the parking spot in front of the winery, letting the wheels slip on the gravel, and stopped abruptly.

"Good grief," exclaimed Aunt Mary. "Was that really necessary?"

"Sorry." He got out and opened Aunt Mary's door. I didn't say anything. I was too busy checking my neck for whiplash.

"Will you look at all this?" exclaimed Aunt Mary, looking around her.

"All this" was worth looking at. I had been to the winery several times in the four weeks Sabrina and Mark had stayed with me while they house hunted, but I was still impressed. The hillsides that sloped away from us were covered by neat rows of vines. The deep green of the glossy leaves and the lush purple of the heavy bunches of grapes glowed in the fading early evening light. The building we faced, low, sprawling, made of stucco and brick, was reminiscent of a California mission. It seemed to command the hilltop, quietly reigning over the grape vines and the view beyond them. I half expected to see a friar come through those heavy wooden doors, sandals on his feet, cowl covering his head. Instead we got Sabrina.

"Thank goodness," she sputtered. "I don't know what to do. You have to help."

"Oh, dear. Is it that awful chef you've been so upset about?" Aunt Mary took a step toward Sabrina, alarm widening her eyes.

Sabrina threw her arms in the air, causing her crimson skirt to swirl and her comb to loosen its grip on her hair. She reminded me of a firecracker about to explode. "No. Yes. Partly. Mostly it's Frank."

"Frank," repeated Dan, looking from her to me.

"Frank? Mark's father Frank?" I asked.

"The very one. The great Frank Tortelli. Tortelli's Restaurante. San Francisco." Sabrina tossed this bit of information over her shoulder and started back through the heavy door. "Come on. You've got to stop him."

"How?" I asked, following her.

"Stop who from doing what?" asked Aunt Mary.

"No kidding," Dan said in a reverent tone. "Wow. He's Mark's father?" He pushed the door open and stepped aside, waiting for us to enter. "Some detective I am. Of course. Tortelli's. Best place to eat in San Francisco, and that's saying something."

I had heard of Tortelli's, of course, but had never been there. It was obvious Dan had. But then, he had lived and worked in San Francisco for years.

"Was the food really that good?" I heard myself ask as I passed Dan. I couldn't help it. I was hungry.

"Yes." That one word said it all.

We followed Sabrina into the entryway of the winery. The walls were covered with medals won by previous winemakers for Silver Springs. Interspersed were pictures of them standing beside famous people, all holding glasses filled with Silver Springs wine. Bottles of award-winning vintages were displayed on shelves, and in the air hung an aroma that made my stomach growl. The yeasty smell of fermenting wine twirled seductively around me, overlaid with garlic and roasting lamb.

To our right I caught a glimpse of what was by day the tasting room. It had been transformed into a formal dining room, thanks in part to several hours of my help. I had been anxious to show it off to Dan and Aunt Mary, but that wasn't going to happen immediately. Sabrina was hurrying us down the hallway to the left, past closed office doors, closer to the cooking smells and the sound of raised voices. Actually, one raised voice. A familiar one.

"Help! I, Otto Messinger, do not need help. Especially from one who makes pasta!" There was Otto, now wrapped in a white apron, his chef's hat madly bobbing, stabbing the air with his clenched fist. His face had turned a unique shade of red. You would have thought, from his tone, pasta was a four-letter word.

"Mark is my only son," said a tall, handsome man in an elegant tux. He didn't raise his voice, but the chill in it would have made a polar bear shiver. "This dinner is his debut as a winemaker. It's my duty, and my privilege as a father, to be here for him. To make sure this important dinner is a success." He paused, looked down at the still quivering chef, then, with the smallest hint of a condescending smile, went on. "And pasta is a gift from the gods. To do it right requires talent. You cannot cover up your mistakes with sauces made from canned soup."

The great Otto sputtered, his face turned from tomato to beet red. He clenched and unclenched his fists and flung himself forward over the long table that bisected the room.

"Thanks, Dad. Thanks a lot." I hadn't seen Mark as we entered the room, but I took a good look at him now. Shorter than his elegant father, stockier, more earthy looking, Mark's hair trigger temper was about to explode. "He's leaving, Otto. Right now. So you can keep your promise and get this dinner together. If you two," he glared at both of them, "want to continue this feud, do it after the dessert course. Now, let these guys get on with it."

"These guys" evidently meant the tall thin one I'd seen earlier, as well as the four young men in black pants, white shirts, and tuxedo ties who were huddled around another table at the far end of the room, filling trays with appetizers and trying vainly to look as though they weren't listening.

"No. I must…" Frank started but was stopped by the tone in his son's voice.

"Leave. That's what you must do," Mark said. "Now, Dad."

Otto flashed him a triumphant smile, which was immediately replaced by a deep scowl at the sight of our little group.

"Who are these people? Am I a sideshow, that you parade strange people through my kitchen? You are perhaps selling tickets? Or are they, too, going to pass judgment on my food?"

The hostility in that room was thick enough to slice and serve on plates. The look Sabrina gave Otto did nothing to thin it out.

Frank couldn't leave it alone. "Your kitchen? Hardly. And no one came to see you. You're a has-been. A never-was. The only success you ever had you got by hanging on to my coattails. Try to get tonight's dinner right, if you know how."

Mark gasped and started to say something, but Otto got his shot off first.

"Not my kitchen? When Otto is invited to create, then that space is his. Know how? Coattails? Phuff. You can cook. Maybe. Create? Never. Tortelli's has had only one success, only one dish. And that dish was stolen. From me!"

Now Frank, black eyes burning, lunged toward the table, and it looked like war was in full swing. The thin man backed up, the waiters stopped filling their trays; Mark let out a groan that was almost a growl and grabbed his father by the coat.

"God damn it, will you stop?" he said.

Otto snickered; Aunt Mary and I openly gaped. Dan seized Frank's arm, and Sabrina stepped into the fray.

"Mark, there are guests arriving. Could you please…?"

He started to say something, stopped, glared at both of them again and stomped out.

"Chef Otto Messinger, I believe you met my aunt, Ellen McKenzie, earlier today," Sabrina said, trying hard to pretend nothing outlandish had happened. I took a little bow, but it didn't help much. Otto continued to scowl. "And this is my Great Aunt Mary McGill, and Dan Dunham, Santa Louisa's Chief of Police. Everyone, this is our guest chef for the evening, and we're all so glad he could be here," she finished a little desperately.

"I'm not," said Frank.

"Either he goes, or I do." Otto pulled himself up and puffed out his chest. The puffing part looked as if he practiced a lot.

"Wonderful idea," said Frank, starting to slide out of his coat. "Is there a spare apron around here?"

Sabrina stepped in front of him, pulled his coat back up on his shoulders, and turned to face Otto. "Frank is leaving right now," she said, with menace in her voice, for which one I wasn't sure. Probably both. "And, Otto, the hors d'oeuvres trays need to go out. Now." She turned to include the waiters, who milled around uncertainly.

Aunt Mary, eyebrows raised, nodded approvingly at this firm Sabrina before she looked up at Frank. "You two are acting like a couple of school boys."

Frank smiled down at her, the smile extending to his eyes. Why, he's loving this, I thought. The old rascal. I almost laughed but looked at Sabrina's face and hid it. Unfortunately, not from Frank. The look he gave me was downright conspiratorial before he started again.

"Your manners are as bad as your food. Worse, if that's possible," he told the fuming Otto. He paused to smooth down his silver-streaked dark hair while staring pointedly at the wispy gray tufts sticking out from each side of Otto's hat. "Steal your recipes?" he went on, disdain dripping from each word. "I would not demean myself, or those who come to dine at my restaurant."

He smoothed the lapels of his immaculate tuxedo, buttoned his jacket, then bowed slightly over Aunt Mary's hand. "You must be the gracious aunt who is putting up my son and my beautiful daughter-in-law."

"No, that's…" Aunt Mary started. Frank didn't give her a chance to finish.

"If you will permit, I will escort you to the patio. I believe Mark is going to give a short talk on the making of wine. Perhaps you will find it interesting. We will sip champagne. We know that will be palatable."

One of the waiters gave a nervous giggle. Frank gave him a withering look, whirled Aunt Mary around, and whisked her out the door. She cast a frantic glance back at us, mouthed something, which I thought was a plea for us to follow, and disappeared.

Sabrina watched them go, then leaned up against the wall, muttering to herself, "Why me, God? Why me?"

There didn't seem to be an immediate answer to that or to the implied question in Dan's expression. Anyway, there wasn't time because Otto once again found his voice.

"Imbeciles. That is no way to fill those trays. Can you not follow simple instructions?" He picked up a finished hors d'oeuvre and threw it at the waiter.

Dan said, "Hey, you can't…"; I gasped; the waiter reached for the tray; and it looked like round two was about to begin, but a new voice stopped the action short.

"Otto, the bisque. It's time to add the cream. Should I finish or…" It was the tall man, who, up to now, had said nothing. His eye twitched, then he stood quiet, waiting.

"Of course not. Last time you ruined it. Here. See if you can get them to do this right." With one more "Phuf" for the waiters and not even a glance for us, he pushed through a door into the adjoining room. I had time for a quick glimpse of a pot-laden stove, open shelves filled with dishes, and a surge of smells that almost drove my stomach mad. Then the door swung closed.

The man walked up to me, stuck out his hand and said, "Hello, Ellen. You haven't changed a bit."

Chapter Four

I had no idea who he was. He stood there, waiting, his tall hat gently swaying, an expectant smile on his face, while I grinned idiotically back, trying to come up with a name. There was something vaguely familiar about him, but Dan's eyes bored down on me, which didn't help me place him. Very blond hair, pale blue eyes, long, nicely shaped face with a nose that tipped up just slightly at the end. If he'd had a chin, he'd have been quite good looking, but I still didn't know who he was. The waiters watched while they filled their trays, evidently thinking a new drama was about to begin.

"I'm sorry I didn't leave a number on your machine," he went on, his words coming out breathy and rushed, "but the only phone I have right now is at Otto's new bed and breakfast, and I didn't want to take the chance he might answer. Not that he does, much."

I had a name.

"Larry," I said, "my, ah, I got your messages. What a surprise. After all these years." I stopped, waiting for him to say something. He didn't. "Dan," I finally said, wondering what I was supposed to do now, "you remember Larry Whittaker from high school."

"Ah," was Dan's reply. It didn't matter because Larry wasn't paying any attention to him.

"I've thought about you so much," Larry said, looking at me expectantly. "You're prettier than ever."

I could feel my cheeks burn. I could also feel Dan watching me. "Oh," I said with what I hoped was a little laugh. "We've both changed."

"How have I changed?" he asked, smiling down at me with an intimate little smile I didn't appreciate one bit.

"You've grown," I blurted out.

At first he looked blank, then the smile came back. "I got all my height my junior year. Must have been all that French food."

"That you ate while you were in Paris," Dan put in. He looked Larry in the eye. Larry looked back. Same height, same expressions of suspicion. They stared at each other like a couple of junkyard dogs defending their territory, waiting to see who would back off first. It was Larry.

"I have to go back to work now, but I'll call you. Real soon. We'll do lunch." He turned back to the trays and the waiters. Dan looked at me with an eyebrow raised. I shrugged and shook my head at him. Sabrina was still leaning against the doorjamb, muttering.

"Shouldn't we do something about her?" I asked, anxious to change the subject.

"What?"

"At least get her out of here. Sabrina, come on. Let's go find Mark."

"And Frank," she said bitterly. "Good old Frank. Now you see him, now you don't. Why can't the man show up when he's needed? Or wanted? Of course, then we'd never see him. I could live with that."

"You mean you didn't know he was coming?" Dan asked.

"We haven't heard from Frank for three years. His idea of being a father is to ignore that fact until something interesting happens. Then he appears and steals the spotlight. Remind me to tell you about our wedding sometime."

"How did he know about tonight?" I asked her.

"I've no idea. All I know is an hour ago he walked in and tried to take over. That's what the scene was all about. Now Otto's raging around the kitchen, Frank's loose with our guests, and the evening is only beginning." She took a deep breath, squared her shoulders, and said, "All right. People are arriving, Mark can't run interference all by himself, and someone needs to rescue Aunt Mary."

"We'll do that," I told her. "You go do your job."

She nodded distractedly and hurried out the door. Dan and I followed more slowly. Larry called out, "Bye, Ellen. See you soon."

"Will he?" Dan asked.

"Not if I can help it," I said softly.

Dan gave a soft chuckle. "So a romantic postcard from Paris doesn't have much staying power?"

"Not after more than twenty years, it doesn't."

"What if that postcard had been from me?"

I looked up at him and laughed. "That would be a very different matter."

He grinned and took my arm. One of the waiters passed us, carrying a tray filled with champagne flutes. He paused. Dan carefully lifted off two, handed one to me, and took a sip from the other.

"You know," he said, toasting me with his glass, "I thought this was going to be a pretty boring evening, but it's turning out not half bad."

"I'm glad someone's enjoying it," I told him. "So far, I think you're the only one. We need to find Aunt Mary."

"Mary and Frank," Dan said cheerfully. "By all means, let's go find them." He started to laugh.

"What's so funny?" I said.

"The first act's been pretty good. I was wondering if the second one will be as entertaining."

It was.

Chapter Five

"Will you look at that!" Dan stopped short. "Isn't this the tasting room?"

"It was until sometime this afternoon." I looked around with what I thought was justifiable pride. The tables were elegantly set. The pale green of the tablecloths showed off the cool ivory of the china; the silver gleamed beside each plate. A myriad of sparkling wineglasses reflected the light from the hurricane lanterns set on mirrors, surrounded by pale lavender Cattleya orchids. At each place lay a roll of ivory parchment on which tonight's menu had been imprinted, tied with a pale green ribbon into which a single pink rosebud was tucked.

"It came out nice, didn't it?"

"You and Sabrina did all this?" Dan asked.

"Yep. This afternoon. I'd no idea it was so much work to put on one of these things. You know," I went on a little thoughtfully, "I always thought Sabrina was sort of—"

"Scatterbrained?"

"Timid," I substituted. "But she had everything ready. Tablecloths, place settings, centerpieces, they were all here, waiting for us to put everything together. She'd done things I would never have thought of, and she had the wines, the food, and the wait staff all under control."

"And you're surprised?"

"Yes," I admitted, "a little. Aren't you?"

"I guess I am. Now if she can just keep Otto and Frank from doing each other in before the evening is over, things should be great."

"I think we're supposed to do that," I said. "Come on."

"All those glasses!" Dan was still staring at the tables. "Anybody that drinks that much wine won't be fit to drive home, let alone find his car."

"Quit acting like a policeman. Besides, you don't chugalug it. You drink a little of each wine because it complements the food. Eat a little, sip a little, and the whole thing takes hours." Four weeks of Mark and Sabrina and one afternoon at the winery had made me an expert.

Dan looked from me back to the glasses, shook his head, and said, "Yeah?" As an expert I was evidently not to be trusted.

"Look. There's Aunt Mary." A group of people were gathered on the deck, looking over the rail at something. Frank and Aunt Mary were standing in the front. Dan and I threaded our way through the tables toward the double French doors and out onto the deck toward the growing group.

"That is the crush pad," Mark said, making a sweeping gesture toward the concrete pad below us. "The grapes are brought here from the vineyards in large gondolas. Large boxes. Then they're dumped in the hopper."

He pointed down toward a wicked-looking piece of machinery as he started his lecture. "This is used for red wine only. It de-stems the grapes before they go into the crusher. We want the juice, but the skins and the pulp help to give the juice flavor."

"That thing looks like my grandmother's old meat grinder," said a young lady in a too short purple velvet dress.

"Wine making is often old fashioned," Frank told her, with a gallant nod. He slipped Aunt Mary's arm under his. "Now you would have a food processor, but here, the old way is the best."

"Not only in wine making." Aunt Mary's tone was a little tart. I wondered if she were thinking of her own meat grinder.

Mark allowed himself one quick glance at his father and went on.

"What comes out of the crusher is called "must." We pump it into those stainless steel tanks for preliminary fermentation." He waved toward the towering, tightly covered tanks visible through the open roll-up cellar door. "That takes about seven to ten days, sometimes longer. During that time, all of the seeds and skins float to the top of the juice, forming the "cap." We ferment in closed tanks, pumping the juice from the bottom over the cap to get the most flavor out of the skins, and that's called a pump over."

Mark paused and looked directly at me and grinned. I grinned back. How about that. I had heard him right.

He went on, "Look down at this platform. This is an old-fashioned tank. We like to keep this big old wooden one open to show you how wine used to be made." Mark pointed down to a shorter tank on a platform directly below us. The top of the tank wasn't more than a few feet from the railing where we stood. There was a set of stairs that led from a double gate on the deck down to the platform, and another ladder led down to the crush pad. The thick cap Mark had been talking about lay on top of the fermenting wine in easy view. "See those paddles?" he went on. "They are used to punch down the cap. Any of you hear stories of crushing the wine by stomping on it? Well, they were punching it down. We don't go quite that far."

There were "ohs" and "I never knew that" through the crowd and several questions.

"How thick does that stuff, what did you call it, get?" asked a portly man.

"The cap."

"Yeah. Cap. How thick does that get?"

"Several inches, and it's pretty tough." Mark was really into his lecture, but his audience, lured by loaded hors d'oeuvres trays and the offered refills of champagne, was starting to fade away. It was Frank who came up with the one last bit of information.

"Tough and lethal." He addressed Aunt Mary, but his dramatic tone carried. Several people, whose glasses were once again full, turned back.

"What do you mean, lethal?" asked a balding, red-faced man.

"Carbon dioxide collects under the cap." Frank waved down at the dull red stuff sitting silently in the wooden tank. It looked like overcooked cranberry sauce, and just about as dangerous.

"He's right," Mark said. "It wasn't uncommon for workers to die of carbon dioxidepoisoning when they did it all by hand."

"By foot," Frank corrected. He got a laugh from the crowd, but not from his son.

"I'll show you the cellar floor during the dinner break," Mark said through clenched teeth, "and we'll do some barrel tasting then."

The last of the group faded away, leaving only Frank, Aunt Mary, Mark, Dan, and me.

"Nicely done," Frank told Mark with a little nod. "Mary, we're going to have one of Mark's wines with dinner, one he made while he was assistant winemaker up north. Quite a nice little thing."

"How kind of you to say so." Mark tried to jam his fists into his tux pants pockets, gave up, and clenched them instead.

Frank blinked, as if taken aback by the sarcasm in Mark's voice, but only for a second. "Not at all," he said. He tucked Aunt Mary's arm through his and nodded to all of us. "If you will excuse us, there are some people Mary should meet."

I had never heard Aunt Mary say so little, nor seen her look so, not exactly bewildered, maybe nonplussed. We watched them disappear through the Ffrench doors. A waiter appeared carrying a tray of full flutes and a champagne bottle. Mark grabbed one. Simultaneously, Dan and I held our glasses out to be refilled but Mark took the bottle from him and filled our glasses. The waiter looked a little startled, but, after a quick look at Mark's face, he walked off with his tray.

Mark held up the bottle, squinted at it, shook it a little and grunted, "Empty." He set it on one of the wooden picnic tables, took a large gulp from his glass and stared down at the remaining bubbles.

"Your father's got quite a sense of humor," I said, trying to lighten Mark up a little.

"You think so?" He glanced up at me. "Lots of people have said so." He made it quite clear he wasn't one of them. We all sipped silently for a moment. "I've heard they put you in jail for strangling your father."

Dan nodded. "Even when it's justified." He glanced at Mark with what looked like sympathy, then held up his glass and watched his own bubbles.

"I've got to go talk to people. Why don't you find your table. They all have place cards." Mark drained the rest of his champagne and walked off, twirling his now empty glass in his fingers.

"Should we? Go find our table, I mean," I said.

"In a minute. It's nice out here, especially as everybody else has gone inside. Let's go over here."

I followed Dan over to the railing where we stood, side by side, saying nothing, letting the view set the mood. The early autumn setting sun had put on quite a show but now had slid behind the hills, leaving us with a silver sky dotted with pink clouds. The oak trees on the far hills and the vines close up were standing out like paper silhouettes, giving us one last look before night enveloped them.

Dan leaned on the railing, playing with his glass. What a piece of good luck, finding him again. After twenty years with Brian McKenzie, I'd wondered if I'd ever actually *like* a man again. I liked Dan. He made me laugh, he talked to me, not at me, and he treated me as if I belonged in his life. The fates, or whatever, seemed most of the time to have a malicious sense of humor. But sometimes they forgot themselves and things turned out pretty well. Like coming home to Santa Louisa. Like now.

"That Whittaker guy's not the only one who thinks you look pretty tonight." Dan wasn't looking at me. Instead, he stared intently at the barely visible grape vines.

"Thank you," I said, amused that he'd let Larry get to him and pleased, very pleased, that he'd said something. Compliments had been few and far between when I was married. Dan didn't throw them around lightly, either, but when he gave you one, he meant it. I frowned. A thought I didn't want intruded. Would Dan still find me pretty, or important, when we had been married twenty years?

"What's the matter?" he asked.

"Nothing."

"You sure?"

"Just thinking about Otto, hoping everything's all right."

"Oh. It's fine. Look at that view. Too bad we can't have our wedding reception here."

Wedding reception. Damn. "We'd freeze to death," I said.

He turned toward me, leaning against the railing, sipping slowly from his glass. His face was half hidden in shadow, so I couldn't read his expression. "I'll bet I could keep you warm."

That was not the problem. Being with Dan made me feel things, do things, that, well, parts of me came alive with Dan that had dozed through my whole life with Brian. Oh, yes, he could keep me warm. But how about five years down the road? What then? Would he still want to? I could feel my stomach knot up.

"I talked with Reverend Hanson," Dan went on. "He thought New Year's Eve would be a great time. We can have the church that night. Service at eight, then dinner and dancing in the Inn ballroom. What do you think?"

What I thought was I was going to throw up. Panic clawed at me. New Year's Eve was just over three months away.

"You know, Ellie," Dan said softly, stepping closer and pulling me toward him. "I think I'm going to like being married again." He bent down and kissed me, the kind of kiss that made my knees go weak and all the butterflies upsetting my stomach fly away.

He let me go and took a step back.

"My," I managed. "My."

"Consider that an appetizer." Dan laughed. "The main course will come soon. I promise."

Yeah, I thought. Soon. "You look pretty handsome yourself tonight. I like you in a tux." I reached out and patted his stomach. "A little more here than the last time I saw you in one, but I think it becomes you."

"The stomach or the tux?" Dan asked, one eyebrow slightly raised.

"Both," I laughed. "Too bad there aren't more events in this town where one is called for."

I could hear him take a deep breath before he said, "Not like in your old life. I'll bet Brian didn't wear a rented tux."

"No. He had his own." Where had that come from? Was Dan worried I'd miss my old life? Miss Brian? He couldn't possibly. I didn't miss being married to Brian. Damn. I didn't miss being married. The butterflies were back. I turned toward him, thinking I should say something, something about bad marriages, divorce, scarring, but not knowing what.

Dan took a step toward me. "I love you, Ellie," he said softly, leaning closer to me.

I lifted my face toward his. His mouth, as it came closer to mine, was tender under the neat little mustache that always tickled me. I let my hand drift up to touch it, to trace the shadows down his cheekbones, ready to forget old hurts, hesitancy, and doubts, ready to believe he was right, that married life could be…

"Ouch," I shouted. Dan suddenly crumbled, then crashed against me, grabbing to keep us both from falling. Champagne flew out of his glass, barely missing us.

"What on earth…" I gasped.

"What the hell?" Dan stared accusingly at the picnic table we'd pushed against. It had moved, evidently not caring for people leaning on it. The railing had stopped it from further travel.

"Damn," Dan said. "It could have dumped us right into that tank." He glared at it as though it had moved purposely.

"Grab it!" I shouted.

"What? Oh." Dan dived forward and caught the empty champagne bottle as it finished its slow journey toward the edge of the table. "Got it. That would have made a nice mess."

"Why is the picnic table shoved up against the gate?" Sabrina's voice made us both jump.

"Ah," I started, but she didn't seem to want an answer.

"Can you help me push it back?" She put the dish tray she was carrying down on the deck, grabbed one end of the table, and started to pull. I took the other end and gave it a tug. "Why do we have to do this now? We're not exactly dressed for table wrestling."

"We need this gate free," Sabrina said. "People often buy cases of wine at an event like this, and Hector uses this gate to fork lift it up here."

"How does he avoid the wooden tank?" I asked, looking down.

"It's a double gate, it swings wide." She gave the table another tug, but nothing happened.

"Didn't seem that heavy when we leaned on it," I observed.

"What?" Sabrina said.

"Never mind," Dan replied. He handed me the champagne bottle. "Move," he told us. We did. So did the table. I looked at him and grinned. He grinned back, sort of, reached over and took the bottle out of my hands and set it in the middle of the table. "Is that okay?" he asked Sabrina.

"Fine. Thanks. Everyone is sitting down and we're going to serve the first course in a few minutes. You're sitting at Mark's table with Aunt Mary and Frank. Could you, I'd really appreciate it, I know its hard but do you think that…" The old Sabrina was back.

I looked through the French doors into the dining room at a table in the middle of the room. Frank pulled out a chair for Aunt Mary, got her settled while he chatted easily with a tall, thin man in a beautifully tailored tux and cowboy boots.

"And you want us to baby-sit," Dan stated.

"I want you to keep Frank away from Otto, from all of the other guests, and don't let Mark kill him. Until after dinner."

"You don't ask much," Dan commented. "How are we supposed to do that?"

"Never mind. We'll try," I said quickly. "We'll go in right now."

"How's Mark doing?" Dan asked Sabrina as we all headed for the open French doors.

"Not great." She gave the room a quick survey. "He's feeling about Frank like I'm feeling about Otto, and that's downright murderous. Do what you can. Okay?"

She hurried off toward the kitchen and we wound our way through tables toward our peacekeeping mission.

"Ah, there you are." Frank made a sweeping gesture, a genial host welcoming his guests. Only it wasn't his table and we weren't his guests.

"Have you met Mr. Ian Applby?" he continued. "Ian is the owner of this wonderful winery and a lifelong friend. His wife, Greta, could not be here tonight, a pity, but Ian has graciously offered me her seat."

Mr. Applby nodded gravely. "A pleasure, Frank, as always. Greta will be very upset that she missed seeing you." Then to the rest of us, "Frank exaggerates. I am only a partner."

"The senior partner. The one with all the brains, all the vision, and all the money." Frank laughed generously, inviting us all to join in. Aunt Mary managed a small one, and, much to my embarrassment, I tittered. Dan and Mr. Applby sat silent.

"I do believe this is my table." The voice had a rich, liquid drawl and the woman had a rich, liquid look. Like brandy, and much the same color. Beautifully done honey beige hair, makeup you never see outside of magazines or Newport Beach, and a beige silk, drop-dead gorgeous dress, draped over a figure that didn't look like it had needed to diet.

"Why, Frank Tortelli. I can't believe my eyes. Whatever are you doin' here?" the creature drawled.

"Hello, Jolene." Frank's voice had, until now, overridden everyone else's with its volume and enthusiasm. Now it had neither.

"Frank, darlin', aren't you goin' to introduce me?"

Mr. Applby was already on his feet, pulling out a chair.

"Jolene Bixby," Frank said. He waved vaguely toward the rest of us. "A wine and food writer."

"I'm the rovin' reporter for *Dining Delights*," she told us all as she let Mr. Applby push in her chair. "We're out of Dallas, but it seems I'm just never home there anymore. So many restaurants, so little time."

Jolene's tinkly little laugh sounded like breaking glass. Aunt Mary caught my eye and gave me a "what do you think about that" look. Dan and Mr. Applby just looked. And looked.

"I've been to Tortelli's just so many times, and I've just loved writin' about it. I couldn't believe my ears when I heard that you sold it. That just can't be true, is it, Frank?"

Miss Dallas might have captivated two of our "men folk," but she was missing with Frank by a Texas mile. This was the first anything had been said about Frank selling his restaurant and he didn't look pleased. He looked furious. Why, I wondered. If he'd sold it, why would he care who knew? But maybe, I thought, the deal isn't done yet, and Miss Jolene was doing a little premature announcing.

Mr. Applby's head swung around to stare at Frank. "You sold Tortelli's? I don't believe it. You loved that restaurant. We all loved it. What on earth made you do that?"

For the first time, Frank seemed to have run out of words. "Oh, well, it's, ah."

He was saved by the unexpected and unwelcome appearance of Carlton Carpenter.

"Well, well. Look who's here. Dan, Ellen, Mary."

Carlton pulled out the chair between Jolene and Ian Applby, leaving only one empty one.

"Good evening, Mr. Applby, ah, Ian," he said, rubbing his hands together. I was reminded of Uriah Heep. "It's so nice to see you again." He managed to get himself and his chair pulled up to the table with only one loud scrape before looking around. His gaze slid quickly over Frank and came to rest on the lovely Jolene. "I don't think I've had the pleasure."

He let that hang in the air, expectantly. I said nothing, hoping everyone would ignore him and he'd take the hint and go away, but Aunt Mary, incapable of being impolite, started to introduce him. Mr. Applby got there first.

"Carlton is the winery's newest partner," he announced, causing Dan to choke on his wine.

I could hardly blame him. I hadn't had a chance to tell him of Carlton's elevated status to winery partner. Dan felt about Carlton very much the way I did, only perhaps more so. Sitting at the same table was tolerable, but having to listen to him boast about this latest triumph wasn't going to be on Dan's list of fun things to do. He frowned as he set his wineglass down and shot Carlton a look. Probably the one he reserved for petty thieves and incorrigible teenagers.

"My goodness, Carlton, I thought you had a real estate agency," Aunt Mary said.

"Not much any more," Carlton answered somewhat vaguely. "Now I'm doing investments and, ah, other things."

"Investments?" Jolene repeated. She set down the champagne glass she had just emptied and studied him. "Now, that just sounds so excitin'. And you're part owner of this winery? Imagine that."

"A very minor partner," he told Jolene, but he preened nonetheless. "I bought out Henry Banks' winery shares." He addressed this to Aunt Mary but immediately turned back to Jolene. "Henry didn't leave poor Mildred much and she was glad to get some cash."

"So it was you she sold to," Aunt Mary said. "And, Carlton, Henry left her in fine shape. She was getting a little income from her shares. You should never sell anything that produces income."

Carlton's face got a little red. "I guess she needed cash now. And she was a very minor partner. As am I." He tried out a chuckle, but no one joined in.

The last chair scraped and Mark sat down. Just in time. The waiters were slipping plates in front of us and pouring wine into the goblets closest to them.

"Has everyone met Jolene Bixby?" Mark asked. "Sabrina and I are delighted she's covering our first dinner." He turned to her, raising his glass slightly, as though to toast her. "I hear that you are Otto's first bed and breakfast guest. Are you doing an article on that also?"

Jolene raised her glass, took a large swallow, and beamed at the table at large.

"I certainly am. We just couldn't not do an article on something as important as a new restaurant with Otto Messinger as the owner and chef, and when that new restaurant is coupled with a fabulous bed and breakfast and is in California's newest wine region, well, all I can say is, that is real news."

That was a sentence that took some sorting through, but one fact stood out. The bed and breakfast Otto had talked about this morning really was news.

Mark ignored his father while trying to make conversation with Jolene, who adjusted her cleavage and smiled speculatively at Carlton. Frank paid slavish court to Aunt Mary, who seemed torn between flattery and confusion. Mr. Applby determinedly picked up his spoon and tasted the crab bisque. Dan looked at me, rolled his eyes slightly, and smiled wickedly.

"I love the look on Carlton's face when Ms. Bixby leans in towards him. Reminds me a bit of a golden retriever, slobbering with anticipation, waiting for someone to throw the ball," he said softly into my ear. "Do you suppose Jolene will make the toss?"

"She's ready, willing, and just waiting for her cue," I said, picking up my spoon. "One more peek down her cleavage, and Carlton won't be able to leave the table without his napkin in front of him."

Dan sputtered with laughter. Everyone looked at us and smiled a little expectantly. Everyone except Aunt Mary. There was warning in those blue eyes. We both smiled back.

After the general conversation resumed Dan whispered, "You're a downright evil woman, Ellie my love."

I smiled as demurely as I could and said, "Jolene looks like a cat on the prowl. I'll bet she thinks Carlton has money."

"Should we tell her the truth?" Dan asked in an innocent tone.

I raised an eyebrow as I watched Jolene readjust her dress a little lower over her bosom. She leaned across to say something to Mr. Applby, and, for a moment, I thought Carlton's spoonful of bisque was going down her front, right down his line of sight. He managed to return the spoon, still loaded with bisque, to his bowl. I loved the expression on his face as he waited for Jolene to sit back in her chair before he lifted it again.

"This is better than a Mel Brooks movie," Dan muttered. "Ouch," he said more loudly when I pinched him.

"Hush. They'll hear you."

"Do you care?" He rubbed his arm.

"It'll just make things harder for Mark and Sabrina. Besides, you'll get it from Aunt Mary if she hears you."

Dan grinned. "You're right about that." He put down his own spoon and picked up his wineglass. "You know, this stuff's not bad," he announced, rather loudly.

Mr. Applby gave a little smile and nodded. "We are noted for our Sauvignon Blanc."

"It's delightful," I said, raking my brain to think of some terms Sabrina had taught me. "So fruity," I finished, hoping I had it right.

"The soup's good, too," said Dan, trying to keep a straight face.

"It is bisque," Frank told him severely.

"What's the difference?"

Unfortunately, Frank started to tell him. We were saved by the plate change.

"What is this?" Dan looked down at his plate, suspicion clearly etched.

"Hum. He has tried the ahi tuna with macadamia nut crust and shitake mushroom." Frank was poking the beautiful concoction gently with his fork. "The bisque was passable. This dish is a little harder. Let's see if he has succeeded."

"Mushrooms. And red tuna. Who would have thought," murmured Dan. He watched everyone start and, brave man that he is, took a forkful. "Wonderful," he said, a smile breaking out.

"This is fabulous, Frank," Aunt Mary said. "I would love to learn how to make it. Is it hard?"

"It takes practice, my dear Mary. And, of course, an expert teacher. I volunteer." Frank smiled at Aunt Mary a little like Jake, my cat, smiles at a mouse before he pounces. He made me nervous, but she actually seemed to enjoy it.

"We'll have to arrange a time." Frank gingerly tasted the salad. "Not quite the right flavor in the vinaigrette. We'll do it better, together."

Spare me. Jolene must have been thinking something similar, because she was frowning down at her plate. Or maybe she didn't like tuna.

"Sabrina did a good job," Carlton pronounced, carefully inspecting the centerpiece. "I was a little worried, she seemed so nervous, but then, she is new at this."

Mark looked up, startled. I was afraid he was going to respond to that implied insult, but Mr. Applby got there first.

"Sabrina is a talented girl. We were lucky to get her, and you, Mark." He nodded in Mark's direction, but it was Frank who preened. "And so far everything seems quiet in the kitchen. I was at the last dinner Otto did and that was a disaster. I was afraid this one might be too. I told Sabrina, but she was determined. So far, so good."

"What do you mean, a disaster?" I asked.

"Our Otto does have a temper." Jolene had been sipping the wine with enthusiasm and was looking a little flushed. "I ought to know; I've been to just hundreds of his dinners."

"And did you give him hundreds of kind reviews?" There was something in Frank's tone that made both Dan and me do a double take.

Ian Applby smiled at Jolene. "Miss Bixby is kind even when the review isn't. I've had the pleasure of reading many of her articles and am extremely flattered that she's here tonight." Jolene simpered, and Mr. Applby went on. "Otto's temper is legendary, but manageable, when he confines it to the kitchen. Only sometimes…the last dinner of his I attended, he came storming out of the kitchen, insulted the host and several of the guests, then walked out. His staff managed to get the main course and the dessert on the table, but you can imagine."

"How does he get anyone to work for him?" asked Dan. He looked down at his plate as if he couldn't believe it was already empty.

"The only one I know who has stuck more than one night is Larry Whittaker," Mr. Applby told him.

"Right," Dan said, eying my half full salad plate. "Larry Whittaker. You going to eat all that, Ellie?"

I silently exchanged plates with him.

"How is everything?" Sabrina appeared, her smile looking somewhat strained. She leaned over Mark's shoulder, giving it a little pat. I didn't think her question was confined to the food.

"Wonderful. Just wonderful," Aunt Mary told her. "It's all so pretty, and the food is…well, I thought I was a good cook, but now I know what it means to be a chef."

I gave Sabrina a thumbs-up. I wasn't sure she noticed. She was too busy whispering instructions to a waiter who was removing plates. She paused only long enough to glare at Frank and pat Mark once more before saying, "The main course is lamb. It's wonderful. I managed to sneak a taste in the kitchen. When Otto's back was turned, of course."

"How is Otto behaving?" asked Mr. Applby, his tone tinged slightly with apprehension.

"Otto." Sabrina's smile turned grim. "That man is a scourge upon the earth. I don't know how Larry stands it. I'd have run him through with a carving knife by now. But he is a genius."

She took a bottle from a passing waiter and poured refills into all of our glasses. No one lifted one but Jolene.

"A genius? Not quite. Good, sometimes, but never great," Frank said. He carefully swirled the wine in his glass, then picked it up and held it to his nose.

"Frank is right," gushed Jolene, who had already polished off half of hers, not bothering with the subtleties of aroma. She handed a waiter her untasted ahi. I heard Dan quietly moan.

"And I'm just sure it's that wicked temper of his that keeps him from greatness. Don't you think so, Mr. Carpenter? Or may I call you Carlton?"

"I would be honored," Carlton said, leaning toward her again. Ian Applby, who had been watching all of this, looked pained. Dan looked like he was going to laugh. I kicked him in the ankle. Softly, of course.

Sabrina paused to whisper in my ear, "It's going to be a long night," then followed the last waiter through the door leading to the kitchen. Mark sighed, pushed back his hardly touched salad plate, and stood. He picked up his glass, struck it with his knife, and waited while the chime hushed the conversation throughout the room.

"Ladies and gentlemen. Please let me welcome you all to Silver Springs Winery and thank you for coming. Many of you have been to dinners with the winemaker at Silver Springs before, so I am sure you are aware that my wife, Sabrina, and I are recent additions. We hope that this, our first event, hasn't disappointed you."

A smattering of applause and Mark went on.

"Of course, the true credit goes to our chef, who needs no introduction, but I would like him to come out of the kitchen so we can thank him personally. Otto Messinger, ladies and gentlemen."

This time a bigger round of applause and Otto appeared.

"Will you look at that," Dan whispered. "The guy can smile."

"It's a wonderful thing, applause," I said.

"Check out Frank," Dan whispered. "Otto's not getting any applause from him."

He wasn't getting any from Jolene, either. I hoped that Otto wouldn't notice but would have bet even money that he did.

"Thank you, Otto," Mark continued, neatly cutting off the speech Otto looked like he was about to deliver. "Now, ladies and gentlemen, please join me in the cellar. We will do a little barrel tasting, a sneak preview of next year's releases, and I will try to answer any of your questions about wine making. I'm sure we all need a little stretch before we try the wonderful main course Otto has for us, and he tells me dessert will be a big surprise. I will join you in the cellar."

Chairs were pushed back, laughter and chatting resumed, and people started to move. Most headed toward the stairway that led down to the cellar floor; others headed for the restrooms. Frank assisted Aunt Mary with her chair; Carlton was on his feet heading for Jolene's. Too late. Ian Applby got there first. Dan and I grinned at each other and started to push back our own chairs when Otto descended.

"I trust you are all enjoying the meal?" He stood there, arms folded across his chest, jaw sticking out, tall hat quivering.

"It's magnificent, Otto," Ian Applby told him. He reached out and steadied Jolene. "One of your finest efforts."

"You are right. Although I am sure it has not received fine comments. Not around this table full of thieves and liars." He glared up at all of us except Aunt Mary. She was the only one at his eye level.

"I would be very careful, Otto. Someday my good temper will fail me." Frank's low, soft baritone seemed somehow more threatening in comparison to Otto's unfortunate squeaky tenor, which now went up in pitch.

"I am not only a great chef; I am an honest man," Otto went on, ignoring Frank's threat. "This one," he pointed to Jolene, who now slipped her arm through Ian Applby's, "has no palate to taste the wine, no discrimination for the food, and no talent for the writing. Bah! Hypocrite!" Finished with Jolene, he turned back to Frank and with a sweeping gesture included Mark. "It is only too bad she doesn't write about the Tortellis as they really are. As thieves. Like father, like son."

"Now hold it," Mark exploded.

"How dare you!" Frank said.

"How dare I? Easily." Otto folded his arms and nodded, making his hat tremble.

"That is a terrible thing to say," stated Aunt Mary.

"It is a terrible thing to do," persisted Otto. "Mr. Applby, you are supposedly an intelligent man. Why then have you chosen for yourself a nest of vipers?"

"I think you had better explain." Ian Applby's tone was low, but grim. He still held onto, or propped up, Jolene, but his glare was directed at Sabrina, who now appeared behind Mark.

"Frank Tortelli made his reputation on one of my recipes. That is a well known fact," started Otto.

"Known only to you," Frank said, through gritted teeth.

"No. To others, as you well know. And his son, his son steals wine!" finished Otto, triumphant.

"Steals—I knew it." Carlton Carpenter had been uncharacteristically quiet up to now but evidently could no longer contain himself.

"Ah, the real estate man. The investment advisor," Otto sneered "So, you are here, also. Are you looking for other clients to cheat?"

"What are you talking about?" demanded Ian Applby, ignoring Carlton. He stared at Otto before swinging around to face Mark. "What wine? What is he talking about?"

"The man's a raving lunatic." Mark threw down his napkin. His expression was furious, but something flickered in his eyes. "I have a barrel tasting to do."

"Yes. We know that," said Mr. Applby. His eyebrows drew together as he frowned, his eyes moving back and forth between Mark and Otto. "But what about this wine business?"

"There's nothing to it. Just a misunderstanding. I'll explain it later." He looked directly at Ian Applby. "To you. When we have some privacy."

Mr. Applby nodded, but he didn't look happy as Mark stomped off. Sabrina started after him, paused, looked back at us, flung her arms out into space and said, "Otto, please."

"Phuf," the genius said, glared at everyone, gave his head a toss, which made his hat go wild, and stalked back toward the kitchen.

"That man is impossible," Mr. Applby said. "We are lucky his little diatribe was confined to this table alone." He turned to Sabrina with an expression of grim dissatisfaction. "I hope that next time you will follow my advice." His tone was low but it had the impact of a whip on bare flesh. Sabrina flinched, the color drained out of her face, but she said nothing. "My dear Miss Bixby," he went on, "shall we join the others in the wine cellar? It will be very instructive to see how Mark conducts this little tour. And the tasting."

Ian Applby and Jolene headed for the stairs, followed closely by Carlton, the partner. Frank's eyes were blazing, but the smile he gave Aunt Mary was bland and sunny.

"Shall we join them? I have heard many good things about next year's Syrah and am anxious to taste it."

Aunt Mary gave us a quick glance, received Dan's slight nod and moved off with Frank, listening to his impromptu lecture on the virtues of Bordeaux wines.

"Otto's going to get us fired, I just know it," Sabrina said. "Why, why didn't I listen to Mr. Applby? And everyone else who said he was awful? The article in *Food and Wine* raved about him. When I heard he was here, in Santa Louisa, I was thrilled. Temperamental? No problem. They're all temperamental. Look at Frank. I had no idea I couldn't control that vicious little humpty dumpty."

"Mr. Applby seems like a reasonable man," Dan told her. "I'm sure everything is going to work out fine."

"Yeah?" Such cynicism would do justice to the current Middle East peace negotiator. "I'd better get back to the kitchen. All these tables have to be reset and Mark's barrel tasting won't last long."

Sabrina hurried off.

Neither of us said anything for a moment.

"I thought you promised me a fun evening," Dan finally said.

"It's had its moments," I told him a little faintly.

"That it has. Want to go see Mark siphon wine out of barrels?"

"Not especially. What I really want is a cup of coffee. At home. On my own front porch."

"With Jake in your lap?" laughed Dan. Jake, my big yellow tomcat, had a real fondness for laps.

"He's more likely to be in yours," I sighed. "As long as Mark and Sabrina's poodle is around, he won't be in either of our laps."

"Paris is a good dog, but Jake sure does hate him. That reminds me. Any word on Mark and Sabrina's house hunting? Not that I mind them being there, of course," he said hastily.

"Sir," I told him with mock seriousness, "I think I have good news. Come on, let's go downstairs, and I'll fill you in on the latest."

We slowly descended the stairs to be met with the coolness of the cellar floor and the yeasty richness of fermenting wine. There was a low murmur of voices, a laugh loud in the cavernous space. Someone handed us each a glass with about a swallow of ruby red wine.

"This cabernet sauvignon is only two years old, but what a nose it has. Here, try it."

I obediently held the glass up to my nose and swirled the liquid around, watching the wine as it dripped down the inside of the glass.

"What are you doing?" asked Dan.

"Looking at the 'legs,'" I told him.

"The what? Why do you do that?"

"I have no idea," I answered, "but this is what Sabrina told me to do, so—"

"Are you going to drink that stuff?"

"I doubt it. Are you?"

"No. Here. Let's go over there."

Dan took both glasses, emptied them into the open concrete drainage line that ran along one side of the cellar floor under the tall stainless steel tanks, put the glasses down on an upright barrel and started to lead me away. We could see Mark standing in the middle of a small group, with what looked like an oversized meat baster in his hand, pointing at the oak barrels stacked up to the ceiling.

"That stack of barrels is 'racked,'" he said. "The wine is resting, picking up flavor. It should be ready for bottling next year."

"There are several people here tonight who might be improved by racking. The kind they did in the middle ages," I muttered.

Dan laughed. "Remind me to stay on your good side."

We were at the other end of the cellar, standing beside huge stacks of boxes, labeled with the famous Silver Springs logo. No one was around, and the voices that had echoed so annoyingly were muted.

"Ellie, have Mark and Sabrina found a place yet?"

The abruptness of Dan's question startled me. "Yes. That's what I was going to tell you. They put a deposit on a house this morning." I paused and asked, "Are you glad?"

"Oh," he started, trying to be nonchalant. "I just wondered. Jake really does hate that dog. And we have so much to do the next couple of months, to get ready for the wedding and all." He grinned somewhat sheepishly, then, without looking directly at me, went on. "When are they moving out?"

"Next weekend probably. Are you glad?"

"Well." Dan still wasn't looking at me. "They have been staying with you almost a month." Now he did look at me and smiled. A corny kind of smile, half hidden under his mustache. "It's put a crimp in our love life."

"It's been awkward, but…"

"I know, I know. Sabrina is your niece, you have a large house, it's the house you and your sister grew up in, and you could hardly refuse when she called and asked if they could stay."

"Could I have? This job came up so suddenly, and they didn't have time to find anything. Besides, I've enjoyed them. It's given me a chance to get to know Sabrina. Catherine never came home to California much, and Brian and I somehow never made it back East. I thought you liked them, too."

"I do like them. They're great kids. But a month's a long time. And I've missed you."

I didn't say anything for a minute. I knew what he meant. I'd missed him, too. Long, lazy evenings, waking up the next morning with him warm beside me, sharing coffee and the news paper over my kitchen table, those things hadn't been the same with Mark and Sabrina wandering through the house. I'd loved those times. Oh, Dan had continued to stay a couple of nights a week, and I'd spent a few nights at his condo, but that hadn't worked out. His next-door neighbor, Mrs. Bloom, a friend of my mother's, made a point of being on her front porch each time I left. I felt as if I were back in high school. It wasn't much better at my house. Moving over politely for Mark and Sabrina in the kitchen, making sure we didn't dawdle in the bathroom, ignoring closed bedroom doors, having to get dressed for breakfast. I knew exactly what he meant and looked forward to having my home back, and, sometimes, to being in it by myself.

"You see me every day," I said.

"We're never alone," he said. "I like cuddling with you on the couch, watching dumb movies and eating ice cream."

"We still do that." Blast the man. He made me feel guilty because, deep down, I suspected I'd used Mark and Sabrina to slow things down. I loved Dan, but our wedding date was roaring toward me like a freight train run amuck.

"Yeah, but then I either go home or tiptoe around like some intruder. I like going to bed with you and getting up with you," he said pointedly. "I like talking to you at midnight without wondering if I'm waking anyone else, and I don't like sharing a bathroom. With anyone but you, that is." He reached over and ran his finger slowly down my jaw and under my chin, tilting my face up toward his. "Nothing's been the same." He dropped his hand and looked away from me. "Anyway, I'm glad they've found a place. Do you think they need help moving?"

I stared at Dan for a moment, then burst out laughing.

"What's so funny?"

"You," I managed. "You're as transparent as tissue paper!"

"Maybe so, but Ellie, if they're out on Saturday, maybe Sunday we could."

"So, this is where you're hiding."

The voice in my ear almost made me jump out of my skin.

"Hello, Carlton," Dan said. If it were true looks could kill, Carlton would be in his coffin on his way to the grave.

"Isn't this a wonderful dinner?" boomed Carlton, oblivious to danger. "And the wines!" He held up a glass with a little red wine in the bottom, made a show of holding it to his nose, then inexpertly swirled it. "What a stroke of luck Mildred wanted to sell," he said, oozing self-satisfaction.

"And another that you had cash in your pocket, just ready to buy," I said in my sweetest voice. Dan smothered a nasty laugh.

"Yes. It was," Carlton answered. The look he gave me was uncertain, almost scared, but he quickly replaced it with his usual overconfident one. "I'd gone over to Mildred's to see if she wanted to sell her house, we got to talking, and the next thing I knew, I was a winery partner."

"You told me." Carlton didn't notice the sarcasm in my voice. Dan did. "I thought you weren't in real estate anymore," he said, but it was me he looked at. I could tell he was holding back a laugh.

"I do a few deals," Carlton said, examining his wine instead of looking Dan in the face. "Special ones."

"Didn't I read that you represented Otto when he bought the old Adams house?"

"No," I corrected Dan. "Carlton had the listing. He represented the sellers." I remembered how surprised everyone in my office had been when we found out Carlton had gotten the listing on that wonderful antique mansion. Not only was Carpenter Real Estate a one-man office, but old Mrs. Adams had hated him. Something to do with one of her granddaughters when we were all in high school.

"I had both the buyer and seller. It wasn't fun," he said, frowning.

That I was willing to believe. I wondered if his commission had bought his winery shares.

"I don't see how you got the parking requirements met for a restaurant," Dan went on. "The town is usually pretty strict about that."

Carlton's eyes shifted, and he swallowed hard. Our whole office had wondered about that parking, but there would be no answer tonight. Parking was not what Carlton wanted to talk about.

"Ellen, I told you Mark had stolen wine. What do you think now?"

"Mark didn't steal anything," I said in my coldest tone. "You heard him. It was a misunderstanding."

"I'm not so sure," Carlton said slowly, looking at everything but us. "You know, there are some pretty important people who are partners in Silver Springs. Cappy Lewis, the western singer, Nona Pickert, who was in that movie, some period thing."

That was about all I could take. "She was in *Pride and Prejudice* and won the Oscar. What's your point?"

"Well, I feel responsible. After all, I live here. No one else does. Why, we could get robbed blind if someone doesn't keep an eye out. Dan, I thought you could do some kind of background check. Don't you think that's a good idea?" Carlton was back to his pompous self.

"No." Dan didn't bother to soften the single word. "Whatever happened is between Mark and Ian Applby. If he's satisfied with Mark's explanation, then you should be, also."

Carlton flushed a little. Embarrassment? Frustration? Anger? I didn't care. The man irritated me in the best of circumstances, and irritation was about to give way to plain mad.

"Well!" Carlton glared at both of us. We glanced at each other before looking blandly back at him. He repeated, "Well! Then I will take this matter up with my partner." He turned on his heel and walked back to the group, many of whom were starting up the stairs.

"What a jerk," I said.

"He gets first prize," Dan agreed.

"Mr. Applby seems like a reasonable man. I wonder how he feels about Carlton as a partner."

"If the expression he's worn all night is any indication, he's less than thrilled. I think he's already discovered that Carlton's a not-too-bright, name-dropping leech."

I burst out laughing. "No one can ever accuse you of not calling them as you see them." But my amusement didn't last long. I watched Carlton disappear into a small group of people and watched a couple of them fade off into other groups who had started back up the stairs into the dining room. "Poor Mark. Poor Sabrina. First Otto, now Carlton."

"I wonder," Dan said, "what do you suppose that whole wine stealing thing was all about?"

"What? Is this the policeman in you showing through? Mark wouldn't do anything like that and you know it."

Dan slipped my arm through his and said, "I'm sure you're right. Shall we go upstairs and partake of lamb?"

We, too, climbed the stairs, laughing as we reentered the dining room, but tucked away in the back of my head was a little thought: What had happened at Mark's last job?

Chapter Six

Aunt Mary was the only one at the table.

"Where's Frank?" I asked her. "He hasn't had his hands off you since we arrived."

"Really, Ellen." Her tone was reproving, but there was a little self-satisfaction in those blue eyes. We never outgrow flattery, and if it comes by way of a handsome man, or woman, so much the better.

"Where is Frank?" asked Dan. "And everyone else? Don't tell me they're not coming back for the second act."

"We should be so lucky," I said.

We seated ourselves, and Dan started to count the new wine-glasses on the table, shaking his head, and mumbling a little.

"For heavens sake," I told him. "There are two more courses and then dessert, and there are eight people. Makes for a lot of glasses."

I looked around the room, wondering if I should excuse myself and check on Sabrina, when I spotted Carlton boring a small group that contained our state senator and the newly elected mayor, who looked longingly at his chair. Ah, the trials of public office.

"Where is everybody?" I asked again.

"Jolene was in the ladies' earlier. Trying to put on fresh lipstick." Aunt Mary's own lips pursed a little.

"Let's hope she hasn't passed out in one of the stalls," Dan said. "Sabrina wouldn't be pleased."

"Really, Dan," said Aunt Mary.

He grinned. So did I. "It will be interesting to read her review of this dinner," I said, "since she hasn't had more than three bites of it."

"You can tell a lot from three bites," Dan said, laughing.

"Where is everybody?" It was Ian Applby's turn to ask as he sat down, nodding to each of us. "Ah, yes, there's Carpenter. And Miss Bixby? Has anyone, ah—?"

"Last spotted in the ladies'," I said irreverently. I heard a soft "meow" from Dan's direction. I ignored it.

"Good, good. And Frank? Where is he?" Ian Applby addressed this to Aunt Mary, who flushed faintly.

"I lost track of Frank right after Mark's wonderful talk. I met the Jensens. I had no idea they came to these things, and we got to chatting, and well, I haven't seen Frank since."

"A fine man, Frank," Ian Applby said. "I've known him for years. I can't for the life of me understand why he sold Tortelli's. That restaurant was his life's blood."

I wanted to know more about Frank and his restaurant, but before I had a chance to ask there was a voice in my ear. "Ellen. There you are." A hand rested on my shoulder. I jumped badly. Thank goodness there was no glass in my hand. "Hello, Mrs. McGill, Mr. Applby, Dan. Ellen, how do you like the dinner so far?"

It was Larry Whittaker. I had forgotten all about him, but here he was, smiling that proprietary little smile.

"It's wonderful, Larry."

"Good. I'm especially looking forward to your opinion of the dessert. That is my creation, no matter what Otto says. You will let me know how you like it?"

"Of course." I barely got that out before he rushed away. His hat didn't bob as much as Otto's. Why, I wondered, but quickly decided I didn't want to find out.

"It seems you have an admirer," Ian Applby smiled.

"No. Larry and I knew each other in high school, that's all." I took a look at Dan out of the corner of my eye. He wasn't paying attention to us. Instead, he was looking at the picture window that looked out on the wine tanks.

"Did you know there's some kind of catwalk up around the top of those tanks?" Dan asked.

"Yes," I answered.

"You can barely see it. I'll bet you can see the whole cellar floor from that window, though," he went on. "What a great idea. You can watch the winemaker, or whoever, do whatever he does."

Mr. Applby smiled. "It's especially interesting when they are blending the wine, putting the raw juice into the tanks, or emptying the tanks into the barrels. You can watch the whole thing from the comfort of the tasting room, glass of the finished product in hand."

I thought Dan was going to get up and take in the view, but the waiters were filling glasses and serving plates. The lamb course kept him in his seat.

Jolene sat down, fresh lipstick in place, followed immediately by Carlton.

"I was talking to the mayor," he began in a ponderous tone.

"We saw you," said Dan. He took his first bite of lamb. It must have been good. He paused, took another bite, and smiled.

Aunt Mary examined Jolene carefully and said, "Are you all right? You were a long time in the bathroom."

Jolene looked startled. "I'm fine, just fine." She reached for her wineglass. "It was my hair. It just wouldn't cooperate at all. You know how that is." She smiled at me.

I wasn't prepared for that little barb, so my usual snappy comeback didn't come. Dan, however, came to the rescue. He leaned over the table toward Jolene. "Tell us your opinion of the meal, so far. Is this up to Otto's usual standard?"

Jolene, who hadn't as yet tasted anything on her plate, looked a little surprised and quickly snatched up a fork, gingerly dipping it in the sauce. She hadn't had a chance to do more than that when Frank slid into his place, looking harried. He was followed closely by Mark.

"What have we here?" Frank took a deep breath and picked up his fork. "Hmm. Lamb, the sauce is a little tricky. You can overdo the mint. Stir-fried vegetables, they don't look too bad, and Mark's wine. Shall we try it?"

We did. Conversation stopped. The lamb disappeared; the fromage course arrived, and all plates, except Jolene's, were empty before it started again.

I had leaned back a little in my chair, blocking out the talk, when I saw Sabrina. She was outside the now closed French doors, waving at me frantically.

"What now?" I pushed back my chair.

"Where are you going?" asked Aunt Mary.

"Outside. I need a little air." Sabrina was still signaling, but with more gestures. Now her finger was over her lips, and she was shaking her head. Then she pointed to me and shook her head some more. Evidently I was to come alone.

"I'll come with you," offered Dan. His back was to the doors and he hadn't spotted Sabrina.

"I'll be right back." I smiled brightly at his puzzled face and headed for the doors. Sabrina had disappeared.

"What's going on?" Sabrina was over by the railing, looking down at the crush pad. There was a tray with several empty glasses on our picnic table.

"Look." The tragedy in her voice would have made Lady Macbeth proud. "Tell me I'm seeing things, because I don't want to believe this."

"Believe what?" I walked toward the edge of the deck, to where one side of the gate that had been securely fastened a short time ago now swung open, and looked down. She didn't have to explain, and she wasn't seeing things. There was Otto, half submerged in the fermenting tank, the thick cap the only thing keeping him from sinking. One side of his head dripped a trickle of bright blood into the duller, dark red juice. His tall hat, no longer white, lay quietly beside him. On his other side was the champagne bottle.

"Oh my God," I got out.

"Mark will be so upset," Sabrina said, shock making a blank mask of her face. "I don't think they will be able to use that wine now."

Chapter Seven

Frozen, I stared down at Otto, or what had once been Otto. The sound of the French doors opening and the scrape of footsteps defrosted me quickly.

"Ellie? What's going on? Sabrina?" Dan's voice was merely curious.

"Don't come over here!" Sabrina jumped between Dan and the railing.

"Why?" Dan caught her by the shoulders and gently moved her aside. "Okay, Ellie. What's wrong?"

"Oh, lots. Look down there."

"Son of a—How did he get in that tank?"

"How would I know?"

"Sabrina?" Dan asked.

"I don't know." Her hands flew to her face, and she gasped. "The dessert. It's time to serve. Damn that Otto. I just knew he meant to ruin everything."

"I doubt if he meant to do it by dying," Dan said.

"Are you sure he's dead?" But I knew better.

"Am I—Come on, Ellie. Look at the man."

I already had.

"I need to call it in. Sabrina, I need Mark's office. That one?" He pointed toward one of the closed doors. She nodded. "You two, stay here. No, don't stay here. Come with me."

"Dan. Don't call it in yet." Sabrina was almost in tears. "Let me finish the dinner. This will ruin everything."

"Sabrina, the man is dead. And something about the dent in his head makes me think he didn't jump. I am a cop, remember? What's more, I am the Chief. Come on."

Sabrina and I followed Dan back through the dining room. I rolled my eyes at Aunt Mary as we passed our table. She started to push back her chair but I shook my head at her, and she stopped. She looked puzzled and a little alarmed. Exactly how I felt. It was clear Dan didn't think Otto had hit himself on the head and then jumped into the wine tank, which left murder, and that meant a long and uncomfortable night.

"In here?" Dan asked Sabrina, pushing open one of the doors.

"Yes. Can you at least ask them not to come with sirens blaring?"

A reasonable request, I thought, but Dan didn't respond.

"You two, don't move. And if anyone asks you any questions, don't answer. I'll be right back." He closed the office door behind him.

"Sabrina." It was Larry Whittaker. "We've cleared all the plates, and I think we should serve the dessert, but I can't find Otto."

"Oh, Lord," Sabrina said faintly.

"Is something wrong?" The anxious look he'd worn when Otto was having his temper tantrum in the kitchen had returned.

"Why don't you go ahead," I said. "I'm sure Otto won't mind." I was more than sure. I was positive.

"How true," murmured Sabrina. "Go on, Larry. Serve it."

"If you're sure." Larry looked doubtfully from one of us to the other.

"I'm sure," Sabrina told him. "Very sure."

"All right." He started to leave, stopped, and turned back. "What are you doing out here? Ellen, I really want you to try this dessert. Aren't you going back to your table?"

"Oh, yes. It's just that Dan had to make a phone call. I'm waiting for him."

"Oh. Well, all right." He finally left, and we could hear muffled voices and clinking plate noises from the room next to the kitchen. Almost immediately, the first waiter appeared with a loaded tray.

Dan appeared at the same time, almost knocking the waiter down.

"What are they doing?"

"Serving the dessert. You aren't going to let any of those people go until your minions arrive and you've had a chance to question them. They might as well be happy until then."

He scowled and started to say something, thought better of it, and nodded. "Not a bad idea. People have a tendency to leave if they think they're going to get mixed up in something unpleasant."

"And you think this is going to be unpleasant?"

"It already is. Come on. Let's go revisit the folks at our table."

◇◇◇

Full dessert plates, dessert wine, coffee, and Larry were waiting for us.

"I couldn't wait to see how you like this. It's my own creation."

I had no choice but to take a mouthful of rich, yummy, unwanted dessert. Mousse, made of both light and dark chocolate, rested on a bed of raspberry sauce, topped with fresh raspberries surrounded by tiny green leaves. Any other time I would have been in ecstasy. Now, I could hardly swallow it.

"It's wonderful. Best I've ever eaten." I hoped he'd go away, or at least stop leaning over the back of my chair. Sabrina was directing the waiters, helping to pour coffee, and smiling at guests who kept stopping her. I didn't know how she did it. Maybe reality hadn't set in yet. It had for me. My hand was shaking as I picked up my coffee cup.

"What's the matter with you?" asked Aunt Mary.

"Nothing," I said, switching to Muscat Canelli. "Nothing at all."

"Oh, yes, there is, and you'd better tell me. Dan, what's going on? What are those sirens?"

"We have a little problem." Dan now had the attention of everyone at our table. "It seems that Otto has met with a mishap. The sirens are the ambulance and my police."

"Mishap?" asked Ian Applby. "What kind of mishap?"

"Ambulance? He's hurt?" Mark asked.

"Apoplexy. I knew it would happen some day," said Frank, holding up the wine to the light.

"Counn." Jolene paused, refocused on her wineglass, and managed to connect with it, then tried again. "Couldn't happen to a better guy. Appa, appoploxy. Appaplexy?"

Mr. Applby pulled away from Jolene a little; his face a careful blank. Carlton waited to move in.

"Now, we don't know yet what happened," he told Jolene, in one of those condescending "let's not upset the little woman" tones. He turned to Dan, fake concern in his voice. "I hope he's going to be all right?"

"Actually, no," Dan said. "He's bobbing around out in the fermenting tank, dead. You're all going to have to stay here while we try and find out who helped him into it."

"The fermenting tank? My fermenting tank? No. He can't; he wouldn't," Mark said. He looked horrified. He started to push his chair back, but Dan, who was already on his feet, put his hand gently on Mark's shoulder, forcing him back down.

"I doubt if it was Otto's idea," he said, shedding the last of his party demeanor and putting on his official deadpan expression. "It's time for me to go to work."

The sirens, which had gotten very loud, stopped. The room filled up with uniforms. The other guests started to get up, panic and excitement in their voices. Dan walked to the end of the room, in front of the French doors, and in a commanding voice explained to the crowd that there had been an accident, and, if they would all be patient, someone would come around to each table to get their names and phone numbers. They would need to know where each person was sitting, and would they all please hold themselves available for questioning.

"Why?" someone called out.

"We always need to place our witnesses," was his cryptic reply.

"What does that mean?" I asked Aunt Mary.

"I have no idea," she said.

"Otto dead!" Once more Larry made me jump. He had taken Dan's chair, and I hadn't even noticed.

"Who will take over the restaurant? Or the bed and breakfast? Our grand opening dinner is scheduled for a week from Saturday. Jolene was staying with us just so she could cover it."

"S'right," Jolene acknowledged.

Aunt Mary eyed Jolene a little quizzically. "You're staying there, aren't you?"

"S'right," Jolene said again.

Aunt Mary and I looked at each other. She raised one eyebrow, and I shrugged. I thought they hated each other. Evidently Aunt Mary did also.

"Grand opening?" Frank sounded surprised. "I didn't realize Otto had come so far. Hmm. That soon."

"I suppose I could do it." Larry was sitting rigidly upright. "I do most of the prep anyway, and I know all Otto's recipes. What do you think, Ellen? Do you think I could?"

How would I know what you can do, I wanted to snap. Last time I saw you, we were trying to figure out how to do geometry. And how could he talk about cooking when his employer was bizarrely dead in a wine tank?

"This will not do the winery any good," Ian Applby said. "This kind of publicity, good God. Think of the headlines. And the TV cameras! Somehow we've got to keep them away. Sabrina. That should be her job."

"Where is Sabrina?" Carlton jumped right in. "She should be here, taking charge."

"The police seem to be doing a good job of that," Mark said. Stress lines were deepening around his mouth by the minute.

"Still, Sabrina should be here, doing something."

"Shut up, Carlton." I gaped in amazement. I had never in my life heard Aunt Mary use that phrase. But she had spotted

Sabrina, and so had I. She was standing against the wall next to the kitchen, her expression terrified, her eyes teary, watching a grim-faced Dan come through the French doors. He carried the empty champagne bottle, dripping red wine, on the end of a pencil, and headed straight toward her.

Chapter Eight

Voices seeped through my sleep-soaked brain. A dog barked. Someone shushed it. The phone rang. Someone quickly picked it up. I turned over and pulled the pillow over my head. It didn't do any good. I was awake.

I rolled back and looked at the clock. Seven o'clock. On a Sunday morning I didn't want to face. Last night had been horrible. Police all over the place, asking questions, taking notes. Dan put on his official face and hid behind it until, somewhere around two o'clock, he seemed to run out of questions and let us go. Frank had taken Aunt Mary home earlier, so it was Mark, Sabrina, and me. None of us had said anything; there was nothing more to say. We all climbed the stairs, fell into bed and, in my case, instantly fell asleep. But the sun was up, so were Mark and Sabrina, and I had better be also. Sighing, I slipped on my long terrycloth robe, knotted the sash, and headed for the kitchen.

Coffee. Fresh made. An omen. Probably the only good one this day would offer, but I was prepared to take it. I paused long enough to let Jake out the front and shove Paris out the back before joining the others in the kitchen.

Mark was on the phone, running his fingers through his hair, and pacing around the kitchen table where Sabrina sat staring into a mug. She looked up briefly as I entered, then again looked down. Her eyes were red and puffy, the way they get when you're exhausted. Or when you've been crying.

"Okay. Pete is between crushes. I can use his? Great," he said, jamming the phone into its cradle. He barely glanced at me as he said, "Hi, Ellen. See you." The screen door slammed, then immediately reopened.

"Here. Keep this dog in until I leave, will you?" and he was gone. Paris immediately lay down in the middle of the kitchen floor.

"What was he talking about?" I asked, stepping over the dog to get to the coffeepot.

"He has grapes coming and no place to crush them. The police still have our crush pad, the tasting room, the whole damn winery shut down. Pete Brown over at Oak Valley is letting him use his pad. Mark's been on the phone since five trying to find something."

"They're still there?" I asked, meaning the police, not the grapes. "When are they going to be through?"

"Who knows?"

"Who knows what?" The screen door slammed again and Aunt Mary sailed in.

"When Dan's people will let everyone back into the winery. Coffee's hot." I pulled out a chair and sat across from Sabrina. Aunt Mary took a mug off the hutch, filled it, stepped over the dog, and took up residence beside me.

"Why don't you ask Dan?"

"I haven't seen him."

"You will," Sabrina said grimly. "And soon."

"How do you know that?" Aunt Mary asked.

"Because he thinks I killed Otto," Sabrina said, letting gloom drip from every word. "Not that I wasn't tempted. Only I would have waited until dinner was over. Now everything is ruined. Mark will probably be fired. I know I will be, and neither of us will ever work again."

Aunt Mary and I looked at each other. I shrugged. She said, "That seems a little, well, dramatic, Sabrina. After all, none of last night was your fault."

"Do you mean the murder?" Sabrina asked bitterly, finally looking up from her coffee cup, "or Frank's sudden appearance.

Or perhaps you're talking about getting stuck with Jolene Bixby? Of all the luck. And then there's that prize partner, Carlton Carpenter, telling everyone who'll listen that Mark is a thief."

I must have shown my surprise because Sabrina almost smiled. "Oh, we know what he's saying. It's not true, of course, but rumors can do as much damage as truth. More. And believe me, we know."

"How? How do you know?" I paused, looked at Aunt Mary, who nodded encouragement, and proceeded to press my point. "What happened at the last winery; what was it?"

"Lighthouse," supplied Sabrina.

"Right. What happened there that has everyone in a flap?"

"Nothing." She looked down into her mug again, a light flush staining her cheeks. "But I'm sure Mr. Applby thinks something did, thanks to Carlton. And Otto. He never let up all night about how he was going to ruin Frank Tortelli and his whole family. I'll be held responsible for all that. Going to jail might even be a relief after last night." She put her head in her hands and groaned. A really good groan.

Something had happened at Lighthouse Winery, but I decided to ignore it, and Sabrina's self-pity, for the moment, and instead picked up on something that interested me. "What do you mean, getting stuck with Jolene? I thought she was some hotshot wine and food writer." I wanted to know about Frank, also, but Jolene and her relationship with Otto had me confused. I didn't get an answer. Instead, the screen door slammed. This time it was Dan.

"Have you seen your front lawn?" he asked, reaching for a mug and emptying the pot. "You're out of coffee."

"What's wrong with my front lawn?" I took the pot out of his hand and started to fill it with water. He didn't answer right away, just handed me the coffee out of the refrigerator, topped his mug off with cream, and opened the cupboard next to the sink.

"The sugar is on the table. What's wrong with my front lawn?"

"It's full of reporters. Also, one TV truck, and I'm pretty sure I spotted another coming over the bridge."

"Probably waiting to see you take me out in handcuffs," Sabrina muttered.

"Dan, you're not going to arrest her!" Aunt Mary exclaimed. "Why, you wouldn't!"

"I'm only going to talk to her," Dan said, his gaze steady on Sabrina's face. "But, Ellie, if you want to save those pink flowers you've got out under the elm tree, you'd better get going."

"What?" I almost yelled. "My petunias. What are they doing to my petunias?"

"Walking on them."

"Oh. Oh!" I headed for the front door, Aunt Mary right behind.

Dan was right. There were people milling around on the sidewalk, chatting with each other, scribbling something in notebooks, peering through camera lenses toward my front door. No one was in my flower bed, but that looked temporary. I reached for the front door handle.

"You can't go out there." Aunt Mary grabbed my hand.

"Why not? It's my lawn they're on."

"Because you're not dressed. Look at you."

She was right. No one was going to see me in this disgusting old robe.

"Stay here and keep an eye on them. The first one steps in my flowers, let him have it."

"With what? And what are you going to do?"

"Get dressed. Yell at them. Threaten them. Tell them we have the police chief in the kitchen and we'll turn him loose on them. Sic Paris on them."

"Nothing would make that dog happier than to pose for pictures. He'd probably end up on every news broadcast from here to Atlanta." She looked down at the dog. He looked back, his tongue rolling out of the side of his mouth. Aunt Mary sighed. "Go on, get dressed. I'll stand here and watch."

I ran up the stairs, pulled back the bedroom curtain to get a better view of the slowly building group, said a really good four-letter word, pulled on some pants and a tee shirt, ignoring my hair and abandoning any thought of makeup. I had reached the bedroom door when I remembered what Aunt Mary had said. Pictures. Newspapers from here to Atlanta. That certainly included Southern California. I knew people down there. Brian and his girlfriend lived down there. Damn. Back to the bathroom I went, ran a comb through my hair, checked the mirror to make sure I didn't look as beat-up as I felt, and raced back down.

"They aren't doing much," Aunt Mary observed. "And they're staying on the sidewalk."

"Hmm. Well, I guess we can go finish our coffee. But we had better keep checking. I can't believe all this. Why are they here, anyway?"

"I told you." Sabrina was sitting alone at the table. "They think they're going to see the murderer, me, come out the front door in handcuffs."

"Where's Dan?" I asked.

"Gone." No basset hound in the world ever looked sadder. "He said what he had to say and left."

"He left?" I asked. His empty mug, still sitting on the table, was proof she was right.

"What are you talking about?" Aunt Mary asked. She walked over to the table and took a closer look at Sabrina. "Have you eaten this morning?"

"Eaten?" She looked as if she'd forgotten what that meant. "No."

"No wonder your nerves are frazzled. Ellen, do you have any juice?"

"In the refrigerator. What did Dan say?"

"I don't want any juice. That my fingerprints are on the gate latch."

"You're having some anyway." Aunt Mary put a full glass of apple juice in front of her. "Drink. Now. Did you touch the gate? You must have. When?"

Sabrina drank. She finished half the glass before she answered. "Right before I saw Otto in the tank. I was on the cellar floor collecting empty glasses. I remembered I'd left a dirty dish tray on the deck." She paused. "Remember, Ellen? We set it down on the deck when we moved the table, and I forgot to take it inside."

I thought back and nodded.

"And then what?" pressed Aunt Mary. She put a glass of juice in front of me, also, and headed for the stove with what was left of my bacon.

"I walked up the ramp past the crush pad and over the lawn onto the deck. The gate was slightly open, so I put the glasses on the tray and went over to close it. That's when I saw him."

"But," Aunt Mary said, looking puzzled, "that's not enough to arrest someone." She turned down the fire under the frying pan and faced us. "Besides, what about other prints? Surely lots of people have opened that gate."

"Evidently mine were the only ones."

"Aunt Mary's right. That's not enough to arrest anyone. But it is odd." I thought back. Had either Dan or I touched the gate? I couldn't remember. "What else did Dan say?"

"That the champagne bottle wasn't the one that hit Otto on the head."

"Sabrina, if you don't stop this and tell us everything, I'm going to do a little head bopping of my own." I didn't bother to hide my irritation. My nerves were starting to go fast. Murder, reporters, my niece a possible suspect; the smell of cooking bacon was the only normal thing about this whole morning.

Sabrina actually smiled. "You sound just like my mother."

There was nothing to smile about in that statement. "I have never sounded like your mother. How do you know it wasn't the champagne?"

"They've already done some tests. No blood or tissue on it."

By tissue, I assumed they meant part of Otto's skull. Yuck. "Then what was he hit with, and how did he get into the tank?"

"That's what Dan asked me." One look at my face and she hastily went on. "He thinks it was another wine bottle. He was asking me questions about how we track the wine we pour, and what we do with the empty bottles."

"What do you do with them?" asked Aunt Mary. The bacon was out of the pan and draining on paper towels. My last four eggs were about to be scrambled.

"Put them back in the case boxes. They aren't corked anymore, so we know they're empty. We count them later. It's the same system we use at tastings. We know how many bottles we start out with, what varietals, so we know how many bottles of wine we used."

"So you'd know if a bottle was missing?"

"Sure. We have to keep close tabs on our inventory. Alcohol, and wine is alcohol, is something the government takes seriously, and we have to report all sales."

"Okay," I said. "So how would you go about finding a missing bottle?" I thought for a minute. "Or, more to the point, if you were a murderer, where would you stash a bottle you just used to bash in someone's head?"

"Well, you wouldn't drop it casually in the dumpster," said Aunt Mary. "Ellen, can you get some plates?"

I got up, went to the hutch and took down three. I also took out the toaster. She started serving eggs and bacon. "Do you have any more of that apricot jam I made? And make some fresh coffee. We're going to need it."

We were all back at the table, munching, before she returned to the wine bottle. "Could you wash a bottle off and put it back in the box?"

"I've no idea," said Sabrina. She laid down her fork, her eggs barely tasted. "All I know is I had nothing to do with Otto's death, and neither did Mark."

"Mark?" I asked. "Who said anything about Mark?"

I glanced over at Aunt Mary, who was looking at Sabrina with a puzzled expression. "What makes you think Mark might have done it?"

Sabrina lifted her chin indignantly, a great gesture spoiled because her eyes met neither of ours. "I don't think anything of the kind." She put more jam on her toast, looked down at it, then fed it to Paris. "But that dreadful Otto kept saying things, 'like father like son,' and Carlton kept dropping nasty comments about Mark, so he could be—" She stopped and looked around helplessly.

"A suspect?" I finished.

"No one in their right mind would suspect either one of you." Aunt Mary picked up Sabrina's plate, looked at the food left on it, shook her head a little, picked up her own empty one, and put them both in the sink. She watched the coffee slowly dripping into the pot, then turned and headed back for the table, almost tripping on Paris, who had followed her, evidently hoping for more leftovers. I thought she was going to grab his collar to pull him out of the way, but she walked around him and sank heavily into her chair.

Sabrina absently watched Paris abandon hopes of toast to stare at Jake, who was on top of the refrigerator, making soft growling noises. I stared at him, too. Who had let him in? Dan, of course. Sabrina shook her head slightly and went on. "I can think of lots of people who wouldn't have minded bashing Otto, people with better motives than Mark or me, but I can't picture how anyone did it."

"What do you mean?" The coffee had finished and was sitting in the pot, inviting me. I wondered if my already jangled nerves could handle another cup. Why not? I'd eaten my toast. "What's so mysterious about it? Someone snuck up behind him, bashed him with a wine bottle, opened the gate, and shoved him into the tank."

"No," said Aunt Mary slowly, "she's right. First, why was Otto on the deck when he should have been in the kitchen overseeing the waiters? Second, why didn't someone see something?"

I had no answer to the first question, but an answer to the second came to me, unbidden and unwelcome. Sabrina had been on the deck. She'd come up from the cellar floor. And everyone else was back in the dining room behind closed French doors. I hadn't seen her, and I didn't think anyone else had either.

"We don't know why Otto was out there." I refused to let that thought go anywhere. "But we know he was good at tormenting people. It had to be someone he'd pushed too far."

"Who might that be?" asked Aunt Mary.

"Everyone who ever knew him," answered Sabrina.

"That's not very helpful. Everyone who ever knew him wasn't there last night." I set my coffee mug on the table and sat back down. "How about Frank? He was there, and their feud was famous."

"Another of my favorite people. Wouldn't it be nice if it turned out to be Frank?" Sabrina looked wistful. "Only it wouldn't help Mark if Frank went to jail."

"Sabrina!" Aunt Mary said. She set her cup down with a bang. "Surely you don't mean that. Why, Mark would be devastated. After all, Frank is his father!"

"Unfortunately. But Mark devastated? I don't think so. Father is as father does, and Frank has been really good at not doing."

Aunt Mary did not look pleased. How late had Frank stayed last night, I suddenly wondered. I took another look at her. She did look better than usual. Her navy blue knit pants hardly bagged at the knee and the oversized white tee shirt was subdued by her standards. It did have a huge peacock across the front, but the colors were not totally garish, and it didn't say NBC or anything.

"I don't believe that Frank Tortelli is capable of murder," Aunt Mary went on firmly. "Besides, he doesn't have a motive."

"You've got to be kidding," I said. "You were there in that kitchen. They hated each other, they've hated each other for years, and Otto accused him of stealing. That sounds like a motive to me."

"Frank told me all about that," Aunt Mary said. "Everyone knows Otto was jealous of Frank. Tortelli's became a huge success after they broke up their partnership."

"I thought Otto was a big name chef also."

"He is," Sabrina said. "Was. Famous for his food, more famous for his temper."

"Did you know that before you asked him to do last night's dinner?"

"I'd heard about his explosions but didn't really believe it," she said. "From now on, I'm going to believe every rumor I hear."

"Right." I tried to read her face. I gave up and turned to Aunt Mary. "And what else did Frank have to say about Otto?"

"That no one believed all that nonsense about the recipe, and that Otto didn't bother him in the least."

"Yeah?" That may have been Frank's story, but I wasn't buying. And what was all that about him selling Tortelli's?

"Frank wasn't the only one who didn't like Otto," Aunt Mary stated, perhaps a bit more emphatically than necessary.

"True," I said, distracted from my thoughts of Tortelli's sale. "Carlton Carpenter, for one."

"Why would he want to kill Otto?" asked Aunt Mary.

"He said something funny last night, something that made me wonder."

"Oh?" asked Aunt Mary. "And what was that?"

"What's with this guy?" asked Sabrina. "Everybody acts as though they smell something bad when they see him coming. Really handsome guys don't usually affect people like that."

"They do if they act like Carlton," sighed Aunt Mary. "He uses his looks to get out of trouble and get in with what he considers the important people. He, well, he doesn't always use good judgment in how he goes about it. And the namedropping gets very tiresome."

"What she really means is," I said, "he's not very bright, his ethics are murky, and the only talent he has is to make sure someone else takes the fall when one of his scams falls apart."

"Ellen, really," Aunt Mary said, but she didn't say I was wrong.

"Which brings me back to last night. He told Dan and me that he represented both Otto and the Adams family in the sale of their old house."

"So?" Sabrina asked. "Is that unethical?"

"Not at all. As a matter of fact, as long as both buyer and seller agree, it can be an advantage to have only one agent involved. But if that agent doesn't disclose something he should have, then both sides can get hurt."

I got up, drained my cup into the sink, and filled it with fresh coffee. After all, caffeine can be bracing in times of crisis. I held the pot aloft, waiting for any takers.

"Here. I'll have some of that. Pour this cold stuff out, will you? What didn't Carlton disclose?" Aunt Mary picks up stuff fast. On the other hand, she'd known Carlton for years.

"Parking. The city requires plenty of parking before they issue permits for a restaurant. Evidently Otto got the permit, but I wonder how."

"So that's what…" Sabrina stopped, nodded, then shook her head. "No thanks, Ellen. My nerve endings are twanging fine. They don't need more help. You know, one of the things Otto was screaming about yesterday was the cost of having to put in a parking lot. I ignored him; after all, if you're going to have a restaurant, you have to have parking. I figured he was just having a good time complaining about one more thing. But if Carlton didn't tell him he had to put one in, and he wasn't prepared for all that extra expense, he had good reason to complain."

"About the cost and also about Carlton," said Aunt Mary slowly. "Ellen, if Otto complained to the Board of Realtors, could Carlton get in trouble?"

"Probably." I leaned up against the stove and thought about it. "It would depend on lots of things, but Carlton has been slapped on the hand before. It sure wouldn't be good for him, but I don't know if it would be serious enough for him to commit murder."

"You both think Frank could murder someone over an old partnership and a recipe," Aunt Mary said with a defensive sniff. "Sabrina, you keep making remarks about this Jolene Bixby, and Frank made a couple also. What about her?"

"Jolene's a lush."

"You don't say," I said.

Sabrina looked a little startled, then laughed. "It isn't hard to pick up on, is it? But she's a charming lush. At least, certain types of men think so. Most chefs don't."

"I thought she was a famous writer," said Aunt Mary.

"She would love to have you think so. She used to freelance, lots of the most prestigious food and wine magazines bought her stuff, but now she only writes for that Dallas-based one. But it's a great magazine, and Mark was really excited to think we'd have our dinner written up in it."

"Why is she staying at Otto's place?" I asked. "There sure didn't seem to be any love lost between them."

"Don't know, don't care," Sabrina said. "She'd just better give us a glowing review, that's all."

"How's she going to do that when she never touched the food?" I asked.

"Judging from her performance last night, she'd better be pretty imaginative." Aunt Mary pushed her chair back, stepped over the dog, who was once again stretched out in the middle of the kitchen, and headed for the sink. "Let's get this kitchen cleaned up."

"I'll do it. You got breakfast." I started loading the dishwasher.

"Do you put your pans in that thing?" Aunt Mary asked.

"Absolutely. I've made a new rule. If something doesn't go in the dishwasher or the washing machine, it doesn't get to live in my house." I added soap and closed the door.

"I'm going to have to get one of those," she said.

Sabrina watched us without moving. Usually she was the one cleaning up, moving nervously around the kitchen, doing something, anything, incapable of relaxing. That had almost driven me crazy, but it was better than this inert Sabrina, immobile under a cloud of depression. She seemed to do better when she was talking, so—"Why did Frank get all frozen when Jolene appeared?" I asked.

"I have no idea," Sabrina replied.

"So, Jolene came here to do an article on last night's dinner and on the grand opening of Otto's bed and breakfast and single seating restaurant, and she was staying with him? But they seemed to hate each other. What was that all about?" asked Aunt Mary. "And what does single seating mean, anyway?"

She sat down across from Sabrina. Paris, who had wanted to help us rinse off the plates with his tongue, resumed his place in the middle of the kitchen floor. It was my turn to step over him.

"There is one set menu each night and only one seating. The diners are often the people staying at the bed and breakfast, but if there are openings, sometimes others can get a reservation. Dinners usually are served only three or four nights a week and, in most places, are special."

"My," said Aunt Mary. "Sounds wonderful. And expensive."

Sabrina nodded, but she didn't seem to be thinking about Otto's dinners. "I didn't know Jolene was staying there. I wonder how she managed that." She pulled her own bathrobe closed over her shoulders as if she were cold. "I only heard him mention her once. He seemed livid with her. But since Otto was livid most of the time and making threats was what he did best next to cooking, no one paid much attention."

"I wonder if Jolene did," I said.

"You can't possibly think Jolene killed Otto," protested Aunt Mary.

"Why not? Someone did, and I would a whole lot rather have the police arrest her than Sabrina. How would I explain that to Catherine?"

Sabrina actually laughed. "I'd love to hear that phone call. And I'd hate to be the Police Chief that has to face the wrath."

I had a mental picture of Dan facing down my older sister, when I realized that all that noise wasn't Catherine yelling. It was raised voices outside my front door. Paris jumped up from the middle of the floor, banged into the table, and charged into the hallway, adding his voice to the din.

"What on earth?" asked Aunt Mary.

"My petunias!" I exclaimed and ran after Paris.

Frank was giving a press conference on my front steps. Larry Whittaker was standing beside him, but Frank was doing all the talking.

"What's going on?" asked Aunt Mary. She was too short to look out the glass in the door and was trying to pull aside the lace curtains on the long entryway windows.

"Your precious Frank is holding the press enthralled," Sabrina said. "It looks like he's coming in here. I think I'll go take a shower."

"What about the dog?" asked Aunt Mary. I could hardly hear her above Paris' barking and the shouted questions outside.

"Let him out the front door," advised Sabrina. "He can help Frank."

I have to admit I was tempted, but before I got the chance, the front door opened. Larry was propelled in, followed by Frank, who turned to pause in the doorway for one more round of pictures.

"Frank," said Aunt Mary, "what on earth are you doing?"

"My dear Mary." He took her hand and pressed it to his lips. Aunt Mary flushed. I snorted and Larry cleared his throat.

"I have been busy this morning." Frank let go of Aunt Mary's hand and looked around. "Where is Sabrina? And Mark?"

"Sabrina is taking a shower and Mark is out at some winery someplace trying to get his grapes crushed," I said.

"Oh." Frank looked disappointed, but not for long. "I have an important announcement to make and rushed right over here to tell them, and you, of course, my dear Mary." He now graciously included me with a sweeping gesture. "However, when I arrived and saw the members of the press so fortuitously waiting for some tidbit, I knew it was fate."

"Fate," murmured Larry. It was the only word he had spoken so far, but his eye twitched, and the anxious expression seemed to have become a permanent part of him.

"Exactly," Frank said, basking in satisfaction.

"All right, Frank. What is this announcement?" Aunt Mary asked. I was glad she was the one doing the asking. I couldn't have done it and kept a straight face. Frank so obviously loved all this drama. Larry so obviously hated it.

"I have talked to Otto's estranged brother, who is his only relative. He lives in New York. He is also a chef. We met when Otto and I were partners, and, of course, he knows what I have done since. He has asked me to take over the restaurant and bed and breakfast until the estate can be settled. Since no one knows if Otto left a will that could be months. Years!"

"You're joking!" Sabrina stood on the bottom-to-last step, wearing cutoff jeans and a white tee shirt. Her still damp hair, pulled back off her face with a headband, was left to fall over her shoulders in soft, light brown curls. She looked like her mother, right down to the scowl.

"My beautiful Sabrina. No, no. No joke. I'm going to stay here, in this charming small town, and make fabulous meals. I will also finish that lovely old house in a style befitting it. I must admit, I'm amazed Otto has started off so well, but with Mary to help me, we'll do even better, much better. And, of course, the worthy Larry will be my right hand. Otto could not do without him and neither can I."

I have never seen anyone look less thrilled at a prospect than the worthy Larry, unless it was someone whose stay on death row was about to end.

Sabrina didn't look too thrilled either. "I don't get it." She came down another step. "You sold Tortelli's, which you swore you would never do, and now you're going to jump into another restaurant? Why?"

Frank looked a little uncomfortable but immediately covered it up with a smile. However, he ignored the question. "My first triumph will be the grand opening dinner. Otto has invited a small group of important people; people who can help make this restaurant, this bed and breakfast, truly world famous. Each dish must be perfect, and it will be, it will be."

"He's changed the whole menu," Larry blurted out. We all whirled around to look at him. It was his first contribution since uttering "fate." He glanced at Frank as though this was a personal affront.

Frank smiled benignly back. "It will be much better, you'll see. And think of what you'll learn."

Larry didn't look convinced. He looked caught between fury and despair. "Now we'll have to change the wine menu. Nothing we picked out will do." His eye twitched again, and he took another deep breath. "I'm sorry, Sabrina," he went on, deliberately, "but the wines you delivered will have to go back. Frank has chosen two others of yours. Could you get someone to deliver them?" The "Frank" was emphasized a little, and the look he directed at him was not one of fondness. Why, I wondered. Frank seemed like fun. Opinionated, vain, but fun. He couldn't be worse to work with than Otto. Could he? I hoped not. Poor Larry. Working with chefs, at least these two, seemed to leave him a nervous wreck.

Sabrina glared at Frank but softened it for Larry. "I'll do it. The tasting room is closed, but the storage area's open. I can still get to the case goods. I can't do anything else, so I might as well. This afternoon? Get me a list of what you want and how much."

"I'll call you as soon as we get back." Larry took another deep breath, and transferred his worried attention to me. That proprietary smile was back, the one that said we'd known each other before, and it was time to take up where we'd left off.

"Ellen, why don't you come with Sabrina? I could show you what we're doing." He smiled that smile again. This was the first time I'd seen him without his chef's hat, and I examined him more closely. His blond hair was a little thin on top; he was a little thin everywhere. A nice tan on his naturally pale face, light blue eyes framed by surprisingly dark lashes, a great improvement on the skinny, sunburned, awkward boy I barely remembered. He must remember me as a scared, flat-chested, awkward girl who had just graduated from braces to a retainer. So why did he keep looking at me like, like, he made me nervous. I didn't want to hurt his feelings, but I didn't want to go with Sabrina.

He'd called me several times, left messages that seemed to say we were old friends, maybe more. We weren't. We'd shared a geometry class for several weeks, one movie, and a postcard, all when we were fifteen. That was it, and there wasn't going to be any more now. I needed to say something to make that clear. I didn't get the chance.

"What a nice idea," piped up Aunt Mary. I could have kicked her. "Ellen can keep Sabrina company and see that beautiful old house at the same time. I've always loved that house."

"It's settled then," Frank boomed. "We'll see you girls later, and, Mary, don't forget about tonight."

With that little comment, Frank pushed Larry out the door, beamed at the cameras that still remained on my sidewalk, and headed for his car. Sabrina and I stood in the hallway, facing Aunt Mary.

"Tonight?" I asked. "What about tonight?"

"Watch out for him," Sabrina warned. "He's a, a, snake in wolf's clothing."

"You are mixing your metaphors," Aunt Mary said serenely. "We're having dinner. That's all."

"Where?" I asked.

"Why, my house, where else?"

"Your house," Sabrina repeated. "And what time does Mr. Frank Tortelli plan on leaving?"

"I don't think that's any of your business." Aunt Mary blushed.

Chapter Nine

In its day, the old Adams mansion had been beautiful. It sat high above the street, sweeping lawns like green velvet skirts spread round it. A brick pathway gradually climbed toward the pillared front porch that ran the length of the house. The front door still held its original glass, as did the French doors that opened from rooms on either side of it, but the doors, and the shutters that flanked them, needed paint. White wicker rockers and low tables were scattered along the porch, waiting for cushions. Empty ceramic flowerpots sat beside them. Tree trimmers had cleaned out the dead branches from the ancient oak that guarded one side of the house, but a pile of leaves and twigs remained.

"If they're going to be ready for guests by their grand opening dinner, they'd better hustle," Sabrina said, juggling a full wine carton while she reached toward the crank doorbell.

"Uhmhp," was all I managed. I had a wine carton also, and it was heavy.

The door flew open, revealing Larry wrapped in a white apron. "Oh," he said, not moving out of the doorway. "Those look heavy. Maybe you should—Sabrina, you shouldn't be lifting—Oh, Ellen, let me…"

"Move over, Larry," Sabrina ordered. "Where do you want these?"

"The kitchen," Larry said, pointing into the dim interior of the house. "That will be fine."

Sabrina brushed past him, got to the staircase rising against the entryway wall, balanced her box on the handrail to get a better hold on it, and proceeded down the hall. I handed my box to Larry.

"Where's the kitchen?" I asked him with artificial brightness.

"Oh," he said again, staggering a little under the weight of the box. "Down here, follow me."

The hall was long, narrow, and dim. I caught glimpses of rooms off each side of it, all in the disarray of redecoration.

The kitchen was a pleasant surprise. Large, sunny, gleaming with modern conveniences, it felt warm, friendly, and finished. A brick fireplace took up one end of the room, an indoor gas barbecue grill built in beside it. A long, narrow table, flanked by armless Windsor chairs, sat in front of it. The soft white cupboards on the other end of the room were interspersed with open shelves stacked with plates, bowls, glasses, and pitchers. The counters were a mixture of wood, marble, and Corian, with the largest chopping block I had ever seen in the middle of everything. Pots hung on a rack above it; knives, lots of knives, fit into slots on the side of it.

"Isn't it great," Larry breathed into my ear. "Otto designed it. He really was a genius."

"Maybe he was," I admitted, looking around.

"See." Larry put the wine carton on the chopping block and pointed toward a huge stainless steel stove. "That is a Viking, it has six burners, a warming rack, and two ovens. The grill is here." He pointed toward a monstrous stainless steel thing. "And this is the prep sink. The washing up sink is over there."

"What's that door?" Sabrina asked. She had set her own carton down on a counter and was also looking around, admiration obvious.

"Our pantry." Larry threw the door open. "Storage for everything and, of course, wine racks."

There were lots of wine racks, most of them full. I wondered why we had brought more but was distracted by Larry showing us the next marvel.

"Not only do we have a Sub-Zero refrigerator, but look at this!" He stood in front of a heavy stainless steel door with a lever handle. He pulled it up and the door slowly opened. "A walk-in freezer!"

Cold air filled the kitchen. I took a step closer and shivered.

"Go on in," Larry insisted. He hit a switch on the wall by the door, letting a soft glow flow over the contents. Big enough for one person to step in and maybe turn around, the freezer had shelves on two sides, bins on the third, all filled with plastic containers or wrapped packages, neatly labeled. "We make our own sauces, soup bases, lots of things, then freeze them for later use. That wall is different kinds of meat."

I'd seen enough and backed up, right into Sabrina. "Sorry."

She didn't seem to notice me, just continued to stare into the freezer. "Efficient, isn't it."

"Close the door," I pleaded. "That thing is frosting up the whole kitchen." I could see puffs of blue air floating around the up-to-now warm kitchen and shivered again.

Larry laughed, pushed the heavy door shut, and pulled down the lever, locking it in place. "Have you ever seen a better kitchen?" He waved proprietarily around. He had a silly grin on his face, like a proud father staring at his newborn through the nursery window.

I had to admit I hadn't. My own kitchen, which I'd thought I'd made pretty modern with a new dishwasher, range, and refrigerator with automatic icemaker, suddenly seemed hopelessly old fashioned. On the other hand, I reassured myself, I had no intention of producing the quality, or quantity, of food for which this kitchen was designed.

"I want to show you something else." Larry reached for my hand. It was a fumbling gesture, but he connected. I could feel his thumb run over the back of my hand, and the "just you and me, babe" smile was back. Involuntarily, I stepped back, taking my hand with me.

His face fell. "Oh," he said, a stricken look on his face. "I'm sorry. I didn't mean, don't think, oh."

For a moment, I felt as embarrassed and flustered as Larry looked. I'd rejected him when all he'd—wait a minute. Of course I had. And he should be embarrassed. I was a happily engaged woman, and he had no reason to think—I hadn't given him any reason to—this was ridiculous. He'd obviously gotten all this wrong, but that wasn't my fault, and I wasn't going to hold his hand, let alone let him stroke it. I turned a little, trying to think of something distracting to say.

Swinging doors at the other end of the kitchen stood open, and I walked quickly into a bright, sunny room that smelled of fresh paint and furniture polish.

"What's this room?" was what I came up with. "Is this what you want me to see?"

There was a large bay window that looked over the side yard. A graceful serving cart, inlaid with mother of pearl, sat in the bay. On top of it was a fragile-looking china coffee server, beside it a number of tiny cups and saucers. They looked old and expensive. A round table sat in the middle of the room, surrounded by ladder-backed chairs with flowered cushions on their seats. A massive sideboard, empty of plates or serving pieces, stood along one wall; a graceful, and obviously old, lady's writing table was placed against a far wall. An open laptop computer sat on it looking utilitarian and out of place.

"This is beautiful." I walked around the room. "Are all these things real?"

"Do you mean, are they real antiques?" Larry laughed a little. "They are. Lovely, aren't they?" Again that silly grin. He couldn't have looked prouder if he'd owned the whole house and everything in it. "This is the morning room. When we start taking overnight guests, this is where we'll serve breakfast. It's almost finished. That," he pointed through a doorway to a much larger room, "is the restaurant dining room. We'll serve dinner three nights a week, and there will be only one seating. Each dinner will be something special."

The dining room was huge and bare. Scuffed hardwood floors, chipped paint on the crown moldings and the French doors that led to the front porch, and red flocked wallpaper half stripped off the walls; it had a long way to go before it would be ready for company.

"This is where your grand opening dinner will be?" I asked. I hadn't meant my tone to be so incredulous, but I couldn't help it. This room needed everything.

Larry's eye started to twitch, and the anxious expression returned. I winced, but he didn't seem to notice. Only my implied criticism.

"We'll be ready. You'll see. You're coming to the dinner, aren't you?"

"No," I said. "Somehow Otto overlooked inviting us. Besides, I had enough trouble dragging Dan to the winery dinner. I'd never get him to this one."

"Actually," Larry's expression softened, but his eye still continued to twitch. He took a deep breath, then let it and all of his words out with a rush. "I wasn't thinking about Dan. I thought you might like to come as my guest. Sort of be my hostess."

His hostess? His date? I could feel my mouth drop open, but nothing came out.

"I've heard that you and Dan are engaged, but I don't believe that. He's not really your type at all. Not nearly sensitive enough. So, you might as well come."

"What are you talking about?" I finally managed. "Dan and I certainly are engaged. And I fully intend to marry him." Well, maybe. But what business was that of his? "And," I said stiffly, "I wouldn't consider going anywhere without him."

"I'll arrange it all with Frank." He went on as if I hadn't spoken, smiling that damned "you and me" smile. "It will make me so happy to have you come. Just like old times."

I didn't know what to say. Old times had never consisted of dinner, and new times weren't going to either. I could feel my teeth grind. This was all Aunt Mary's fault. If she hadn't tricked me into coming with Sabrina I wouldn't be in this fix. Now, how did I get out of it?

"Come on, I'll show you the rest of it." Larry reached for my hand again. This time I wasn't quick enough. He dragged me out into the hallway and started up the stairs.

Aunt Mary won't live to see tomorrow, I vowed as I stumbled after him.

"This is the only finished room," Larry said. He dropped my hand and stared through a partially opened door. He looked so sad that curiosity got the better of me. I pushed up against him to look in.

"Well," I said after a minute, "the wallpaper's pretty."

The four-poster bed was not only unmade, it was strewn with clothes. The quilt was on the floor in a tangled heap. Spilled cosmetics, empty wineglasses, and what looked like the remains of a pizza littered the lovely cherrywood dresser. A filmy nightdress hung over the slipper chair, a bra was draped over a doorknob, and discarded panties, intertwined with a still damp bath towel, were on the floor just inside of the door where we stood.

"Jolene's room," Larry said unnecessarily. "She's supposed to clean up after herself. We don't have any staff yet, and she's getting the room free."

"Ah, yeah," was all I could think to say. Poor Larry. It was going to take a lot to clean up that mess. No wonder his eye twitched.

He moved out of the doorway into the hall and, not knowing what else to do, I followed, but a question had formed. "Why was Otto letting Jolene have a free room? It sounded like they hated each other. Or that Otto hated her."

Larry stopped and looked at me, eyes sad. "I think he wanted a glowing write-up in her magazine. It had been a while since he'd had a really good review." He shook his head and started down the hall again. "Sad, sad." I didn't know if he meant Otto's lack of reviews, his death, or that he had given Jolene a free room.

"I'm glad you're coming to the dinner," he said suddenly. He stopped again and stared at me for a second. I opened my mouth to tell him once more I wasn't coming, but he interrupted me. "It really is going to be nice. Let me show you the other bedrooms."

Larry smiled down at me. Any embarrassment he might have felt in the kitchen was gone. The "you and me babe" thing was back, and he seemed to be trying to add a little something extra. Some intimacy kind of thing that made the smile seem more like a leer. Uncomfortable is way too mild a word for the way it made me feel. I had no idea what he had in mind; actually, I was afraid I did, and being alone with him in a bedroom, even one with no furniture, was, I decided, not on my agenda. Too late. He threw open the next doorway.

"Hey!" a voice said. "Watch it!" I caught a quick glimpse of a man on a ladder, paintbrush in hand. Larry had narrowly missed him.

"Sorry." Larry quickly closed the door. He retreated to the middle of the hall, looking indecisively at the other closed doors. "Those rooms will be finished by next week," he finally said, moving down the hallway, "then we'll have six bedrooms and four bathrooms ready for guests. Later, we plan to add three more bedrooms and two, maybe three bathrooms on the third floor. Have you seen this?"

It was another door. Dark wood, white porcelain knob, old-fashioned keyhole, it looked like all the rest.

Larry threw it open with a flourish. "The servants' staircase."

Dark, steep stairs descended, and another set went up. I reluctantly stepped on the landing and looked down. Being a servant in a Victorian home couldn't have been much fun under any circumstances, but having to climb those stairs would have been downright painful.

"How interesting." I could feel Larry's breath on my neck. I had no intention of going down those stairs, but if I stepped back, I'd probably land right on Larry's toes. Oh well.

I had started to shift my weight when something smashed onto the front porch, shaking the front of the house. The tinkle of pottery breaking followed.

"Shit!" said a voice.

Larry paled, turned, and ran down the hall, taking the front stairs two at a time.

Sabrina reached the hallway first and flung open the front door. The porch was filled with a huge roll of carpet, pieces of broken ceramic flowerpot, and a very bald, very angry man.

"I tripped on that," he said, pointing to the pieces. "Could have killed myself. Could have wrecked the carpet. You shouldn't leave stuff like that around."

He gave Sabrina a long look, glanced up at me where I had stopped halfway down the stairs, then told Larry, "Move. I've got to get this in. Where does it go? Upstairs? Then she'll have to move, too."

I moved. Down the stairs and into the hallway, dragging Sabrina with me.

"We'll let ourselves out, Larry. Thanks for the tour," I said, heading for the kitchen.

"What's the matter with you?" Sabrina asked, trotting to keep up with me. "You act like—oh. He came on to you."

"Not really. Well, sort of. And I'm not waiting for a repeat performance. Let's get out of here. I've seen all the kitchens and all the bedrooms I need for one day."

"Who would have believed." Sabrina followed me out the kitchen door, past the swimming pool, around the side of the house, and down the path to the street. "First Aunt Mary and dear old Frank, now you and Larry. And it's not even spring."

"It's not funny," I said.

"Sorry." Sabrina kept on smiling. "I'd love to see Dan's face when you tell him you're going to the dinner, but he's not invited."

"A privilege you won't have since I have no intention of going to that dinner," I said somewhat sourly.

"Are you going to tell Dan about being invited?"

"And have him roll on the floor laughing along with you?" I asked. "I don't think so." This had to stop. I took a deep breath. "Look, Larry is nervous, probably lonely, and for some reason thinks we had something going in high school and that I still like him. I probably could like him, as a friend, of course, if he backed off a little. And if you're thinking Dan would be jealous, forget it. He has other things on his mind."

Sabrina's face immediately lost its smile. "Like Otto's murder."

◇◇◇

"Has he come any closer to finding out who did it?" Mark asked. We were all in his office, the police having opened up all of the winery except the cellar floor and the fermenting tank where Otto died. He was behind his desk; Sabrina and I were lounging in high-backed chairs, and Paris took up the remaining floor. They each had a glass of white wine. I had a glass of water.

"I haven't seen him," I replied. "I've been a little busy."

"Hmmm," he responded. I wasn't sure he really heard my answer and was positive he hadn't heard a word about my adventures with Larry. He looked exhausted and worried. Maybe a little more than worried.

The phone rang. Mark picked it up. It was on speaker, which he quickly clicked off. "Yeah. Okay, sure. I understand. Well, thanks for trying. Yeah, I will." He hung up the phone, stared at it for a moment, then looked at Sabrina, and very slightly shook his head. She looked stricken.

"Who was that?" I probably shouldn't have asked, but curiosity overcame me.

"An old friend." It hadn't sounded very friendly, and I wondered again about Mark and Sabrina, and what it was that they weren't willing to talk about. They talked to each other, though. They were doing it now, Sabrina looking anxious, both eyebrows raised, eyes asking some kind of question, Mark responding with slight reassuring nods. Their closeness had never been more evident, and I envied it. Brian, my ex, equated closeness with sex. Talking to each other, being in tune with my feelings, sharing his, were not things that would ever have occurred to him. Nasty cracks, hurling them like tiny arrows, waiting for them to wound, hoping they would bring tears so he could feel he'd "won" again, were his specialty. I had never understood what kind of war he thought we were fighting, consequently had never been able to defend myself. Dan wasn't like that. It mattered to him how I felt, and I would do anything to make him happy. We also were close. Of course we were. We were about to be closer. Much closer. But how would it end? Like Mark and Sabrina or like what I had with Brian? I shuddered. That I couldn't go through again.

The door flung open, and a rather large girl with long blonde hair burst into the room. All thoughts of relationships fled as she furiously stated, "He's doing it again. Mark, you have to come out here. You, too, Sabrina. He wants all this stuff, and I have no idea what to do." Her face was blotchy red, her hair in disarray where she had run her fingers through it. She looked like she was going to burst into tears any moment.

"What?" Mark pushed his chair back hard. "Who?"

"I'll bet it's Frank," Sabrina said grimly. "What's he doing now?"

"It's Carlton. Mr. Carpenter. He's in the office, has been for an hour. It was bad enough having the police, but at least they were polite."

Dan would be glad to hear that.

"What does he want this time?" Mark was on his feet, moving around his desk toward the door.

"Everything." The girl threw her arms out dramatically. "Inventory lists, reports, he wants to go through files, and to know who works here and how much they get paid. He even wanted to know how much we pay you two. Right now he's trying to break into my computer!"

"All right, Nikki, calm down," Mark said soothingly, but his face had a red tinge under his deep tan. "I have no idea what Carlton thinks he's up to, but I'll take care of it."

"Tell him to get lost," Sabrina said. "What right does he have poking his nose into everything?"

"He's a partner." Mark's voice was still mild, but the lines around his mouth were hard.

"None of the other partners ever come in here messing up the office." Sabrina's voice was tinged with hysteria. Then she turned to Nikki. "Do they?"

"No, never. We hand out quarterly reports, they ask questions at the partners' meetings, and that's it. Why is he doing this?"

"I've got a pretty good idea." Mark's stride as he left the office was a little faster and a little longer than usual. Sabrina was right behind him, Nikki practically on Sabrina's heels. I brought up the rear.

"Can we help you?" Mark stopped in the middle of the main office, towering over Carlton, who sat in a desk chair, flicking the mouse at anything on the screen. "You're going to freeze the whole thing if you keep doing that. If you want something, I'll have Nikki or one of the other girls get it for you."

Carlton got to his feet. He took a step toward Mark, who didn't back up. Carlton looked a little surprised, then ran a hand over his Ken-doll perfect hair and thrust his chin into the air. "I want the inventory records and then I want someone to take me downstairs so we can check everything off."

"Why, Carlton?" Mark asked, his voice much too quiet. "Do you think I've been stealing wine?"

"I didn't say that," Carlton stated belligerently. He took a good look at Mark's face and took a step back. "As a partner, I have a right to check up if I want to. Besides, I'm the only partner that lives around here. It's my responsibility."

Ah, Carlton had learned a new word. I wondered if he'd figured out what it means.

"The partners are all very important people," he went on, seeming to gain confidence from the thought of associating with celebrities. "Someone has to look out for their interests."

I could hear Sabrina sputter. I put my hand on her arm, hoping to remind her to keep her mouth shut.

Mark didn't say anything for a moment. He didn't have to. The rigid shoulders, the tight lips said it all. Finally he spun around and told Nikki, "Print out a complete inventory list for Mr. Carpenter, and then take him down to the cellar. Tell Hector he wants to count cartons and wine bottles. Make sure he gets a gallon count on the wine stored in the tanks and in the barrels. However, Hector doesn't have to stay with him, only show him where things are. I'm sure Mr. Carpenter will be glad to report back to you with the results of his inventory. Then I want you to write a report of his findings for the other partners." He turned back to Carlton. "This could take some time. Better plan on coming back tomorrow. We close at five thirty."

Carlton's mouth was open, and he was stammering. "You don't have to—I don't think we have to bother the other partners—I'm sure everything is fine, just wanted—"

"Give him the inventory." Mark turned on his heel and stomped out. Sabrina and I followed, but not before I took a quick peek back at a very red-faced Carlton. Embarrassed or outmaneuvered, I wasn't sure. Either way, Carlton clearly wasn't sure what to do next. I almost felt sorry for him. Almost. Why was he trying so hard to make Mark into a thief? And, if he really had any information, why didn't he share it with someone? Like, for instance, Dan. Or had he? I wondered if Dan would tell me. I wondered if he was coming for dinner tonight. If he showed, maybe we'd have a little talk about Carlton Carpenter.

Back in Mark's office, Sabrina threw herself into a chair. She got up, grabbed the tissue box, blew her nose noisily, and collapsed into the chair again.

"Why, oh why, did we ever come to this miserable town? I'm about to be arrested for murder, and now Carlton the schmuck Carpenter is going to ruin your reputation. You'll never work again as a winemaker. You'll be branded!"

"Sabrina." Mark bent down, his hand pushed the hair out of her eyes, and he tried to draw her to him, but she pushed him away.

"We can always look on the bright side," she said bitterly. "They don't charge you rent on a jail cell."

"For heaven's sake," I said. "No one believes anything Carlton says. Mark's not going to lose his job and you're not going to jail."

"Yeah?" she asked as she mopped at her eyes.

"Ellen," Mark said, never taking his eyes off Sabrina, "could we meet you at home later?"

I got the hint, loud and clear. He'd been through these upheavals with Sabrina before, probably lots of times, and he wanted to handle it his way. And alone.

"Right." I grabbed my purse and fled.

Home, I wanted to go home. No one was there, not Mark and Sabrina, not Carlton, not Jolene, not the exuberant Frank or the uncomfortable Larry, not even Dan. I was suddenly bone tired, and I wanted more than anything to sit on my front porch, all by myself, sipping a glass of wine, and forget all of them. Not Dan, of course. Well, maybe for a while. I'd coped with houseguests for a month, I was getting married almost before I knew it; we had a murder that seemed to involve people close to me, and to top it all off, someone I barely remembered wanted to take me on a tour down memory lane. I'd had it. If Dan showed up, we'd order in. If not, a bacon, lettuce, and tomato sandwich was going to be dinner, followed by a large cup of hot chocolate and a long bath. I wouldn't even call in for my messages. Yes, I would. But, for the first time ever, I hoped I didn't have any.

Chapter Ten

I had decided that Tuesday morning was mine. Mark, who hadn't been fired, was at the winery. So was Sabrina, who hadn't been arrested, and they had Paris with them. Jake and I were going to clean house. Monday, I had taken two listings, written one offer, and then spent the evening alone with Jake, sitting on the front porch. I wondered what had happened at Lighthouse Winery that had Mark and Sabrina so upset, why Frank had sold his restaurant, why Otto had let Jolene stay at his place for free, and why she wanted to. Mostly I wondered what Dan was doing.

I was to hear this morning if yesterday's offer was accepted, so I turned on the answering machine, meaning to monitor my calls. Larry had called three times the day before, each time asking me to come to the grand opening dinner. Each time I'd said no, and I had no intention of repeating that performance today. It never occurred to me he might just show up.

"Hi, Ellen." There he was, standing on my front porch at nine thirty in the morning. "Hope you don't mind me stopping by like this."

Mind! I certainly did, but years of conditioning by my mother and Aunt Mary took over and instead of slamming the door in his face, I heard myself say, "Larry. Of course not. Would, ah…"

"Thanks. I'd love to come in. Boy, this place looks wonderful." He followed me through the living room, into the dining room, and stepped into the kitchen, looking around avidly. "Better than when your folks lived here."

How could he know that? He had, to my knowledge, never been in my house.

"Would you like some coffee?" Why was I being so damn polite? "I think there's some left."

"I would love some." He pulled out a chair, sat himself down at the table, leaned back, and looked around. "I love your hutch. Is it built in? And the little hanging rack for wineglasses, that's a great touch. You need a wine rack, though."

I didn't say a thing, just took two mugs off of the hutch and walked over to the coffeepot. There were very few outlets in this old kitchen, so it sat beside the sink. I looked out the window, not seeing the yard, just willed myself to be patient, poured coffee into both mugs, and set one of them in front of Larry.

"You certainly were lucky your folks decided to move to Scottsdale, and that you got to come back and live in this house. I've always loved this house. It's so much nicer than my grandmother's old one. You remember it, don't you? The little blue one down on Fourth Street?"

If he kept this up, the stranglehold I had on my patience would give. Of course I didn't remember his grandmother's house. I barely remembered Larry. But we were sure making up for that. "Cream and sugar?"

"No. Just black. You know, I didn't just stop by. I wanted to talk to you."

You have been, I said silently. Over and over. Aloud I said, "I really can't come to that dinner with you." I turned to face him and leaned back against the sink, holding my mug in both hands. If I didn't sit down again, maybe he'd get the hint and leave. "Ah—clients, you know. We have an offer pending and—ah—Sabrina. And Mark. They're getting ready to move, and I'm helping them and…"

"Actually, Sabrina's why I'm here." His eye was going a mile a minute; so was the spoon he was twisting through his fingers. "I wanted to apologize."

"You want to—what?" I was so surprised, I pulled out a chair and sat down without thinking.

"Apologize. You know. About Sabrina."

I didn't know. "You've lost me. What about Sabrina. Why are you apologizing to me?"

"Because of what Jolene told the police, and, of course, I had to back her up. And because she's your niece."

Now I was really confused. The only thing clear to me in that garbled sentence was that Sabrina was my niece, not Jolene. And getting Larry to explain was beginning to look like an all-day job.

"Exactly what did Jolene tell the police? What did you tell them?"

"About Sabrina's fight with Otto, you know, before she dragged Jolene out of the kitchen." He carefully put down the spoon, lining it up neatly in front of the sugar bowl. His eyes were on it, not on me. "Last Saturday night. And what she said. I'm really sorry, but I was there and could hardly lie. Could I?"

"What fight?" Damn. This didn't sound one bit good.

"The one they had right after the break." He finally looked up at me, leaning a little forward in his eagerness to tell his story. "Otto threatened to walk out. He did that, you know. Jolene had come into the kitchen. He ordered her out, and he was being pretty awful about everything. He said Jolene was of no use, and she had to leave his house as well as his kitchen, and if she didn't, he was going to walk out on the dinner. Sabrina told him if he did anything to spoil the dinner, anything more, she would kill him. She said Mark's future depended on this dinner going well, and then she told Otto what she would do to him." Larry paused, his eyes dropped back down to the table. I could have sworn he blushed. "It involved portions of his personal anatomy."

It didn't take much imagination to know what Sabrina had said. Any other time I would have been amused at Larry's prissy description of Sabrina's threats. "Jolene told that to the police?"

"Yes. I backed her up. I had to."

"What happened after Sabrina said all that?"

"She grabbed Jolene by the arm, and they both left the kitchen. Otto stormed around for a while, mostly getting in the way, and I finally suggested that he go up onto the deck and cool off. Only I put it more politely. He never came back."

I thought about it for a moment. It didn't seem like much. "Was there anything else? Did Sabrina have a wine bottle in her hand? Did she come back into the kitchen for any reason?"

"No, no, she didn't. And I would have known. I never left the kitchen until I saw you in the hall, right before we served the dessert."

I really didn't see how dragging Jolene out of the kitchen and threatening Otto with bodily harm could propel Sabrina into the role of chief suspect, but something else Larry had said…

"Otto told Jolene she had to leave? Without doing her article on his grand opening?"

"That's what he said that night." His eye started to twitch again, and he looked away from me. He picked up the spoon, and it started going round and round in his fingers. I had an almost overpowering desire to snatch it out of his hand. "He probably would have changed his mind."

"You seem to have been the only one who got along with Otto. How did you stand it?"

"He was going to make me a partner." Larry seemed to think that said it all. Maybe it did.

"And now? What happens now?"

"You mean now that Frank has wormed his way in? I don't know. I just don't know." Larry pushed his chair back, stood up, and reached over the table for my hand. He crushed it between both of his and said, "I'm sorry you can't come to the dinner. I know you'd enjoy it. I'm going to do most of the cooking, at least that's the plan right now." His smile faded. "Like everything else, it's subject to change at any moment." His thumb started roaming over the back of my hand again. "But I want to cook for you anyway. Next week for sure, after Mark and Sabrina move out. I'll call you." He gave me another of those intimate smiles, my hand another hard squeeze, and walked out of the kitchen toward the front door. I didn't move until I heard it close.

Damn! This was getting out of hand. I slumped back in my chair and thought about getting a headache. How did I go about getting rid of Larry? At least convince him that I had no feelings for him, amorous, lecherous, or anything close. I was engaged. In love. Going to be married. Married. I got a mental picture of myself walking down the aisle of St. Anthony's, holding my father's arm, feeling the smiles of everyone in this blasted town, and shuddered. I shook the vision out of my head and pushed back my own chair, gathered up the coffee mugs, stopped, looked at the spoon and added that to what was going in the dishwasher. Why was life so complicated anyway? Then I thought about what Larry had told me and reached for the phone, meaning to call Sabrina and find out about that fight. But that wasn't happening right then. The agent who had the listing on the house my clients had offered on was on the line.

"That was fast," she stated, laughing. "Anxious, or what?"

I didn't think her joke very funny, but, since my offer had been accepted, I forgave her. The next hour was spent talking to my lucky buyers, congratulating them, explaining what would happen next, and opening the escrow. It was close to noon before I finally remembered Sabrina.

Chapter Eleven

I wanted to blast Sabrina for not telling me she had engaged in a three-way battle with Jolene and Otto on Saturday night, but I wasn't the police, and she had no obligation to tell me anything. And wasn't that a bummer! So, I tried to edge my way into the subject.

"Larry was just here, and he said…"

"I know what he said," she interrupted, "and speak of the devil, guess who's driving up right now?"

"Not Larry," I said, surprised. "He didn't say anything about going out to the winery. What does he want?"

"He called this morning. He's bringing back the wine Frank doesn't want. In our rush to leave, we forgot it."

I laughed. "We did exit in a bit of a hurry. It's nice of him to make a special trip."

"Evidently there are some pots or something that he left here the night of the dinner. He wants them back, which is fine with me."

"Why didn't he tell us Sunday? We could have brought them."

"No idea. Besides, I haven't been here long enough to know what belongs to the winery and what's the chef's. They always bring their favorite something. He can rummage around to his heart's content until he finds his precious pots."

Sabrina didn't sound as if she were in a very good mood. Maybe I'd wait until tonight to ask her about Otto and Jolene and—everything. But she was one jump ahead of me.

"You want to know what happened in the kitchen Saturday night, don't you?"

Put that way, it sounded like meddling, misplaced curiosity, or none of my business. But I did want to know. So I simply said, "Yes."

"Damn that Larry."

Unfortunately, that didn't answer the question, so I said, "This could be serious. What happened?"

"Jolene barged into the kitchen and started in on Otto about something. I walked in just as he was ordering her out of the kitchen and out of his house. She was yelling he couldn't do that, he'd be sorry, and he was yelling right back that yes he could, and he could walk out of this kitchen right now as well and no one could stop him. So, I told him how I'd stop him. Then I grabbed Jolene and dragged her out the door. I almost knocked Frank over. Served him right for hanging around in the hallway. I got Jolene into the ladies' room and left. She evidently spent some time."

I almost laughed. The mental picture was wonderful. Otto with his round beet-colored face, Jolene losing her Southern charm to a little too much Southern Comfort, Sabrina besting them both. Sabrina. She was turning out to be something of an enigma. Either that, or rage gave her courage I'd doubted she had. But another thought intruded.

"Why was Frank outside the kitchen? I thought you told him to keep away from it."

"I did, and I don't know."

"Did he go into the kitchen?"

"I don't know that either. I told him to go back into the dining room, but I had my hands full with Jolene wailing about how awful Otto was treating her and that she wasn't going to put up with it. All I thought about was getting her somewhere quiet, where she couldn't make a public scene. I never thought about Frank again."

"Have you told this to Dan?"

"Of course," she said. "I didn't kill Otto. I never even thought about killing him. Although, in hindsight…"

"Don't say that," I said hastily. "I know you didn't, but you don't need to run around giving yourself a motive."

"I already had one. Ask Dan. Listen, I have to go, the tasting room is filling up and I have to help the girls."

Nothing like a good murder to bring out the morbid in people and bring in the customers. Oh well, as long as they spent money. "See you tonight?"

"Late, we'll be late," she said and hung up.

I hung up also and sat for a moment thinking about our conversation. I hadn't learned anything and there was a bunch I wanted to know, starting with Otto and Jolene. What was that all about? They evidently hated each other, but Otto was letting her stay in his unfinished bed and breakfast for free and she seemed to be happy to be there. Why? What had changed? And why was Frank hanging around in the hallway outside the kitchen? Listening to the fight? Had he gone back into the kitchen after Sabrina and Jolene left? No, he couldn't have. Larry would have said something. But another thought started to form. Sabrina. She wasn't an enigma. She followed a pattern, a behavior pattern. When she was at the winery, doing her job, and Mark wasn't around, she was Miss Efficiency. When Mark was around, she became either a helpless little female or a fierce tiger, ready to do battle protecting her—what? Mate? Territory? Wasn't that interesting? It was more than interesting. If she thought she was protecting Mark, would she have followed Otto out onto the deck, fought with him, and in a fit of desperation, swung at him with the wine bottle? It seemed possible, and the thought made me a little sick. What did I do now? Call Aunt Mary, of course.

Chapter Twelve

"The man is going to drive me crazy!" was the way she answered the phone.

"Who?" As if I didn't know.

"Who do you think?"

"I thought you liked all that attention. You sure weren't crying the blues on Sunday," I said. I hadn't talked to Aunt Mary for a couple of days and the last thing I expected was this explosion over the phone.

"Saturday night, Sunday, yes. They were fun. But then there was Monday. Today is Tuesday, and thank God, he has something he 'can't get out of' tonight, but what am I going to do about tomorrow?"

"What exactly is Frank doing?" I quickly swallowed what was threatening to be a belly laugh. This was so unlike unflappable Aunt Mary, the organizer of half the charity events put on in this town. Dinner for two hundred homeless, a Fourth of July picnic for four hundred, a church bazaar that hosted six hundred, none of these made her turn a hair, so whatever Frank was doing, it must be pretty good.

"He's…he's….he's here!" she sputtered. "In my kitchen! I can't get to my own pots and pans."

The fatal sin. He'd taken over Aunt Mary's kitchen. I would bet even money he was telling her how to do everything. Gallantly, with grand sweeping gestures, but telling her nonetheless. After all, he was the "great" Frank Tortelli.

"I thought he was busy taking over the restaurant. Isn't there a lot to do?"

"Oh, yes. Lots. But he's doing most of it on my phone. My dining room table is full of fabric pieces and wallpaper books. My sofa is piled high with restaurant catalogs. I have strange people calling me, giving me quotes on sides of beef and crates of vegetables. I'm scared to death to open my door. It'll probably be some man with a truckload of potatoes."

This time the laugh wouldn't stay in. "I've got to come over and see that."

"It's nice someone sees the humor," I was told, with no small amount of bitterness.

"Okay, Frank's definitely—anyway, the restaurant part of the bed and breakfast will be open soon. The big dinner is a week from this Saturday. Then he'll be too busy to be under your feet. Now listen, you're not the only one—"

"You think so? I don't. He'll just give that poor Larry more to do, no credit at all, and camp in my kitchen, writing out menus and telling me how great he is."

"Speaking of Larry…" I tried again.

I heard a pot clank. "That poor boy." Aunt Mary's voice sounded a little hollow, then there was a faint whoosh. The refrigerator door, I assumed. "I don't know how he puts up with it. First Otto, now Frank. He must have the patience of a saint."

"He has the persistence of one. You have Frank; I have Larry, and he's driving me nuts."

"What are you talking about?"

"Larry. He keeps calling me. Wants to cook me dinner, wants to take me to lunch, he even stopped by this morning."

"He's got a crush on you. Probably has since high school." There was a banging noise. "But, he's lonely, and you should be nice to him. He's really quite nice looking. He'll make someone a good husband."

"Did you have someone in mind?" I waited but got no reply. "He's not lonely. He's horny. And I'm not amused. If he tries stroking the back of my hand once more, I'll smack him. With a wine bottle. He's making me crazy."

"What does Dan think of all Larry's attentions?"

"We haven't talked about it." I started to doodle a stick man with a top hat.

There were splashing noises. "Too busy talking about the wedding?"

"Well," I let the word sprawl a little, "we haven't talked a lot about that either." A stick woman with a veil found her way next to him.

"Ellen." She sounded almost exasperated. "You have three months. That's not a lot of time. If I didn't know better, I'd think you were dragging your feet." There was a pause filled with faint banging noises. "You're not, are you?"

"Of course not," I replied hotly. And that was true. More or less. "Dan's been a little busy."

"Wait a minute." I could hear peculiar noises interspersed with "stupid slippery things." She came back on the line. "Sorry."

"What are you doing?"

"Cooking," she answered.

"Cooking what?"

"Food, of course," she said, a bit grimly. "Now, why did he stop by?"

"Who?" I asked, still trying to identify the strange sounds.

"Larry, of course. What's the matter with you?"

"Nothing. Sabrina. He wanted to tell me about Sabrina. Actually about Jolene and what she told the police."

"And what was that?"

When I had finished, there was a long pause. "Are you suggesting that Sabrina's removal of Jolene so that Otto would continue to cook makes her a suspect?"

"No, I'm not. Not exactly. She had a motive to want him dead, but a stronger one to keep him alive to finish the dinner. It's something else."

"What?" Aunt Mary asked. A series of hollow thumps followed.

"You know how sometimes Sabrina is so nervous? How she seems to be anticipating trouble? Then an hour later, she acts as if she could run the United Nations without mussing her hair?"

Aunt Mary started to laugh. "Not exactly the way I'd put it but, yes, I've noticed that."

"Have you noticed when she's a nervous wreck?"

"When she's worried about Mark."

I didn't say anything for a moment. "How do you do that?"

"Do what?"

"Know what I'm going to say before I get the words out?"

"I've been watching Mark and Sabrina for a month," she stated. "It wasn't hard. So, you think what exactly?"

"That if Otto were going to bail on the dinner, knowing how much it meant to Mark, she may have lost it and banged him over the head with a wine bottle."

"Then pushed him into the fermenting tank and tossed the champagne bottle in to do—what? And what did she do with the bottle that actually killed him?"

"So you don't think it was her?" I so didn't want it to be Sabrina.

Kitchen noises resumed. I recognized water running but couldn't identify the pounding noises. "I think what you have right now is pretty thin," Aunt Mary said, then, "Damn."

I couldn't stand it any longer. "Okay, what are you making?"

"Lasagna," Aunt Mary said, a little defensively. "I just dropped the onion on the floor."

I almost made the mistake of laughing. She had reclaimed her kitchen. Out loud I asked, "You going to feed it to Frank?"

That was ignored. "When did Sabrina take Jolene into the ladies' room?"

"I'm not sure, but everyone was still downstairs, tasting wine out of the barrels." I thought for a minute, listening to the cooking noises coming over the phone. Something had started to sizzle. Sausage maybe? Or onions, green peppers and garlic? I could hear chopping, probably tomatoes and fresh basil. She'd put the stockpot filled with homemade sauce on the back burner to simmer until the lasagna was ready to assemble. My mouth started to water. "Jolene was late getting back to our table, wasn't she?"

"Yes, but if you're thinking of her as the murderer, think again. She could barely stand up, let alone swing a wine bottle."

"Don't be so sure," I told her. "She looked pretty steady when I saw her. And the bathrooms are in the front of the building. It would have been only too easy for her to slip out the front door of the winery, walk around to the deck, spot Otto, and attack. She could have gone back the same way. Maybe she hid the wine bottle in a bush."

"And maybe some of us have too much imagination," I was told. "If you want to make up stories, make up one about Carlton."

"All right. But you're going to have to get me started."

"Carlton was going up the back stairs, the ones that lead to the offices and the kitchen, right about the time everyone else was going up the main stairs, back to the dining room."

That wasn't a story, it was front page headlines. "How do you know that?"

"I saw him," she answered. "Do you want some of this lasagna? I certainly can't eat it all."

"No. Yes, of course I do. I'll come get it later. Tell me more about Carlton." I'd been doodling a poodle but stopped right in the middle of a topknot.

"There's nothing to tell. I was going up the main stairs, back to our table, and I just happened to see him on the other staircase, the one that leads to the offices. I paused on the landing to catch my breath, you get a good view of it from there."

"Was he alone?" My pencil was poised, ready to take notes.

"Yes. Probably why I noticed him. That's got to be some kind of first."

"Do you think he was going up to see Otto?"

"I have no idea. All I know is what I saw. He was going up the stairs."

"He could have gone into the kitchen. He could have—"

"What?" she asked. "Think. Otto was killed on the deck, not in the kitchen. So how did Carlton get him onto the deck?"

"Yeah," I said slowly. "Besides, Larry didn't mention anyone else coming into the kitchen. But he could have seen Otto on the cellar floor and followed him and—"

"Why would he? I don't think much of Carlton, but I don't see him as a murderer."

"You know, I think I have an idea why Carlton might have been very upset with Otto, and I think I know how to find out. What time will the lasagna be done?"

"Come by about five," she instructed. "And you can tell me some more stories."

Five it would be, and if I were right, I'd have a much better story to tell than she was expecting.

Chapter Thirteen

The real estate office where I had worked for almost a year, Santa Louisa Home and Land, was owned by an old friend of my family, Bo Chutsky. Bo and my father had played golf, gone to Rotary, and played poker once a month with "the boys" the whole time I was growing up. Bo knows everybody in town and has handled most of their real estate transactions over the last forty years. He also knows where all the bodies were buried, but getting him to tell you anything he isn't ready to relate is a bit like trying to pry open a clam guarding its pearl. That's why I stopped by Hazel Chutsky's desk for a nice cozy chat.

Plump, sweet-faced, Hazel had raised two children and was supervising the rearing of her six grandchildren. Several years ago, she moved from housewife to office manager. She keeps the files, pays us our commissions, yells at us if we make a mistake, and soothes and comforts us if a deal goes south. She knows as much about this town and what goes on as Bo, but she's much more willing to talk. So, when I asked her what she knew about Carlton Carpenter and his handling of the sale of the old Adams mansion to Otto Messinger, I struck gold.

"I never understood that whole thing." We'd settled down at her desk, her with a cup of tea, me with a cup of coffee. "Abigail Adams—she was so proud of her name, you know, but she wasn't any relation to the John Adams family even if she did give herself airs—anyway, she hated Carlton. He's so darn good looking;

he was always getting into trouble with some girl when he was young, and I guess one of Abigail's granddaughters got smitten. I think there was a baby, but it got so hushed up, I was never sure." She clucked in sympathy for the unfortunate Abigail, took a sip of tea, and went on. "Anyway, you could have knocked me over with a feather when I heard he got the listing on that old house. I bet Abigail turned over in her grave more than once when that listing got signed."

"How did he get Otto as a client?" I asked.

"No idea, but we've all sure wondered. That Otto must have had a ton of money, though. I hear they've torn the whole kitchen out and put in a new one, refurbished the pool, and added a deck. They've just completely redone the whole house. Even filled it with real antiques. Doesn't make any sense to me, but whatever floats your boat."

"How did Otto get around the parking requirements?" I asked. "The city is usually pretty strict about that kind of thing, especially in the historic areas."

She started to laugh. "That Carlton. He thinks he's so sharp, but this time he cut himself."

"What do you mean?"

"Well, this is gossip, so don't tell anyone I told you, okay?" She leaned toward me and lowered her voice. I put my arms on her desk and gave her my full attention. "You're right about the parking and it seems Carlton 'forgot' to mention that it might be a problem. When that Messinger man went down to the city to get his restaurant permit, they refused him because he didn't have enough parking spaces around the house. So, the way I heard it was, he stormed into Carlton's office, screaming at the top of his lungs, threatening to sue, to have Carlton's license, or maybe just cut him up into little pieces and stuff him down the meat grinder. I guess Carlton was so scared he just about wet himself."

"So then what happened? The bed and breakfast is set to open, including the restaurant part, so they must have resolved it some way."

"Yep. Carlton bought the lot next door to the Adams mansion, the one with the little ol' red teardown house, and deeded it over to Otto."

"No kidding," I said, stunned. "That must have cost Carlton a bundle."

"Close to one hundred thousand," she said, more than a little satisfaction in her voice.

Non-disclosure is the cardinal sin in the real estate business, and to have both ends of a deal and put your client in the kind of jeopardy Carlton had put Otto in, was inexcusable. Not to mention a potential lawsuit, a certain reprimand by our board of realtors, and a real possibility of much harsher punishments. I couldn't believe Carlton would be that stupid. The unethical part didn't surprise me much.

"Where did he get the money? He bought himself a partnership in Silver Springs Winery about the time the escrow on the Adams place closed. Unless Carlton's changed a lot, that should have been about all the cash he had."

"He hasn't changed. I don't know how he swung it, but it got Otto Messinger off his back for a while. That man could really carry a grudge. I hear he was still going to sue Carlton and was telling everyone in town who'd listen that he was going after Carlton's real estate license as well. Don't know if he could have made it stick, but he sure could have made Carlton's life a living hell. "

"Yeah," I said, my brain churning ideas like a bread mixer. "Yeah, a living hell. Well, better get back to work. See you later."

"Ellen," she stopped me, "you got your ads done for those new listings you took?"

I assured her I did and handed over the photos I had taken, and then we went through the file to make sure all the signatures were in the right places before I finally got back to my desk. I sat for a few minutes, going over everything in my mind. Sabrina was out. She had to be. Carlton was our man, I was sure of it. So Otto was going to sue him and, worse, try for his license. That meant Carlton couldn't work. He was probably broke; he had to hate Otto, and he was going up the back stairs, alone, the night of the dinner. All I needed to do now was confirm he had been in the kitchen with Otto and that they had fought, or that somehow he knew that Otto was on the deck. Then I'd be ready to spring my theory on Dan.

I picked up the phone to call Larry. He would know if Carlton had talked to Otto. No answer. I let it ring. Please, pick up, I thought. I wanted that one piece of information before Dan arrived that night, and I wanted it on the phone. I did not want to track Larry down in person. I hung up. Where could he be? Outside, talking to workmen, no doubt. I flung myself back in my chair. Which did I want more? To not see Larry or get the information I needed before I saw Dan tonight? I thought about getting trapped in a bedroom, about Larry constantly reaching for my hand, about how awkward it would be if I had to—oh well. Information gathering won. I sighed, picked up my purse, put my phone on voice mail, and headed for my car.

Chapter Fourteen

The place was swarming with workmen, but there was no sign of Larry.

"Hey, Ellen," called a stocky, balding man, brown muscled arms showing under his local wine festival-emblazoned tee shirt. "What are you doing here? Trying to get a listing?" He laughed heartily at his little joke. I didn't find it especially funny, but I joined in. Ed McNamara and his crew did a lot of small termite and repair jobs for me, often with little or no advance notice, and I needed to keep them on my side.

"Hey, Ed. I didn't know you were doing this place."

"Yeah, and it's been great. I think."

"What do you mean?"

Ed walked over closer and lowered his voice. "It's been great in some ways, sure has paid well, but that guy's loony."

"Too demanding?" I asked sympathetically.

"Can't make up his mind. Wanted French doors in that little dining room where the bay window was. No problem. Only he changed his mind three times, and we ended up not doing them. I've mixed six colors of paint for one upstairs bedroom. We've changed moldings, moved bathroom cabinets around, rehung shelves—the guy's crazy. But the more time we spend here, the more money I make." This last he told me with a large grin. "It's the decorator lady he really drove nuts. I think she finally ignored him and just went ahead. Said she'd never get the fabric ordered if she waited on him. Anyway, after we finish that deck out there, we're done."

The deck extended out from the breakfast room, around an old oak tree, and wound around the back of the house where broad steps led down to the pool. It was going to be fabulous for summer morning breakfasts or late Sunday afternoon wine sipping.

"Otto was difficult," I told Ed, "but the final product is great."

"Otto. That was the guy who got killed, wasn't it? No. I mean the other guy."

"Frank?" I asked, surprised.

"Frank's the other old guy, isn't he? I'm talking about the nervous one, the guy with the twitch."

I almost laughed out loud. Frank wouldn't have been pleased to know that he was the "old guy." I was surprised, though, that Larry was making all of the decisions, first for Otto, now for Frank. No wonder his eye twitched. Only that didn't sound like Frank. I couldn't see him giving up running the show, whatever that show might be. However, I wasn't here to worry about new doors, fabric, or porch railings. I was here to find out if Carlton had come into the kitchen Saturday night, and if so, why? While I was at it, I'd ask about Frank. I was sure Larry would have said something, but it didn't hurt to ask.

"Where is he?" I asked Ed.

"Which one?"

"Larry. The one that twitches."

"Coming your way."

There he was, rushing towards me, hands outstretched, ready to grab mine. I could see Ed out of the corner of my eye, amusement and amazement plainly written on his face. I was going to take a lot of heat the next time he visited the office. The temptation to turn and run was strong, but the thought of Carlton and how I was about to prove him guilty of Otto's murder rooted me to the spot.

"I didn't know you were coming," he started, fumbling for one of my hands. "I was going to call you. Everything is turning out so nice, and I wanted you to see it, especially the dining room. Come look."

Ed's face was a study. He knew Dan, knew we were going to be married, everyone in town knew it, and here I was being practically mauled by someone else. The small-town news network was about to go into warp speed. Damn!

"I thought you might have changed your mind about coming to the dinner next Saturday," Larry said, evidently oblivious of our audience. "Come on." He tightened his grip on my hand and started pulling me toward the house. Short of sitting down or screaming, there wasn't much I could do, so without a backward look, I let Larry lead me inside.

Someone had worked a miracle. The dining room had been a shell Sunday. Now it was magnificent. Wood floorboards, polished bright, were partially covered with a jeweltone oriental rug. Silk window hangings hung at the sparkling-clean long windows, freshly painted crown moldings set off the high ceiling, and there was no trace of the flocked wallpaper. An antique landscape painting hung above the hand-carved mantel, from which all traces of soot had been removed. A beautiful Chippendale sideboard overflowed with delicate china and freshly polished silver.

"Aren't these elegant?" Larry asked, waving at the three round mahogany tables that graced the room. Each had eight intricately carved chairs around it. "See how beautifully the tablecloths complement the rug and the wall hangings." Larry's beaming face turned anxious as he faced me, and his eye started to twitch again. "I picked it all out."

"They're gorgeous," I said. "The room—the whole house—is fabulous." Larry's eye stopped twitching.

"I'm so glad you like it." He looked around the room with the same proprietary air he'd had when he showed us the kitchen. "This whole thing, cooking with someone as talented as Otto, creating this house, has been like a dream come true."

I must have looked a little surprised, because he smiled at me, that same smile that made me so nervous, and gently picked up my hand before I could hide it. He started the stroking thing again, but it seemed different. Distracted. "You know, all I ever really wanted to do was be a chef. My father thought that was for, well, not for a real man. I told him over and over that cooking, real cooking, was like great art, but he didn't believe me. All those years in France, and he didn't understand. But I got my chance. Otto gave it to me. Some people thought he was difficult, but I thought he was a great man."

I was so surprised I forgot to pull my hand away. Otto great? That wasn't the way I'd heard it. But if Larry thought so… I wondered what he thought of Frank.

"Let me show you the rest of it." We stepped further into the room and, retrieving my hand, I slowly followed him around, ending in front of the sideboard.

"Good grief, Larry," I exclaimed. "Where did you get this silver? It's sterling!"

"I know. We'll only use it for the formal dinners. I have something a little less ornate for every evening and for the breakfasts. Come on."

Stunned, I let Larry lead me through the rest of the house. Where had all these antiques come from? And the carpets! A bone china tea service sat on a low table between two silk-covered chairs in one of the bedrooms. I picked up a cup. Limoges. Why would anyone put out something like that for a guest to break? Or steal? But the house was beautiful. Larry threw open each bedroom door with a flourish, making sure I noticed the hand-made quilts, the antique brass headboards, the museum-quality highboy. All the bedrooms were exquisite; all the bathrooms offered gleaming porcelain and plush towels. All but Jolene's. Her door was closed, and, this time, Larry didn't offer to open it. He didn't mention her.

"There are two more bedrooms to finish before next Saturday, but I'll get them done. I'll have fresh flowers in all the rooms, of course, and I have flowers planned for those little tables as well."

Larry pointed at small tables set in the hallway. A collection of silver salt dishes sat on one of them, a leather-bound book on another. If the food turned out half as good as the decorating of the house, there would be glowing reports in magazines and newspapers from coast to coast.

"Come on downstairs." Larry pulled me toward the only other closed door. He pushed it open and announced, "This was the old servants' staircase. You saw it Sunday, but you didn't have time to go down. It leads right into the kitchen. It's going to come in handy again for, oh, all kinds of things. Hurry up. I want to show you the menu."

He led me down the steep flight of stairs, not saying anything. I followed more slowly, clutching the railing, placing each foot carefully on the steep treads. He ducked under the low doorframe and turned to watch as I navigated the last step. We had arrived in the kitchen, just next to the pantry.

Between my admiration of the house and struggling with my personal problems, I had almost forgotten Carlton. As we walked into the kitchen strewn with half-unpacked dishes and stacked wine crates, thoughts of him returned. How was I going to work in my questions around Larry's enthusiastic explanations of his dinner plans?

"What do you think?" He spread out handwritten menus all over the counter, shuffling them like a deck of cards. "Do you think the fumé blanc is good with the clear soup? Or should I have a rosé? Wait, you can tell me what you think."

He jumped up and practically ran to the wine rack. Before I could protest, he had the cork out of a bottle and had poured a little into two glasses. Handing one to me, he held the other up to the light, swirled it, watching it as it coated the inside of the glass, buried his nose in it, breathing the aroma, then came up for air. "The pairing of wine and food must be perfect. Don't you agree?"

I'd heard Mark and Sabrina talking about pairing, about acidity, fruitiness, nose, all terms I had not understood. I wasn't about to join Larry in some strange discussion where I was lost before I began. Besides, this wasn't giving me what I wanted to know. So I put down my untasted glass and blurted out, "Larry, about Saturday night."

He stopped abruptly and stared at me. "What?"

"Last Saturday night," I repeated, "you said Sabrina was in the kitchen and Jolene came in. Is that right?"

"Sabrina wasn't there when Jolene came in. She came in after Otto and Jolene had started to fight."

It was my turn to pause. "Right. That's what Sabrina told me. But did anyone else come into the kitchen? Like, after they left?"

"Who?" He put his own wineglass down and stared at me, apparently confused. I felt irritation rising. This was not that hard a question.

"Like Carlton, for instance. Did he come into the kitchen? Did he speak to Otto? Did they argue or anything?" If this were a trial, my questions would have been thrown out of court, but, since Larry seemed so obtuse, I felt a little witness leading was needed.

After a couple of minutes, he replied, "Otto was gone."

"What? Are you saying Carlton did come in?"

"He stuck his head in the door, that's all," he told me slowly.

"What did he say?" I was getting more and more impatient. "And what did you say?"

"He wanted to know where Otto was." He dragged out each word. "I told him he was out on the deck."

"And then what?" I was getting excited. This was exactly what I needed.

"Nothing."

The man was maddening. "What do you mean, nothing? Something must have happened."

"He went away."

"He went away," I repeated. "Is that all? He just went away?"

"Yes."

"Did you see him again?"

"Not until we served the dessert course. He was sitting at your table."

I knew that. What I didn't know was where Carlton went after he left the kitchen. I had an idea, but no proof. "You don't know where he went?"

"No. Why are you asking all these questions? Do you think Carlton killed Otto?"

I didn't know what to say. I thought there was a better than even chance Carlton had picked up a wine bottle, sneaked out the front door and around to the deck, smashed Otto over the head, opened the gate and pushed him in, then tossed in the champagne bottle, hoping the police would think it was the murder weapon. But it somehow didn't seem an appropriate discussion topic with Larry. Dan, yes, Larry, no. So I wracked my brain and came up with, "I have no idea who killed Otto, but I thought it would be a good idea to know who was where."

Larry stared at me. "I've told the police most of this. They know Mark was looking for Sabrina, and they know all about Frank."

Frank. "What about Frank?" Sabrina had said he had been in the hallway when she dragged Jolene away from her argument with Otto, but I had been so convinced Frank hadn't entered the kitchen I had almost forgotten about it.

"He wanted to talk to Otto." Larry didn't seem very interested. "You know, I really didn't want to work with Frank. I don't like him much. But he's really good. Otto taught me a lot, but I think Frank is even better than Otto. I'm going to learn a lot, and when I'm ready to go solo, I'll be better than either one of them."

I had no idea that being a chef, a great one, meant so much to Larry. Obviously I'd never thought about it, but he had, lots. There was an eagerness, an intensity in his voice when he spoke about it that made me almost hurt for him. Had I ever wanted anything that much? Susannah maybe. Getting away from Brian. But nothing the same way Larry seemed to want this. I found myself hoping he'd make it, that he wouldn't be hurt. But that still didn't tell me about Frank.

"Larry, did Frank talk to Otto?"

"No. Otto had stormed off out of the kitchen, and I told Frank he was in a bad mood."

"Then what did Frank say?"

"He laughed."

That I could believe. "And?"

"He said he'd catch him later and left."

Something I'd better do as well. I pushed my wineglass away and gathered up my purse.

"Aren't the police supposed to be asking all these questions?" he asked, an anxious expression on his face. "You could get hurt."

Hurt? Me? How ridiculous. "Sabrina's worried," I told him as I pushed back my chair. "That dinner meant a lot to them. Did you tell the police about Carlton?"

"I told them about Jolene and Sabrina. They didn't ask about Carlton." His anxious expression deepened, and his eye twitch returned with a vengeance. "Can you forgive me?"

"There's nothing to forgive." I headed for the front door.

"And you'll think about coming to the dinner?"

I could feel myself stiffen. Slowly I turned and looked at him. "No," I said, hoping my tone was kind, hoping more that I was finally getting the point across. "I am not coming to the dinner. Thanks for the information and, ah, the wine."

This time I made it out the door and into the car. Irritation surged through me. What did it take to make Larry realize I wasn't going to date him, go to dinner with him, or do anything else with him? But one good thing had come out of this afternoon. Oh, did I have a lot to tell Dan. As it turned out, he also had a few things to tell me.

Chapter Fifteen

Once again Mark and Sabrina would not be home for dinner. They would be at their new house unpacking boxes that they had stored in Aunt Mary's garage. There were plenty more in mine, but one thing at a time. I knew this because Aunt Mary told me when I stopped by to pick up the lasagna. She said she was going to help them line cupboards, unpack books, and no doubt feed them as well.

"Why are you doing all this?" I'd asked, suspicious by the look on her face.

"Because Sabrina is my great niece and I want to help," she'd answered, so innocent.

"Why are you really doing this?"

"Because you and Dan need an evening alone," she'd said. "Really, Ellen, sometimes I wonder about you. You have a wedding in three months, and you haven't even looked for a dress. The only thing that's done is the church, and Dan arranged that. Tonight you can talk. Make decisions, discuss things like flowers, invitations, the rest of your lives."

I left her house clutching my lasagna, feeling more torn than ever. I loved Dan a lot; I was more than willing to admit that, but I also liked my life the way it was. Finally. Divorcing Brian hadn't initially been my idea, but it turned out to be one of the best ones that had ever landed on me. I liked my job, I liked this old house where I had grown up and now had made my own, I liked this town, growing pains and all. I especially liked my independence. Marriage to Brian had been a whole lot more like bondage. Would it be like that with Dan? Maybe not. Probably not. But this little feather of doubt kept tickling me. Would I, once again, be giving up all the things I'd worked so hard to accomplish? I sighed. I'd better get this straight in my head soon, because time was running out.

The screen door slammed, and there he was. "It's nicer tonight. Fall's trying to fool us, make us think it's summer and it's going on forever."

I got a kiss before he got a beer. The top snapped open, and Dan took a long swallow. "What a day," he said when he was able. He spotted the dip bowl, took a chip, and filled it with guacamole. "This is good. What did you put in it?"

I really didn't think he wanted the recipe, so I ignored that and took a good look at him.

"You look tired." His eyes had lines around them, the gray in his sandy hair seemed to show more than usual, and his usually tidy mustache needed a trim.

"I am. What do they say, when it rains it pours?"

"What do you mean? What else is happening?"

He didn't answer. Instead, he stood still in the middle of the kitchen, listening.

I listened too, but couldn't hear a thing. "What? What are you listening to?"

"The quiet. Don't you hear it?" He grinned at me, then set his beer can down on the table and reached for me. "There's nobody here but us, is there?"

"There's Jake," I told him.

"Jake I can handle. Besides, he knows when to keep out of the way."

I let him pull me into his arms, let his hands slide around my waist, let my face reach up to meet his, let his lips find mine. The kiss was long and very satisfying. Dan kept holding me, nuzzling my ear a little, running his hand up my back, through my hair. My hands did a little exploring of their own. The nuzzling dropped down toward my neck, and I heard a little sigh.

It was me! Oh well, I thought. It may be a while before we get around to eating.

Then the doorbell rang. So did the phone.

"God damn it," Dan hollered, right in my ear. "I might as well try to make love to you at the bus station."

The doorbell rang again. So did the phone.

"Go answer the door," I said. "I'll get the phone."

The call was for Dan. He came back into the kitchen carrying a large basket of flowers, slammed them down on the kitchen table, growled, "Who the hell is sending you flowers?" and picked up the phone.

"Yeah?" was his initial greeting, but his expression evened out and he started to look interested.

"Unhuh," he said, then, "unhuh, you don't say, okay, unhuh, got it. Thanks."

"Who was that?" I asked. Cryptic conversations always make me curious.

"My office. With the results of some lab tests. Who sent you flowers?"

"What lab?"

"The fingerprint lab. Who sent you flowers?"

"I don't know. What was so interesting about the fingerprints? What fingerprints? Where were they?"

"You'd know if you looked at the card."

"What?" I asked. "How would I know—?"

"The flowers. Look at the card."

"Oh." I picked the card off the little spear and opened it. "Oh."

"Who sent them?" Dan reached for the card, but I held it out of his reach.

"Larry Whittaker."

"The school boy from Paris? Why is he sending you flowers?"

"Be kind. He's been calling me all week. Wanted me to go to that dinner they're doing next Saturday. That reminds me. He came by this morning and I wanted to talk to you about what he told me. He said…"

Dan took the card out of my hands and read it aloud. "The invitation to dinner still stands. I will call you tomorrow and we will plan when we can be together. Always, Larry.

"What the hell is that all about? He was here this morning? He's been calling? Now he's sending flowers?"

"Oh for heaven's sake. You could hardly think I'd be interested in Larry."

"Actually, I don't." He grinned. "Not when you can have me." His grin faded as he stared at the card. "But he seems to be making a nuisance of himself. Can't you get rid of him?"

"I'm trying. And he was just trying to cheer me up, I'm sure. About this morning, Larry said that Jolene said that Sabrina…"

"Why do you need cheering up? If he wants to cheer up someone, have him send flowers to me. I could stand some. So could my whole staff. But not pink roses; bright red would be appropriate." The refrigerator door opened, and Dan disappeared inside, reappearing with another beer and the lasagna. "We might as well cook this. If I try to kiss you one more time, city hall will probably blow up. I'd hate to be responsible."

Frustration is not a strong enough word to describe how I felt. Dan disappeared into the backyard, not answering my questions about the phone call, not letting me ask him about Sabrina, and not willing, or ready, to start again what the phone and door had interrupted. I looked at the basket of pink roses, stuck my tongue out at it, put lasagna in the oven, opened the refrigerator myself and removed the bottle of chardonnay. I tucked it under my arm, picked up a glass and the platter of chips and guacamole, and went outside. I had a right to know about Sabrina; she was my niece, and city hall would not blow up if I got kissed again. At least, I didn't think it would.

One look at Dan's face told me I wasn't the only one suffering from frustration. Work or me, it didn't matter. This was not the time to push the issue. Any issue. So I set down the bowl where he could reach it easily and said, "Another beer?" He looked at me suspiciously before he replied. "Not right now. Want me to open that?"

I handed him the bottle and the opener; he poured me a glass, took several chips loaded with guacamole, and visibly relaxed. Jake appeared, the smell of cooking pasta drifted from the kitchen into the backyard, and we gradually started talking, laughing, getting back our comfortable relationship. Dan looked up and smiled, not a trace of the policeman in his eyes. "Jake is going to be one happy man when Paris leaves." His laugh was a little too relieved to be for Jake alone. "So, Saturday's the big day. I'll bet Mark and Sabrina can hardly wait."

That made four of them. Since he'd brought up Sabrina, maybe I could also. I walked over behind him and started rubbing his shoulders.

"What are you doing?"

"Helping you relax," I murmured.

"I can think of another way, one that's lots more fun." He turned around, pulled me close with his free hand, and kissed me. We didn't come up for air until I smelled burning pasta.

"Damn it," he muttered, "every time I start to make love to you, something happens."

"Well, city hall didn't blow up. I'll go get everything else, and we'll eat."

"And after dinner?" He looked at me with a wicked grin.

"Comes dessert," I laughed.

I brought everything out, and we ate on the patio table, agreeing it might be the last time this season. We were almost finished, and both on our second glass of wine, before I broached the subject of murder. "Dan, I'm worried about Sabrina. Really worried."

"Why?" I could see him stiffen a little bit.

"I know you don't want to talk about this, but I need to know. Do you think she killed Otto? Are you planning to arrest her? Sabrina is going crazy with worry, and I'm right behind her."

"I don't see why you're so worried. You're not her mother," he said somewhat impatiently.

"I am her aunt. Remember? And Catherine is my sister. Remember?"

"Remember Catherine? No chance I'd forget. Okay, Ellie, a couple of facts. Then we're going to talk about something else. I am not going to arrest Sabrina."

"Thank God."

"That doesn't mean I'm not still looking in her direction."

"What?"

"You asked. Now I'm going to tell you. Policemen don't run around suspecting people like they do in those mystery books you read. Policemen gather evidence, slowly and carefully, and eventually that evidence tells them something. Like who perpetrated a crime. In this case, most of the evidence we've collected has Sabrina's name on it."

I could feel myself get cold. He couldn't mean this.

"What evidence?" My voice sounded small even to me.

"First, the fingerprints on the gate. Hers were the only ones. That was suggestive, but hardly conclusive. You know about the fight. Again, suggestive."

"Everyone fought with Otto. You were there. You know."

"Exactly. But that phone call tonight, one more suggestive thing. They're adding up, Ellie."

"What one more thing? Come on, Dan."

"That was the fingerprint lab. They finished the tests on the champagne bottle. Even with all the gunk on it, there were traces of fingerprints. Yours, mine, a smudge of someone's we haven't identified, probably the waiter's, and Sabrina's."

Hope built. So did confusion. "But Sabrina's prints would be on the bottle. She was pouring from it."

"Was she? I remember the waiter giving Mark a flute, refilling our glasses, and leaving that bottle on the table. We almost dumped it on the floor. You held it, I picked it up, but I don't remember Sabrina having anything to do with it. Do you?"

"Couldn't she have held it earlier, given it to the waiter, or something?" I asked, maybe a little desperately. Sabrina couldn't have done it. But why were her fingerprints on that damned bottle? And where was the real bottle, the one that had been used to kill Otto? If she'd killed, where had she hidden that bottle? Now was the time to tell Dan about Carlton and find out if he'd considered Frank.

"Dan, listen." I practically grabbed his shirtfront in my eagerness to tell him what I'd found out. "It's not Sabrina. And I can prove it."

He looked at me in complete surprise. "You have proof? What proof? And why haven't you told me before this?"

"Because I just found out, that's why. Now listen."

He did. Only when I was finished, he shook his head. "Sounds like that kitchen had a revolving door, but none of it's proof. It is enough for me to go back and take another look at our friend Carlton, ask Frank a few questions, and I might even talk to Jolene again, although I'm not sure she was in any condition to do it. But I don't want to talk any more about Otto, Carlton, or murder. I want to have another glass of wine and enjoy you and the evening."

The subject was closed, and I found I was glad. I also was enjoying this evening, at least I had been until we had interjected murder, and was glad to leave it alone. Stars were appearing, one by one, as if a heavenly lamplighter was wandering through the sky, turning them on. The smallest suggestion of a breeze had come up, saying autumn was close, enjoy this while you can. Good idea.

"Great dinner," Dan said, leaning back in his chair. "That lasagna's almost as good as Mary's. Where did you learn to make that?"

"You should know by this time I can cook," I replied, giving my blessed aunt no credit at all.

"I do. I do. You're a great cook." He smiled at me from under his mustache. It was the sexiest smile I'd ever seen. I wondered if he knew what it did to me. I hoped the smile I gave him was as inviting as the one he'd sent my way. It must have been. He moved over in his chair a little, set his wineglass on the grass, opened up his arms, and said, "Come here." I did.

"My goodness," I said a few minutes later, when I could breathe again. "You certainly do know how to—let's go inside."

"Upstairs?"

"Yes." I sat up, started to fasten the buttons on my shirt, then quit. Why bother?

"What about the dishes?" Dan asked, doing a little fastening up of his own.

"Tomorrow's another day." I headed for the kitchen door, Dan on my heels.

"What if Mark and Sabrina come home?" he asked, amusement in his voice.

"According to Aunt Mary, the whole town knows you spend a large portion of your nights here. So do they. Besides, we'll close the door."

Dan laughed, a wonderful, warm, comfortable laugh, and grabbed me as I passed the washing machine. He slid his arms around me, his hands inside my unbuttoned blouse. His mustache tickled my earlobe then moved to the nape of my neck. I pushed back, feeling him against me, ready to explode. We might never make the bedroom. I twisted in his arms to face him, my arms around his neck, bringing him down close to me, letting his mouth devour mine, drowning in his kiss.

"We'd better go upstairs while we can," I finally said.

"I've never made love on a washing machine, but it sounds like good clean fun," Dan said in my ear. His tongue followed. I moaned.

"Not funny. I really would be upset if Mark and Sabrina walked in on us—like that."

"Might be a little embarrassing," Dan conceded, but not with much conviction.

"Come on." I slid my hand down into his and led the way into the kitchen. I wasn't planning to stop, but Dan paused and stared once more at the basket of flowers.

"What are you going to do about him?" he asked, emphasizing the "him."

"I'll get him to back off. But I have to do it gently."

"You have to do it quickly." He still had my hand and now he headed for the stairs, pulling me after him. "I have this terrible vision of Larry wandering around after you at our wedding reception, telling everyone about postcards from Paris, trying to get your attention—what's the matter?"

I'd stiffened. I couldn't help it. Wedding reception, wedding, marriage. Damn.

"What's the matter?" Dan tugged at my hand, but I didn't move.

"Nothing," I said, a little too quickly.

"Oh yes there is. The minute I brought up the wedding, you acted like I'd smacked you. And it's not the first time."

"That's not true," I protested, but it lacked conviction.

"You know, if I didn't know better, I'd suspect you of not wanting to go through with this."

"How ridiculous. How can you even think such a thing."

Dan put his hands on my shoulders and held me at arm's length. He looked at me for what seemed like a year, then said, "Ellie, do you love me?"

I started to protest, but the look in his eyes made that seem so false. Truth won out, and I startled myself by saying, simply, "Yes."

"A lot?"

"A lot."

"Then why don't you want to marry me?"

"Oh Dan," I said, trying to get past his hands, which still held my shoulders, and into his arms. "I do want to. But maybe not so soon."

"Why?" His face was still, the warmth gone from his blue eyes.

"Because, well, you know what kind of life I had with Brian and…"

"Don't you trust me?" he asked, so softly I almost didn't hear him.

"Of course I do." Damn it anyway. If he didn't stop this, I was going to break down and blubber. "But, well, why can't we keep things the way they are now? At least for a while? They've been good; we still see each other…" I broke off.

"I don't want to share your table and your bed a couple of nights a week," he said, bitterness ripe in his voice. "I want a commitment, a lifetime of commitments, me to you, and you to me. I want to love you with passion, and I want to love you as your best friend, forever. Don't you get that?"

I didn't. At least, I couldn't make myself believe it could happen. Dan was talking about some idealist kind of marriage, the kind you read about in Cinderella novels. I'd been married, and it sure wasn't "happily ever after." It had meant loss of freedom, loss of self-esteem, of self-confidence. It meant loss of trust, something I wasn't sure I knew how to do anymore.

"What's the matter?" The hurt on his face was unbearable. "Do you think I'll turn into Brian the night after the wedding?"

"No, no, you won't turn into Brian."

"So what do you think will happen?"

I looked up at him, unable to speak, wanting so badly to say, "You'll get busy, you'll get bored, you'll get critical, you'll quit loving me, and I couldn't bear to go through all that again." Instead I said, "I don't know."

"Well, let me know when you figure it out." Dan's hands dropped off my shoulders. He stared at me for a moment and added, "But don't take too long. I love you, Ellie, above everything in the world, but I'm not going to sit around forever while you make up your mind. I'm not going to ride roughshod over you. If you don't know me well enough, love me enough, to know I don't operate that way, then there's nothing left to say." He started for the door, leaving me in the middle of the kitchen, arms hanging loose at my sides, my whole world suddenly upside down.

"Dan," I started. He turned, waited a second, but I couldn't go on.

"Don't forget to feed Jake," he threw at me, then stormed out, letting the kitchen door swing angrily shut behind him, followed almost immediately by the slam of the front door.

It opened again. I jumped, then ran into the living room, ready to throw my arms around him, saying—what?

Mark and Sabrina came in, laughing.

"Hi," Mark said. "We saw Dan storming down the walk. What's he so het up about?"

"Oh dear," Sabrina said. "Something bad's the matter. Is it my fault?"

"No, of course not." I was starting to have a mood change. How dare he storm out of here like that? Who did he think he was? I had a perfect right to decide who, and when, I married. Just because he thought December was a good time didn't mean I did, and I was not, repeat, not going to be told, by any man, any more, ever, what to do. Just because I loved him didn't mean—damn. What had I done?

"I'm sorry, Ellen." Sabrina touched me on the arm. She looked like she was going to burst into tears. That was all I needed. If she did, so would I, and that I refused to do. "You were fighting about me, weren't you? Because Dan wants to arrest me? Is that why Dan was so mad? Because you stood up for me?"

"No, this has nothing to do with you. It's something else…"

I never got to finish my sentence, not that I had any intention of explaining anyway, because Mark jumped in.

"What do you mean, Dan wants to arrest you? That's nonsense, and you know it. If he's going to arrest anyone in this family, it'll be me."

"Why you?" he surprised out of me.

"Because of that missing wine thing, Otto accusing me of stealing, the jerk, and—"

"And what?"

He waved his hand as if to say "nothing" but his face was beet red.

I was curious, of course, but mostly I was tired. Tired of Mark and Sabrina, of murder and murder suspects, of police chiefs, of marriage, of weddings, and of anything remotely connected with any of them. I turned away from Mark and started toward the stairs.

"Where are you going?" Sabrina asked.

"Upstairs." I started up. And when I got there, I was going to either have a raging temper tantrum or a long cry. Maybe both. I didn't do either. Instead, I sat on the bed, letting my thoughts swirl around me like phantoms, swooping down, then darting away. I loved Dan. Maybe I didn't love him enough. But what did "enough" mean? Or maybe I was trying to guard this new, independent life I'd worked so hard to produce. Or maybe I really had forgotten how to trust. Twenty years with Brian meant I was out of practice. Or maybe he was bullying me, and he could just back off. After all, this didn't have to be all my fault. And if we were going to talk about trust, how about him thinking I would miss Brian's money? Sweatshirts and jeans, dinner at Smitty's BarBQue, eating ice cream, and watching old movies, all those things were just fine with me. If he really loved me, he'd know that. Wouldn't he? But what if he'd meant all the things he'd said? Could you really have a life like that? The way he'd described it, like his first marriage. Could ours be like that, also? Damn the man, just look at what he was putting me through! I didn't need him. I'd curl up with my cat and a—where was my cat? Not here. I pushed open my bedroom door, checked to make sure Mark and Sabrina's door was closed, and crept down the stairs. A phone was on the coffee table in the living room. Should I? I stared at it for a long time, but somehow, I couldn't.

"Well," I told Jake as I plucked him off the top bookshelf, trying hard to control the tremor in my voice, "I guess it will be a while before we see Dan Dunham again."

As it turned out, that wasn't exactly true.

Chapter Sixteen

It was four o'clock in the morning when my bedside phone rang. I had spent most of the night tossing and turning, thinking about what I should have done, should have said, trying to figure out what I should do, what I wanted to do, and had just dropped off into an uneasy doze. Dan. It was Dan calling. I fought my way out of the sheets and grabbed the phone.

"Is Mark there?" an anxious voice asked.

"Who is this?" I snarled.

"Hector. It's Hector from the winery. I have to talk to Mark. Right away. It's an emergency."

I was awake enough for the urgency in the man's voice to override my disappointment. "Wait. I'll get him."

Mark answered groggily when I pounded on his door.

"Get the phone," I said. "It's Hector."

I could hear a groan from behind the door. By now I was completely awake, and I wanted to know what had happened. It must be something pretty grim for Hector to call at this time of the morning. Where was he, anyway? At the winery? Questions that needed answers, so, instead of hanging up my extension, I listened in.

"You've got to get here fast," Hector said. "I've already called the police. They're on the way."

"Just let me get my pants on. Take me about ten minutes," Mark answered and slammed down the phone.

I rubbed my ear a little as I hung up. It serves you right for eavesdropping, I thought, then something penetrated. Police. Coming to the winery. Not too many police in this town, and this must be serious. So that probably meant the police chief? Maybe I needed to go with Mark. Yep. Maybe I did.

"Why are you dressed?" Mark asked, as I met him in the hall.

"I'm going with you."

"Why?" asked a bleary-eyed Sabrina.

"Never mind. Let's go," I said.

Mark looked at me strangely but didn't say anything. He just fumbled for his keys and headed down the stairs, followed by Sabrina. I was right behind.

"I can't believe it," Sabrina kept saying as Mark careened the car out of the driveway and down the empty street. "I just can't believe it."

Believe what? I wanted to ask but was too busy trying to keep from flying across the backseat to say anything. Finally I fastened a seat belt, I wasn't sure which one, and managed to keep upright around the next corner.

"What exactly happened?" I asked, a little breathlessly.

"Don't you know?" Sabrina said, obviously surprised.

"No," I said, trying hard for patience. "No. I don't. Only that it's an emergency." Then for the first time a thought struck me. "It's not another body. Is it?"

"Worse," said Sabrina.

"Wine," Mark said. "Someone stole the wine."

I didn't think that was worse than a body. I wanted to ask, "What wine?" but was too busy keeping myself upright to get the words out.

By now we were charging up the hill to the winery. Gravel crunched, tires skidded, and we came to an abrupt halt in front of the huge roll-up doors that led onto the cellar floor. They were up, all the lights were on, and Hector, the dark-haired, sinewy-looking young man I'd met on Saturday, stood on the concrete ramp, waiting for us. He'd been all smiles then; now he glowered.

Mark jumped out of the car and ran up to the doors.

"What happened?" he demanded, grim voiced.

"Come on, I'll show you. The bastards."

They disappeared into the cavernous room, Sabrina and me right on their heels.

The huge fluorescent lights that had burned so bright Saturday night seemed dim. Shadows played around the towering stainless steel tanks; the tall stacks of wooden barrels refused to show their labels. The chill of the cellar caught me by surprise and I shivered.

We stopped almost immediately.

"There." Hector pointed at one of the tanks, indistinguishable from any of the others. "That's the one. They emptied it."

Mark squatted on the floor, examining the huge hose nozzle, reading the volume valve, staring at the drain that ran in front of all the tanks. Only this one showed vivid red drops in front of it, crimson red, blood red. Wine red.

"How did they get in?" Mark asked.

"I've no idea," Hector answered. "But they must have known how to turn off the alarm."

"Then how did you know?"

For the first time, Hector looked almost happy. "I saw them."

"You what?"

"Yep." There was no mistaking the satisfaction in Hector's voice. "I saw a tanker truck coming out the gate. I couldn't figure out why it was here. I didn't think we'd scheduled any bulk wine to be moved, but I wasn't sure. Then I came up here and found everything locked up, no one around. I got worried, so I turned on all the lights, started looking around, saw the wine in the drain, and checked the valve. That tank is empty."

"But why are you here so early?" asked Sabrina. A question that had been running around my mind as well.

"I got a call from the Martinelli brothers about two thirty. They'd finished picking grapes and were on the way. Matter of fact, they should be here any minute, and I haven't even been up on the crush pad. Better do that right now."

"Wait," said Mark. "The police are coming?"

"Called them before I called you. They should be here any minute."

"Minute's up," I said. "Here they are."

Headlights shone in the parking lot and car doors slammed.

"Get going. Get that crush pad ready," Mark ordered. "They can talk to you later."

Hector hurried off and was replaced by two uniformed men. Men I knew well.

"Gary. Sergeant Riker," I said, nodding politely.

They looked a little startled to see me, which was understandable. I usually saw them when I stopped by the station house to collect Dan for lunch. Back in the good old days.

Gary looked around uneasily, then back at me. "You folks didn't find another body. Did you?"

"What we found was an empty storage tank," Mark said, pointing up at the stainless steel monster. He thumped its side. "Hear that? Empty. See that valve? Says empty. We've been robbed."

They both stared up at the tank, then looked around the cellar. Hector had turned on the crush pad floodlights and opened the double doors at the other end. The place was bathed in light, forcing every corner to give up its mysteries.

"What's that smell?" Gary asked.

"Wine fermenting," Mark told him.

"Smells good," Gary commented. "Sort of earthy, maybe like yeast. Would it be yeast?"

Riker gave him a disgusted look, then favored the rest of us with it. "Don't you folks lock up this place?"

"Of course we do," Sabrina said indignantly. "We have an electric gate down by the road, and the whole place is on an alarm system."

"Then how did someone get in? Seems like it would take a while to empty a tank that size," Riker said.

It certainly did seem that way. We were all silent, staring up at the equally silent tank.

"I've no idea how they did it. But yesterday that tank was full of wine; this morning it's empty," Mark finally said.

"How did you find the tank was empty?" asked Gary.

"Hector Munoz, my cellar rat, found it. He came in early to meet a truckload of grapes."

"Cellar rat? That's a funny kind of name," said Gary. He was ignored.

"Hector saw a tanker truck leaving, got suspicious, started looking around, and found this tank empty."

"You people keep strange hours," Riker commented.

"We're in the middle of the crush," Mark said.

Riker didn't look as if that explained much.

"What's a crush?" Gary asked. No one bothered to answer this question either. I was beginning to feel sorry for Gary but was immediately distracted.

"More visitors," said Riker.

We could hear tires crunch and headlights glowed. Several sets, judging from the glow. Voices called, then truck gears groaned, and most of the voices were transferred to the crush pad. Except one.

"Will you look who's here?" asked Dan. His tone left a lot to be desired. "I wonder why I'm not surprised. Find another body?"

"Sarcasm isn't your thing. Stick to billy clubs and thumb screws." I wanted to bite my tongue. Damn! Why did I do that?

Dan glared at me but turned to listen to Riker, who was pointing at the tank.

"This tank is empty. He," he pointed at Mark, "says it was full of wine yesterday. Claims someone stole it."

"What do you mean, claim?" protested Mark.

"Someone did," Sabrina said hotly. "Hector saw him."

"Who's Hector?" asked Gary. Finally someone took note of one of his questions.

"Yes. Who's Hector?" Dan asked. "And exactly what is going on? Will someone please start at the beginning?" The look he gave me made it plain I wasn't the someone.

"Hector Munoz, my cellar rat," Mark looked at Dan's raised eyebrow, "my assistant, got a call that a load of grapes was ready. We weren't expecting them until tomorrow night, so he hurried over here to have the gates open and the crush pad ready."

Dan nodded for him to go on, ignoring Gary's open mouth, ready with another question.

"Hector saw a tanker truck, the kind we use to move bulk wine, driving out our gates. Only we didn't have any juice scheduled to be moved. So he came up here and, instead of opening up the pad, checked the cellar floor. He found this tank empty."

"How did they get in?" Dan asked. "Don't you have an alarm system?"

"A good one," said Sabrina. "And the gate is electric, you have to punch in the code."

"How long would it take to empty a tank that size?" Dan stared up at it, then squatted down to examine the valve.

"Hours," Mark told him. "Whoever it was had to have started around ten, maybe earlier."

"Pretty risky, staying that long, pumping all that stuff," commented Riker.

"Probably not," Mark told him. "Usually the building is locked up by eight and unlocked about seven in the morning. You can't see lights from the street, so if the gate was locked, no one driving by would have any idea someone was here."

"Only Hector showed up at just the wrong time. For our thief," Dan said thoughtfully.

"This time of the year, our hours get pretty erratic," Mark said. "Machine harvesting is done at night, hand picking during the day, and they pick when the sugars are right. It's not uncommon to get a call, like tonight, that grapes we've contracted for are on their way. And, believe me, we aren't about to let them sit around. Like now. Those grapes haven't been off the vines more than a few hours."

We all turned to look at the brightly lit crush pad, where gondolas of deep purple grapes were being poured into the stemmer. It slowly turned, pulling grapes, twigs, leaves, whatever it could get hold of, under its jaws. Twigs and leaves were slowly spit out and the pulp and skins, along with the dull red juice, made their way into the fermenting tanks, hopefully not the one Otto had so recently inhabited. We watched, fascinated, but started as two new voices broke the spell.

"What's going on here? I saw lights. Those are police cars. Why? What's happened?"

I was almost positive I heard "shit" escape from Dan, but it was quickly replaced by "Hello, Carlton. What are you doing here?"

"I, that is, we saw the gate open. The gate shouldn't be open now. Anyone could come up here and—something's going on, and I demand to know what it is."

Carlton advanced toward our group, dragging a disheveled-looking Jolene behind him. Her dress was wrinkled, her champagne-colored hair badly mussed, and her shoes seemed to be missing. Carlton's shirttail was hanging out, his pants were rumpled, and there was a mark on his neck, right about where his ear started, that was rather interesting. The temptation to ask where they had been and whata they'd been doing was almost irresistible.

Dan isn't as polite as I am. It's probably his police training. "Where are you two going at this time of the morning?"

"I was taking Jolene back to her room at the bed and breakfast," Carlton stated with as much dignity as he could muster. "I saw the gate open as we were passing. I thought I had better check on things, so we started up the driveway and saw all the lights. Would you please tell me what is going on?"

"We've had a little problem," Mark said.

"I can see that," Carlton told him. I thought the sarcasm in his tone excessive, even for him. "The police don't usually show up for the fun of it. What is it this time?"

Sabrina gasped, and Mark ground his teeth. I didn't really blame them. Carlton was making it sound like everything that had happened was not only their fault, but that they had thought it all up. Jolene started to giggle, which didn't help things much.

"Carlton got just real upset when he saw that gate open. He takes his responsibilities real serious, don't you Carlton, honey."

Carlton honey looked like he could have done without sweet Jolene's input. He ignored her, along with all the rest of us, and went right to the top.

"Well?" he demanded of Dan.

"Seems there has been a robbery." Dan's tone was mild, but I knew better. Carlton had better watch out.

"Robbery. What kind of robbery? What was stolen?"

"Wine," Mark said. "Someone drained that tank."

Now it was Carlton's turn to stare at the tank. It didn't tell him any more than it had told the rest of us.

"How much wine?" he asked, turning to Mark. "How much was in there?"

"About five thousand gallons."

"Five—Good God. How much money is that worth?"

"A lot. But maybe we can get it back. Hector saw the tanker leave."

"Hector? Who is Hector?" Jolene asked, but she didn't sound very interested. She shifted from one foot to the other, rubbing her bare toes on the leg she was standing on, then she shivered.

"He's my assistant," Mark told her.

"What was he doing here at this hour?" Carlton demanded. "He must have been up to something."

"He was doing his job," Mark said through clenched teeth.

"Well, I think he needs to be questioned," Carlton went on. The man had no eyes. Both Dan and Mark looked like steam engines ready to blow.

"You'll find this Hector had something to do with this," he told Dan, "and you'd better have a long talk with Mark also. This is the second time he's been involved with stolen wine."

I think Mark would have gone after him, but Sabrina grabbed his arm, and Sergeant Riker stepped quickly in front of him.

"Carlton, go home." Dan's tone was a bit strangulated. "Now."

"I'm a partner in this winery and I have a right to be here. Especially in a time like this." Carlton drew himself up and glared at Dan, who glared right back.

"I don't care if you are the President of the United States, the Queen of England and the Pope, you're leaving. Sabrina, so are you. Ellie's taking you. Now. Mark, go get this Hector, and let's figure out just what went on here tonight."

We left. Jolene gratefully, her feet by now a rather interesting shade of blue, Carlton sputtering. Sabrina and I followed, but not until Dan had promised to drop Mark off. When that would be was anybody's guess.

We didn't say much until we got home. The sun was working its way over the eastern hills, the paper was on the walk, Paris was standing by the back door begging to go out, and bed was out of the question.

"Want some coffee?" I asked, filling the pot.

"Why not?" Sabrina sighed. "Life has turned out to be one nightmare after another. I can't decide if I should go to bed and hope I don't have a new one or stay awake and battle through the ones I know about."

"Stay awake," I advised her. "Better the nightmare you know—or is that devil? Anyway, you're going to have to face them sooner or later, and later always seems to make them worse. Now. What do you think happened tonight?"

"I can't imagine." Sabrina reached out for the coffee mug I had filled. "But it had to be someone who knew the gate code and how to turn off the alarm."

"Who knows those things?"

"Anyone who works there. Or has worked there in the past, oh, I don't know, couple of years. Nothing has been changed since we got there, and I have no idea how long those codes have been in existence."

"Which opens up a lot of possibilities."

"You don't think Dan suspects Mark, do you?" Sabrina's face was pinched and white. I didn't blame her. First murder, now this. Dan had better figure this out fast before we all had nervous breakdowns.

"He couldn't possibly," I told her, in my most positive voice.

"Right. Just like he couldn't possibly suspect me of doing in Otto. I wish I had your optimism."

She put down her empty mug and announced that she was going up to take a shower. I watched her go, ignored Paris scratching at the back door, and thought about everything that had happened. First Otto's murder, Frank taking over the bed and breakfast—Frank. He'd been looking for Otto that night. Had he found him? Was Frank's sudden appearance in Santa Louisa, his "availability" to step into Otto's empty shoes, just coincidence? Why did he sell his beloved restaurant? And why was he, too, letting Jolene stay on? For free!

Dan was suspicious of Sabrina. Did Frank know that, and would he let Sabrina take the blame? He didn't seem like that kind of person, but then, he evidently hadn't been a candidate for father of the year. Or father-in-law. Would Frank have any reason to steal wine? He had to know Mark would be the leading suspect. Would he put his son in that kind of position? It didn't seem possible.

But Jolene might. Only, why? She was there to write up the dinner and the grand opening. The only thing she could be guilty of was getting a few freebies. I had to admit, reluctantly, that because I didn't like her didn't automatically make her a thief and a murderer. My every fiber told me the murder and the wine theft were connected. But how? I couldn't see it. Maybe I would ask Dan…right. There was one relationship that appeared to be dead, and I was the one who had killed it. Nice analogy, I thought, and shuddered. Nope, I thought. I don't think so. I love Dan, and he loves me. I'm still not sure about the married part, but damn it, I'm not letting this relationship die. How I'm going to bring it back to life, I have no idea, but I'll think of something. I know I will.

I filled my cup again and went upstairs to wait for my own turn in the shower.

Chapter Seventeen

Over the next several days, not one blasted thing happened. Oh, ordinary things happened. I went to work, and so did Mark and Sabrina. They made arrangements to have their furniture delivered to their new house on Saturday. Aunt Mary bustled around helping them haul boxes out of my garage. Frank appeared on a regular basis, brought food, and offered advice. There was no sign of Jolene, but Larry called me twice a day. Dan didn't appear. No one got arrested for murder. The truck with the stolen wine wasn't found. And we were all left, waiting, wondering what would happen next.

By Saturday afternoon, I was sick of the thought of Otto, murder, bed and breakfasts, restaurants, wineries, Mark, Sabrina, and Larry. Thinking about Dan just made me sick.

"If you don't watch out, every glass Sabrina has will end up in pieces," Aunt Mary told me.

I was pulling them out of boxes as fast as I could, unwrapping them, and stacking them on the counter of Mark and Sabrina's new house. Aunt Mary neatly filled the cupboards.

"What on earth is the matter with you?" she continued. "You've been smashing around here all day, acting like a she bear that's misplaced her cubs."

"Have I?" I paused to lean against the sink. "Maybe I have. I feel, oh, I don't know how I feel. I should be happy. Mark and Sabrina have this cute house, I have mine back, business is good, but I feel…I'd like to kick something."

"Or someone?"

"Maybe a couple of someones," I said, a little more sourly than I had intended.

"Is Larry still calling you?" Aunt Mary pulled her head out of a cupboard and surveyed what was left to put away. "I think we're almost done. I hope Sabrina will be able to find all this stuff. Is he?"

"Yes. And he's driving me nuts. I've done everything but drive him off with an ax, only it doesn't do any good. He seems to have some idea that we dated a lot in high school, keeps talking about all the good times we had and how wonderful it is to pick back up again. We went to one movie before his father swooped him up and took him out of the country. That doesn't qualify as any times, good or bad, and I don't want any now."

"Has Dan called?"

"No." She didn't ask anything more.

"Watch it." Mark's voice made me jump. He backed into the kitchen, balancing a refrigerator on a dolly. "It's going to slide off. That strap…"

"Got it." Only Hector's face and hand appeared as he grabbed a canvas strap and pulled. "Put it down gently. Right. That does it. Wait, let me get this plug in."

The refrigerator slid into place, and Mark and Hector pulled the dolly out from under it and disappeared out the door. Sabrina took their place.

"Now all we need to do is set up the bed, and we're in." She wiped hair out of her eyes. "Wow. Look at this. I can't believe you've done all this."

The kitchen did look good. Most of the cupboards were full. I had removed all of the empty boxes but one, and Aunt Mary had even hung some bright yellow curtains. Their dinette set was in place, and Paris' dog dish was on the floor.

"All I need to do is stock the refrigerator with beer," Sabrina said.

"A little food wouldn't hurt." Frank appeared in the doorway, loaded down with sacks and covered bowls. "Look what I brought."

Paper plates appeared, followed by thick sandwiches, two salads, Greek olives, cheese, and, of course, wine.

"I brought beer, too, and some waters. Although I don't know who would want them," Frank said, lavishly filling plates and handing them around. "Where's Mark?"

"Right here." Mark stood in the doorway watching his father, evidently trying to make up his mind how he was going to react. Finally he smiled.

"Thanks." He took a plate. "This was real nice of you."

Sabrina was having a harder time being generous.

"Shouldn't you be at the restaurant?" she asked him, carefully cutting a sandwich in half. All of the ingredients fell out of one end. She tried stuffing them back in, gave up, scooped the whole thing onto a plate and started eating bites with her fingers.

"We aren't open for lunch. Actually we aren't open for anything, won't be until the grand opening dinner one week from today. Anything that's going on, Larry can handle. Mary, try this salad. It's chicken Thai. A little hot, but worth the fire."

Aunt Mary obediently held out her plate and let Frank pile it full. She took a forkful, smiled, and nodded, then quickly grabbed one of the waters.

"I hope you're willing to part with the recipe for this, Frank," she said after a long swallow. "It's hot, all right, but wonderful!" She took another, much smaller, forkful. "And how nice you have so much time now. After you open, you won't have time for anything but that restaurant, will you?"

Wishful thinking? I couldn't resist grinning at her and got a slightly sheepish one back.

"But you have Larry, and I'm sure he's a terrific help," I said, with probably the same wistful note in my voice. "He won't have any more free time than you will, I suppose." I hoped I was right. That restaurant could be salvation for both Aunt Mary and me.

"Too bad Larry isn't more gifted," Frank said. "Then I could leave more often. But we'll see. Maybe he can be trained."

"Trained?" I asked, surprised. "I thought he was trained. Didn't he graduate from that school where Otto taught?"

"Actually, he went to Cordon Bleu in Paris. Maybe trained isn't the right word." Frank filled wineglasses and passed them around. "He has no flair, no, how shall I put it, no imagination. He follows instructions and can read a recipe. He can cook, but creating takes talent."

I cringed for Larry, thinking how devastated he would be at Frank's assessment. I wondered what Otto had thought of his abilities. "I thought Otto was going to make him a partner," I said, accepting a glass.

"That I don't know about. But Otto wasn't creative either. If Larry had been good, Otto wouldn't have kept him, and Larry wouldn't have stayed. A toast. To my son, who is creative, my daughter-in-law, who is lovely and talented, and to their new home."

We all raised our glasses, and then Paris barked. We heard the front door open, heels tap, and a voice call out, "Yoo-hoo. Where is everybody?"

"Oh, no," said Sabrina softly.

"How did she know where we all were?" Mark asked. No one knew the answer, and it didn't matter, for there she was. Jolene.

"I just knew I'd find you all here. Well now, isn't this—cute. Cozy."

She let her eyes travel slowly around the kitchen, taking in the new curtains, the old cabinets, the out-of-date wallpaper. Sabrina flushed but said nothing.

"A toast?" Jolene went on. "How nice. Are you celebrating moving into this house or something else?"

She picked up a full glass and leaned against the refrigerator, cocking one hip, giving us all a good view of her emerald green jumpsuit and her in it before she took a sip.

"What else would we be celebrating?" Mark asked her. "Nothing else's happened recently worth drinking to."

"I thought you'd gone back to Texas," Sabrina said somewhat vaguely. What she left unsaid hung heavy on the air.

"Why, honey, of course not. I have to cover Frank's grand opening, now don't I? The one that should have been Otto's. And, of course, I have to finish my research."

"Research? On what?" I should have known better but the words were out before I could stop them.

"On dear little ol' Otto himself, of course. I'm writing an article all about him, and I'm especially goin' to tell how he came to this darlin' little town. He was going to make this town famous. He told me so."

"More like infamous," Sabrina muttered.

"Otto? Humph." Frank glowered. He pulled the cork out of another bottle and offered refills. Jolene held out her glass.

"Wasn't that a little presumptuous?" Aunt Mary asked. "Silver Springs Winery is famous, so are several of our other wineries, and we have a lot of interesting history that brings in tourists without them."

"Maybe." Jolene moved away from the refrigerator, making sure all eyes followed her, then struck a pose by the sink. "Still, there's lots to write about Otto." She let that statement hang in the air while she smiled at Frank.

"I thought you were going to do a review of last Saturday night's dinner," Mark said.

Sabrina groaned. "Now there's a good idea."

"I already have, and my editors loved it. Just loved it," Jolene gushed, removing her eyes from an obviously seething Frank.

Sabrina groaned again.

"What did you say about it?" I asked. Visions of ghoulish phrases, ones that had nothing to do with food, skipped through my mind.

"Nothing but good things. And Mark, honey, I praised your wines right up to the skies."

The temptation to laugh almost got the better of me. Of course she had.

"And the food?" Frank asked. Good question. Not easy to review food you never touched.

"Now, how could I give a bad review to Otto's very last dinner?"

How could she, indeed? None of us knew what to say, and the silence lay uncomfortably for a moment. Aunt Mary broke it.

"Where's Carlton?" she asked, all innocence. "Ellen says you two have been seeing a lot of each other."

"Why, I thought maybe that was why y'all were celebrating," Jolene said, lengthening her drawl a bit. "You mean you don't know?"

"Know what?" Mark asked, sitting up straighter in his chair.

Aunt Mary stopped covering up the salad bowl, Sabrina quit dumping empty paper plates into a plastic trash sack, and Frank's hand tightened on the wine bottle. I felt myself get rigid, bracing for something I could feel coming; what, I didn't know.

"Something's happened," Sabrina said slowly. "What?"

"I can't believe you haven't heard," Jolene went on, green eyes narrowing a bit, cinnamon-colored lips pursed in a small smile.

"Believe it." Aunt Mary stood as tall as she could and glared straight at Jolene. "What's happened?"

"Why, Carlton's gone and gotten himself arrested. That's what."

Stunned, we all stared at her. I found my voice first.

"Arrested! For what?"

"For stealing Mark's wine, of course."

Chapter Eighteen

The silence in the kitchen was deafening. Each of us stared at Jolene as if we had never seen her before.

It was Mark who recovered first.

"Carlton? Arrested? For stealing my wine? Are you sure?"

"Just positive," purred Jolene. "I have it on the very best authority."

"Oh no," said Sabrina, shaking her head. "It couldn't be."

"Not that idiot who announced himself a partner at the dinner?" Frank had been pouring himself more wine but stopped in mid-pour.

"The very same," Jolene told him cheerfully. "Poor little ol' Carlton wasn't any too smart a thief. Took them hardly any time at all to catch him."

"I don't understand," I said. "When did all this happen, and how do you know about it?"

Every instinct that I owned screamed not to trust Jolene, but I didn't see how, or why, she'd make up a story this wild.

Jolene rearranged herself so she could hold out her glass toward Frank's wine bottle. He poured a little into it, put the cork back into the bottle, and placed it on the counter, ignoring his glass and everyone else's.

"I just happened to drop by the police station," Jolene said, after a healthy sip. "I thought Chief Daniel Dunham might need company for lunch. He told me."

I could feel bile rise. How dare she. Standing there in her tight green jumpsuit, smiling that secret little smile with her carefully painted-on cinnamon-colored lips, color that hadn't even had the courtesy to come off on her glass. And Dan. The nerve of him, telling Jolene and not the rest of us. Especially me. How could he! Easily, came the answer. Unconquered insecurity, fear, stubbornness, inability to trust my feelings or his, all had helped push Dan away. Damn!

"Jolene, exactly what did Dan say?" As usual, Aunt Mary got straight to the point.

"Only that they had arrested Carlton on suspicion of stealing Mark's wine and he didn't have time for lunch. I asked him if he wanted a rain check." This last with a little sideways glance at me. The cat.

"Why would Dan offer that kind of information?" Aunt Mary persisted. She still held the salad bowl, forgotten, its cover about to slide to the floor. Her eyes bore down on Jolene.

"Well." Jolene paused to take another sip. She avoided Aunt Mary by letting her own gaze flicker over Mark. "Carlton was supposed to take me to lunch. We were goin' over the hill to that little place on the creek in San Luis Obispo. I hear they have a great wine list." Here she gave a little sigh. Regret she was missing great wine? Or chagrin at being stood up? "Anyway, when he didn't show, I thought about Dan. And there was Carlton, in the police station, in handcuffs! You can imagine how I felt, so I asked what was goin' on. Dan, that sweet man, wasn't goin' to say, but Carlton started shoutin' they thought he was responsible for stealing the wine, and, of course, he wasn't. He kept askin' me to go get him an attorney. Can you imagine that? Then they took ol' Carlton in another room. It was downright interestin'."

"Are you going to get him an attorney?" I was pretty sure I knew the answer. Poor Carlton.

"Why, honey, what ever for?" Jolene drawled, then took another long sip of her wine.

"I thought you and Carlton were—ah—friends," Frank said, accusation and incredulity fighting each other. "You certainly gave every indication."

"Why, Frank, darlin', we had a couple of dates. That's all. And you could hardly expect me to have any loyalty to a common thief, now could you?"

Aunt Mary, Frank, and Sabrina stared at Jolene as if she were some strange species that had suddenly appeared under their microscope. Mark had another agenda.

"Where is my wine?"

"What?" replied Jolene. She looked up from examining the empty bottom of her glass.

"My wine. If Carlton stole it, where is it?"

"How would I know?" Jolene told him, a little petulantly.

"Didn't you ask Dan?" pressed Mark.

"Of course not. Now, why would I ask a thing like that?"

"Because…because it's important. I need to find that wine."

"Dan didn't say anything about the wine?" Sabrina asked.

"I told you everything I know." Jolene was getting a little huffy. Losing center stage to something as mundane as stolen wine must be tough.

"Ellen." Mark turned to me, urgency making his voice hoarse. "Call Dan. Find out where my wine is."

"No."

"Why not?" said Sabrina. "We have to know."

"I can't. I'm sorry."

"Dan and Ellen had a little tiff," Jolene said, that nasty, playful little smile back. "Maybe she's waiting for Dan to call her. Or to come over so they can kiss and make up."

"Jolene," I started, hoping threat rang in every tone.

"Jolene, stop it. Ellen, call Dan." Aunt Mary's tone left no argument. Jolene stopped talking, but she didn't stop smiling. I called Dan.

He wasn't in. Aunt Mary eyed me, but I could reply honestly.

"He really isn't," I said.

"God damn it!" Mark glared at me. "I need to find that wine!"

"It's not my fault he's not there. I tried."

"Of course it's not your fault," Sabrina said, watching Mark, who had started to pace. "It's just that if we can salvage that wine —losing it will be a big loss."

"What can happen to it?" I asked. "It's sitting in a nice stainless steel truck somewhere. All you have to do is get it and put it back in your own tank."

"Not quite," Frank explained. "Temperature is vital to fermentation. If the tanker is left where no one sees to the refrigeration and the wine gets too hot, it will be ruined."

"It won't even be fit for vinegar." The expression on Mark's face was as sour as his sentence.

Bang went the back door. No one moved. Bang bang. Mark kept pacing; everyone else watched him. No one even glanced at the door. There was a series of barks followed by more banging.

"I used to think it was cute when he did that," Sabrina said with a sigh. She got up and opened the screen. Paris marched into the room, looked at each of us in turn, then walked over to me and sat.

"Oh, all right," I said and fed him the remains of my sandwich.

Aunt Mary stared at the dog, but what she said was, "Carlton."

Sabrina looked at her as if she had gone mad. "That's Paris," she said. Paris got up, moved over to her, and sat. Sabrina fed him some sandwich. Paris turned his attention to Jolene. She looked back at him and shuddered. The dog immediately plopped down in the middle of the floor and stretched out full length.

Aunt Mary watched it all, but she wasn't seeing any of it. "I wonder."

"What do you wonder?" I asked.

"Why Carlton needed to do something as stupid as stealing. I've never been impressed with him; he even cheated in my Sunday school class. I know he's done some…well…dubious business deals, but I never thought he had the courage to do something like this." She finally realized she had the salad bowl and set it down on the drain board. Paris lifted up his head hopefully. "Forget it," she told him. He dropped his head back down.

"Courage?" I asked. "I think the word you're looking for is 'balls.'"

"That's the word," she replied with a little laugh. "Carlton's a bit of a con man, but stealing, this kind of stealing. That's different."

She had everyone's attention. Even Mark stopped pacing. The room got quiet while we digested this new thought.

"I don't know him," Frank said slowly, "but he seems the type to skim a little off the top of any deal he's in. But Mary's right. He risked a lot by stealing that wine."

"Exactly," said Aunt Mary. "And Carlton isn't a risk taker."

"Then why?" asked Sabrina. "He had enough money to buy into the partnership, why would he steal?"

"Carlton was dead broke."

If Jolene had wanted center stage back, she couldn't have come up with anything better.

"What are you talking about?" I asked.

"How do you know?" asked Sabrina.

"She'd know," Frank said.

Jolene made a little face at him and held out her glass. It was obvious she wasn't going on until he refilled it. Frank picked up the bottle, pulled out the cork, and poured it half full. He started to put the cork back in, looked thoughtfully at the bottle, and poured a little into his own glass.

"Well?" Mark demanded. "What do you mean?"

"Carlton had to pay cash for his partnership," she said.

"We know that," Aunt Mary told her. "But that shouldn't have left him destitute."

"It didn't. But buying the lot did."

Jolene kept staring at the dog as if he were going to explode any minute, jump up and attack her. Not much chance of that, but I might if Jolene didn't quit playing obscure word games. On the other hand, the wine could be taking its toll. If she took smaller sips, maybe we could keep her on her feet long enough to find out something.

"Buying what lot?" Mark's patience was beginning to fray, and from the look on Frank's face, so was his.

"The lot next to the bed and breakfast. Where all the parking is going in." Jolene stopped again. Mark was clenching and unclenching his hands, and I could see Frank grit his teeth.

"Parking lot. Carlton sold Otto the Adams place. And Carlton bought the lot? Are you telling us that Otto made him?" Frank asked.

"That's what happened." Jolene paused for another little sip. "That lot had to be bought for cash. Set ol' Carlton back a bunch."

"Will someone tell me what's going on?" Sabrina asked.

"Sure," I said. "Let's see if I've got this right." I smiled at Jolene. She didn't smile back. "Carlton 'forgot' to mention how touchy the city is about parking when he sold Otto the house. Otto went for his restaurant and bed and breakfast permits, but he couldn't get them without more parking."

Jolene frowned, but nodded. Maybe she didn't like sharing center stage.

"Our whole office wondered how Carlton got by the parking requirements," I went on. "Only, he didn't. So, the way I heard it was, Otto went back to Carlton and demanded he do something."

"He told Carlton that if he didn't buy the lot next door, pull down that old shack on it, and pay to have it paved, that he'd go after his real estate license, take ads out in the local paper saying he was a cheat and a fraud, in general ruin Carlton forever." Jolene took over neatly, making sure all eyes were back on her.

"How do you know all this?" Mark demanded.

"Otto told me." That demure little smile was back.

"Sounds exactly like something he'd do," exclaimed Frank.

"Does, doesn't it," confirmed Jolene. "Actually, Otto told me about the lot, among other things. Carlton told me about being broke."

"People certainly seem to confide in you," Aunt Mary said. I loved her expression.

"That's what makes me a good reporter," Jolene told us all, holding up her empty glass. No one obliged.

"This changes things," Aunt Mary went on. "Do you suppose—?"

"Do you suppose what?" I asked. "Are you thinking what I'm thinking?"

"She's thinking that Carlton had the best motive of all of us to bang Otto over the head, and he had the same opportunity. He's our murderer!" Sabrina's tone was gleeful. "Isn't that right?"

"That's what I was thinking," admitted Aunt Mary. "I wonder if Dan's thinking that also."

"It has occurred to him."

None of us had heard Dan come in the front door.

"Place looks good, but you better do something about that doorbell," he said. "Doesn't work."

"Dan." Mark was the first to react. "Man, am I glad to see you."

"Always nice to have someone welcome you." He bent down and rubbed Paris behind the ears. The dog rolled over on his back and put all four feet in the air.

Was I supposed to respond to that comment, I wondered? Least said, soonest mended, especially as that sly smile was back on Jolene's lips. Its effect on me almost guaranteed I'd say something that would need mending.

Aunt Mary pulled Dan away from the dog. "Dan. For heavens sake, tell us what's going on."

Sabrina was right behind her. "Did you really arrest Carlton? And you think he killed Otto?"

"Sit right down." Jolene was not to be outdone. She waved him toward the one empty chair at the table, but she stayed posed against the cupboards, away from the dog and close to the wine bottle. "You poor man. You must have had just a terrible day."

"Have you had lunch?" That, of course, came from Frank.

Dan looked at me as though expecting me to add something. I wasn't sure what that was, so I kept quiet. He turned to look at Jolene, who made sure he got a good view of the jumpsuit, nodded once, and pulled out a chair. "No, I haven't," he answered Frank. "Or breakfast either. Um, that looks good."

He accepted the full plate Frank handed him, shook his head at the wine, and popped open one of the waters.

Aunt Mary, usually the one providing the full plate, now had no patience with the needs of the inner man.

"Dan Dunham, Jolene tells us you have arrested Carlton Carpenter for stealing Mark's wine. Is that true?"

Dan mouth was too full for him to do anything more than nod.

"Swallow that right now and tell us what's going on."

Aunt Mary's instructions get followed. Dan looked longingly at the half sandwich and remaining salad on his plate, but refrained, at least for a moment.

"Jolene's right. We did arrest Carlton. Mark, we found your wine up in Napa. It's safe, and the winery that called us is taking care of it. They were going to buy it from Carlton, thinking he represented Silver Springs, and would probably still buy it from you, if you want to sell."

"Really?" Gloom was gone; hope was back. "It's all right?"

"Which winery?" asked Frank.

"How did they know to call you?" asked Sabrina.

"We sent out a statewide bulletin, thanks to the information Mark gave us. We figured it had to be offered for sale somewhere. Some smart person in their office actually read it and put two and two together. The driver claims he didn't know the wine was stolen; that Carlton hired him to pick it up, and didn't tell him where it was going until the next day. He had all the right paperwork."

"I can't believe the driver didn't think something was wrong. Someone is always there when we move wine. How did he get into the building?" Sabrina asked.

"Carlton gave him the gate combo and the key earlier that day, told him no one could make it that night, could the driver handle it." Dan paused long enough to grab a mouthful of salad, glanced at Aunt Mary, and put the sandwich down. "The driver is a freelancer, goes all over the state, said, of course, he could, and he did."

"How did Carlton get the keys?" Sabrina asked, visibly upset.

"No idea," Dan replied. "We asked, of course, but he's not saying."

"Who is the driver?" Mark wanted to know.

"Guy by the name of Cassidy. Sean Cassidy. You know him?"

"Yeah. He's done a little work for us. Seemed an all right guy. And we do keep weird hours, especially this time of year," Mark conceded.

"But what about Otto?" pressed Sabrina. "Did Carlton…do you think…what are you going to do about that?" The last of that sentence came out in a rush.

Dan didn't say anything for a minute. "He certainly had a motive, and he had the opportunity. We're looking at it."

"It was Carlton. I know it. It's the only possibility." Sabrina was beaming, shining her smile all around the kitchen. Mark looked about as happy. Why not? He had found his wine, and his wife was no longer a murder suspect. Neither was he. All in all, a good day. For some of us.

"You certainly have been busy, Dan." Jolene left the cupboards and moved in for the kill. The only thing that kept her from hanging over Dan's shoulder was Paris, who sat beside Dan's chair looking hopeful. What a good dog. "I never would have suspected Carlton was that kind of person." She moved around the table away from Paris. "Just gives me chills to think I spent all that time with a murderer."

"I didn't say that," Dan told her firmly. "I only said we're looking at possibilities. All kinds of possibilities."

"It had to be Carlton," Sabrina said. Nothing was going to dent her euphoria.

Frank didn't look quite so convinced. "If he was going to kill Otto, why not do it before he put out all the money for that lot?"

"I doubt Carlton planned it," Aunt Mary said. "I don't think he's the type."

Dan had been watching me out of the corner of his eye, but now he turned toward Aunt Mary.

"You're most likely right. Otto's death was bizarre, but nothing about it seems planned. Probably whoever did it finally had enough, there was a full bottle of wine in his—or her—hand, and before they knew it, Otto was in the tank, followed by the empty champagne bottle."

"My. That sounds just awful." Jolene gave a graceful little shudder and moved closer.

Dan gave her a long look, then turned toward Mark. "Come on," he said, pushing back his chair. "I'll get you in touch with the people who have your wine, and we'll see what we can do. Can I take this with me?"

He wrapped the half sandwich Aunt Mary hadn't let him eat in a napkin, and put the top back on the water bottle. He didn't get far.

"I was just wonderin', Dan honey." Jolene was almost on top of him, long lacquered nails lightly touching his arm. "Since we didn't get to do lunch, maybe we could get together for dinner?"

Dan honey? I couldn't help it. The words were out before I could choke them back. "Dan already has a date for tonight," I told her, in my sweetest sugary voice. "One he's had for some time."

Oh boy, now I'd done it. We'd had a date all right, but I doubted Dan planned on keeping it. For the first time since he'd come in, I looked him in the eyes, but I couldn't read what was there. I held my breath, waiting, for this wasn't about Jolene.

After an eternity, Dan smiled. "That's right. We have a date. See you about six o'clock?" Then he gestured to Mark, who followed him out the front door.

Chapter Nineteen

"I'm going to have to change that gate combination," Sabrina stated. "I don't know how Carlton got it, but I can't take the chance someone else might have it."

"He probably found it when he was driving your office people crazy, demanding all the records," I said, but my mind wasn't on Carlton or gates.

"Oh, I'll bet you're right. We keep a set of keys on a nail inside the roll-up door, and the gate combo is on a card right by them." Sabrina's eyes were wide with surprise. "Why, that—my office people. That's how he got the paperwork. He kept after them to show him everything, what we had to fill out for ATF, what kind of documentation we needed for a sale, who we normally traded with; they couldn't figure out why he wanted any of that. Ha! That…"

"Who'd have thought little ol' Carlton would be that enter-prising," Jolene drawled. She sank into the chair Dan had vacated, smiled at Frank, and twirled her empty glass in her fingers. Frank didn't take the hint, but Paris did. He moved over to stand beside her and sniffed at her glass. "Augh," said Jolene, just like Lucy in *Peanuts*. She got to her feet and moved away from the dog as quickly as she could. "I think I'll just run along." She set her empty glass down on the counter, looked at each of us in turn, letting her eyes rest longest on me. There was the faintest trace of a smile as she turned to go.

"I'm goin' to have to think up somethin' interesting to do this evening, and that might take me a few minutes. Frank, honey…" You could see the speculation in those almond-shaped eyes, speculation that was dismissed almost immediately. "I'll see you later. Maybe we can have a little glass of wine while you tell me all your plans for next Saturday night. Or maybe I'll just ask Larry. See y'all."

I wondered if she noticed no one asked her to stay or offered any ideas for her evening's entertainment.

Frank gathered up his bowls and put them in the refrigerator over Sabrina's protests.

"No, no, you won't want to cook later, and who knows when Mark will be back. I have to go, lots to do. Mary, I'm afraid I won't be over this evening. Tomorrow maybe? Sabrina, tell Mark how happy I am that they found his wine, and also the thief. Everything is working out fine, isn't it?" Frank was out the door before any of us could react.

"Well, that was fast." Aunt Mary stared at the closed door, then shook her head a little. "Not that the idea of an evening by myself isn't welcome, but, how odd."

"Frank's always been odd." Sabrina dismissed Frank with a wave of her hand. "The whole time Mark was growing up, all Frank thought about was his precious restaurant. That was one of the reasons Mark's mother left him. He was never there for Mark, until he found out Mark was going to be a winemaker. Next best thing to a chef, I guess. I was afraid he'd have nothing to do, now that the restaurant is gone, so let's be grateful Otto's project is keeping him occupied and out of our hair."

"She's got a point. That's what you wanted, Frank out of your hair," I told Aunt Mary, giving up any attempt to keep a straight face.

"I know, I know. Still, I wonder what he's planning on doing tonight and why he's acting so mysterious."

"If it's any consolation, I don't think it includes Jolene."

"It's not," she replied tartly, "and speaking of tonight, I think you need to make some plans of your own."

How right she was. Dan was coming over at six, presumably for dinner, and I hadn't bothered to go to the market. Not to mention make time for a badly needed shower and shampoo. I looked down at my nails. Nope, they were beyond hope.

"Hadn't you better go to the store?" Aunt Mary reads minds.

"If I'm going to feed him," I said grimly. "Otherwise he's going to get hot dogs and beans. How about you two? Will you be all right?"

"We'll be fine," Sabrina said. "You've done too much already."

"Go, go." Aunt Mary handed me my purse and car keys. "Dan deserves a good meal, and if he gets something better to look at than those old jeans and that filthy tee shirt, you might get yourself engaged again. If that's what you want, of course." The front door closed on their cheerful chatter, both expressing wonder that it had been Carlton all along.

Mark and Sabrina's troubles were behind them, Aunt Mary had at least one night's reprieve, Paris was settling into her new life by trying to dig up an ancient camellia bush, and I was on my way, I hoped, to put my own life back together. Because, wonder of wonders, I had finally realized, after much agonizing the last few days, that being engaged again, ending with a wedding on New Year's Eve, was exactly what I wanted. Fingers crossed, I got into my car and headed for the market.

Chapter Twenty

The closer it got to six, the more I worried. What had I done? My little outburst had clearly told Dan I wanted, at the very least, our relationship to continue. But how? Should I come right out and say, 'I love you, and I want to marry you'? Or should I let him lead the way? Make the first move? Maybe he'd changed his mind; maybe he wouldn't want to marry someone he thought didn't trust him.

I'd worried about what Dan thought, what he wanted, all through the grocery aisles, all the way home, and all the way through a shower and shampoo. Finally, as I blew my hair dry, I stared in the mirror and wondered what I thought, what I wanted.

"Are you positive you're ready to make the commitment Dan wants, Ellen McKenzie? Do you want it, too? Because if not, you had no right to trap him into coming back over here," I told my reflection. That was when the doorbell rang.

"Hi," was what I got, along with a small peck on the cheek.

"Hi, yourself," I said, trying to sound breezy and normal. "How did it go?"

"How did what go?" His reply, coming out of the refrigerator, where he was rummaging for a beer, was a little muffled.

"Everything. Mark's wine truck, Carlton's arrest, Otto's murder investigation."

"Fine. Everything's going fine."

"Really," I said. "Everything's fine."

Dan popped the lid of his beer can and took a healthy swallow. "Ah, that's better. Yep, Everything's fine." He took another sip and stole a look at me over the top of the can. "Did you want something? Wine or something?"

I knew that look. It was the same one he'd had when we were kids. Dan's guard was up. Now what did I do? Keep it light, I decided. Light and friendly.

"Wine," I said. "I'll get it. How about some chips? I have some new ones I thought we'd try. Got them at the health food store. No fat and no salt. By the way, I was thinking of a large salad for dinner. With non-fat dressing. And maybe yogurt for dessert?"

"Okay," Dan laughed. "I'll tell you. But I'm not giving in to threats. I can smell pot roast. Living room okay?"

I sighed as I followed him. He'd never asked before where we should sit. He'd always just gone in and plopped himself down on the sofa, making sure he left plenty of room for me to cuddle up beside him. This time he took my reading chair. There was only room for one.

There wasn't much to tell. Mark knew all kinds of people in Napa, and his tanker truck, complete with wine, was being well looked after until the winery either decided to buy it or return it. Carlton had hired an attorney and was out on bail.

"Who's his attorney?" I asked.

"Someone from San Luis Obispo."

I didn't need to ask what Dan thought of him. His tone told it all.

"What happens next?" I stretched out my legs to make a lap for Jake. He purred as he settled himself. Nice to know someone wanted to be close.

"Carlton's arraigned, a trial date is set, he's convicted and goes to jail." Dan made it sound easy, but I had a feeling it wasn't.

"How can you be so sure he'll be convicted? It doesn't look that easy on 'Law and Order.'"

"They have to make it look hard or you wouldn't watch. Anyway, Carlton gave the driver a key to the winery overhead doors, as well as the gate combination, and all the supposed paperwork for the sale. He also gave the driver a false name, but he let the guy see him. Not smart. The driver picked him out of a group of pictures immediately. And, just to make things better, Carlton used a local locksmith to have the winery key copied. The locksmith knew who he was and will testify. No, our friend Carlton Carpenter is going to jail."

"How about the murder? Will this lawyer, whoever he is, defend Carlton for that as well?"

"We haven't charged him with that."

"But you're going to, aren't you? It couldn't be anyone else." I could hear the urgency in my voice and felt my neck muscles tighten. "Unless you think Frank might have…he was looking for Otto. Do you think it was Frank?"

"I don't think anything yet. Evidence, Ellie. We're collecting evidence. Speaking of collecting, I think I'll collect another beer. What's that I smell? Not the pot roast, is it?"

"Oh my God. My roast." I dumped Jake on the floor and headed for the kitchen, Dan following.

"Just in time," I told him.

He popped the top of another beer. I handed him the bottle of wine I hadn't bothered to open and a corkscrew.

"Open this, will you, and pour me a glass? I'm going to start the potatoes and you get to snap the beans. If you're lucky, I'll let you mash. Don't you dare stick your fingers in the frosting of that cake. That's for after dinner."

The evening passed quickly. We talked about everything. Local politics, local events, the funny and not-so-funny things that happened in real estate, how Susannah, my college-aged daughter, liked her classes, when my roof might need replacing, and how best to prune my fruit trees. We didn't talk about his job, Carlton, or murder. And we didn't talk about us.

Dan had brought a Steve Martin movie, which we watched over chocolate cake and hazelnut coffee. When it was over, he put Jake, who'd deserted me for Dan's lap, on the floor, stretched, and stood up to leave. He pulled me to my feet, and for a second did nothing. Then he kissed me, gently and feather light.

"It was fun, Ellie. A nice evening. Thanks."

"It was fun," I said, a little disconcerted. "Ah, you'll call?"

"Do you want me to?"

"Of course." It came out a little tentative.

"All right. Shall I take that movie, or can you drop it off tomorrow?"

"I'll take it." I wondered what else I should say.

"Great. Good night. Lock the door after me."

He was gone.

I turned the deadbolt, feeling awful. Here I was, ready to do exactly what Dan wanted, make a huge commitment that still made me nervous, and I wasn't going to get the chance. I walked back into the living room and glared at my reading chair. But it wasn't its fault. It was mine. No, it wasn't. It was Brian's. Because of him, I couldn't shake the feeling that I'd emotionally get the stuffing kicked out of me somewhere down the road if I committed again. But, I'd gathered up enough nerve to give it a try. So what happens? I can't even get the guy to kiss me! Because that peck I'd gotten as he left wasn't even second cousin to the one I got on the washing machine.

"What do you think?" I asked Jake. "What does that mean?"

He looked at me and started to purr.

"Thanks a lot," I said bitterly and started slowly up the stairs. About halfway up, I stopped. What was it that Dan had said that awful evening we fought? Something about how good the silence sounded. I listened a moment, then kept on going. It didn't sound so good to me.

Chapter Twenty-one

I worked Sunday afternoon, showing property to a couple new to our town, and got home around five. I stood inside the front door and listened. Silence. This afternoon it sounded beautiful. After all that had happened in the last month, I needed an evening alone. Please, I thought, don't anyone call, come over, ask me questions, or make me think how I should be feeling.

No one did. The phone didn't ring, the doorbell didn't buzz, no one interrupted my long soak in the bathtub, and Jake, my book, and I went to bed early. I finally put my book down and listened to the quiet, empty house. I wondered if I'd have to get used to it.

Monday was—Monday. For some reason, weekends breed crises, and I spent the first part of the day dealing with them. Right before lunch there was a lull. I found myself sitting back in my chair, congratulating myself on the fires I'd stomped out, when I looked at my watch and thought—time to go to the Yum Yum. Only Dan hadn't called. Should I call him? I would have a week ago, but now...The uncertainty of our relationship chased away any hunger pangs, but the thought of Dan brought up Jolene, the boyfriend thief, and I started to think about her article. Why wasn't it finished? Wouldn't most reporters write the story, go to another location, and then come back for the next event, in this case, the big dinner, if that was indeed going to be a feature? The more I thought about it, the more I wondered.

What was the name of that magazine? It took a minute, but I finally dredged it up. *Dining Delights*. Printed in Dallas, Texas. A quick look at the clock told me that the staff should be back at work after their own lunch hour, and this should be prime time for a game of twenty questions.

Information was, as always, obliging, and even connected me. The soft Texas drawl of the girl who answered the phone sounded friendly. Until I asked about Jolene Bixby. Then it turned downright frosty. "Ms. Bixby doesn't work here anymore."

I don't know what I expected, but it wasn't that. "She must. I just met her out here in California, and she said she's doing an article on chefs on our central coast for your magazine."

"Not for us. She may have gone back to freelancing, but she left us a few weeks ago."

"Are you sure?" I asked, knowing the answer.

"Yes ma'am."

"Will she be back?"

"No ma'am." The answer was quiet but emphatic.

I hung up the phone and stared at it, stunned. This answered a lot of questions about Jolene. Or did it? It sure opened up some new ones. I was pretty sure that Jolene's clout with Otto was the article she was going to write, the great review she was supposed to give him. Had he discovered that there might be an article, but no guarantee it would ever see print? Is that why he wanted her out? Had she killed him because she didn't want anyone to know she no longer had power over chefs, no longer was a "roving reporter"? It made sense. At least, a sort of sense. But where was the connection to the wine theft? I was deep in thought when the phone rang. I picked it up, expecting to hear from a lender that my young buyer's loan had been approved, or maybe Dan suggesting lunch. Instead I got Aunt Mary.

"Ellen, you have to get over to the police station right now." She sounded breathless and dreadfully upset.

"Why?" I asked, starting to feel upset myself. If she were agitated, something bad must have happened. It had.

"Carlton's been murdered and Dan has arrested Sabrina."

Chapter Twenty-two

I sat there, holding the phone to my ear, unable to move. I had heard what she said, but somehow it wasn't processing. Carlton dead? Sabrina arrested? No, not possible. Carlton was the murderer, not the corpse.

"What did you say?"

"You heard me, and you heard me right. Get over to the police station right now. I'm on my way, too. We have to find out what is going on."

It sounded as if she already had, but I said, "I'm on my way," hung up the phone, punched the button that would put it on answering service, remembered to grab my purse, and ran for the door.

"Hey, Ellen," shouted our receptionist, "your lender is on the phone."

"Later. I've got an emergency."

Our police station isn't very large. Today it looked even smaller. The San Luis Obispo County Sheriff's homicide van sat outside the station; several detectives were in the office talking on cell phones. Patrol officers, who I would have thought would be on the street doing something, were hanging around, trying to look inconspicuous while listening to Mark and Frank take turns yelling at the harassed-looking uniformed officer sitting at the front desk. He sat, stony faced, refusing to answer any of the questions they kept shouting at him. He probably didn't know the answers.

"What happened?" I asked, hurrying up to them.

"Oh, Ellen," Mark said in voice strangulated with tears and anger, "these idiots have arrested Sabrina."

"These 'idiots' have not arrested her," a quiet voice stated. Dan. Appearing out of a room almost directly opposite the front desk. "We're questioning her."

"Why?" I blurted out. "What happened? Is Carlton really dead?"

"We're questioning Sabrina because she was found standing over Carlton, holding a knife. The one that killed him." Dan stood quietly in front of the closed door he had just come out of, saying nothing more, just watching us. The little line at the corners of his eyes seemed heavier, and his mouth was set in a grim line. A sobbing sound came out of the room. Dan reached behind him and closed the door. Mark's head snapped up, and he turned toward the room, stopped only by the hand his father put on his arm.

"Dear God," said Aunt Mary.

I whirled around, startled. I was trying so hard to make sense out of what Dan had just said, and what he hadn't said, that I hadn't heard her come in. Now she stood close beside me, looking up at Dan, an expression in her eyes I had never seen before. Fear.

"But, how?" I asked, returning my attention to Dan. "Where?" I didn't seem to be able to get beyond words of one syllable.

"How?" Dan replied. "He was stabbed to death by a French boning knife. Where? In his office. Someone drove the knife right through the back of his throat. A very angry someone."

I felt sick. Really sick. As if I might lose it right there, in the middle of the police station. Carlton dead. Sabrina standing over him with a knife. She must have killed him, but why in such a horrible way? Why kill him at all? He had been arrested for stealing their wine, which cleared Mark, and she was delighted to think he might be Otto's murderer. Which left her with no motive I could see.

"Why?" I asked Dan. "Why would Sabrina want to kill Carlton?"

"She wouldn't want to." Mark had left the officer at the front desk to stand beside Aunt Mary and me and glare at Dan. "And besides, you know Sabrina. Can you see her sticking a knife in someone? She won't even bone a chicken, and the damn thing's already dead."

That argument didn't seem to impress Dan. "These are questions we're asking her. Look, I know you're all upset, but this is going to take a while. Why don't you all go home, and, Ellie, I'll call you later."

"No," stated Mark. His eyes were boring holes in the closed door. "She's in there, all alone, thinking—there's no way she killed anyone, and I'm not leaving without her."

"I'm staying with my son," Frank said.

Mark glanced at his father and shrugged. I took a better look at Frank. He looked worried, tired and worried. His face had taken on a gray tinge, and, for the first time, Frank looked his age.

"I'll stay too," Aunt Mary said. "Frank, are you all right?"

She didn't ask Mark, or me, she asked Frank. Now, what did that tell me? I wasn't sure, but whatever was going on, it was mutual. Frank took her hand and pulled her into the fold of his arms. He dropped a gentle kiss on her forehead.

"Sabrina's not alone," Dan said. "Two homicide officers from the Sheriff's department are with her. One of them is a woman," he finished hastily, glancing at Aunt Mary's face. "They're taking over for now."

"Why?" I asked.

"Evidently, I'm a little too intimately involved to be an impartial interrogator." The narrowing of his eyes and the tightening of his jaw made it plain this was not to Dan's liking. He'd been trained as a homicide detective while with the San Francisco Police Department and had conducted a number of investigations while Chief of Police of Santa Louisa. Not being able to question a chief suspect must be driving him crazy. I wondered if he had voluntarily excused himself or had been pushed gently out of that room. Either way, Dan was not happy.

Another door opposite us opened. Two detectives and Larry came out.

"Thank you for your help, sir," one of them said, but Larry wasn't listening. He had spotted me and rushed across the room. "Oh Ellen, I'm so sorry. It was horrible, finding her there, finding them both there, but I had to tell the police, I just had to. You do understand, don't you?"

No, I didn't. I had no idea what he was talking about.

Dan made the explanation. "Larry walked into Carlton's office and found him dead. Sabrina was standing over him with the knife. He took it away from her. That's how he got the blood on him."

For the first time, I noticed the stains on Larry's chinos. There were stiff spots on his navy polo shirt as well, but they didn't show up unless you looked for them. I wondered if Sabrina had blood on her as well, and how much. I started to feel sick again. Aunt Mary gave a low little moan.

Mark went white. "Shit," he said loudly.

Larry ignored them all. "I'm so sorry, Ellen." He'd grabbed my hand and was giving it little pats.

"It wasn't your fault." I pulled my hand away and glanced at Dan. "I'm sure you did what you had to."

My mind was whirling. Larry had found Sabrina? Why was Larry in Carlton's office? More to the point, why was Sabrina? I kept watching Dan, wondering what he was thinking. Had he asked those questions? Had he gotten answers? His face gave away nothing.

"Let's go get coffee or something," Larry said, grabbing my arm. "I really need some, and I'll bet you do, too."

Coffee with Larry wasn't at all what I needed. Answers, that was what I needed. Answers to about a thousand questions. I raised my eyebrows at Dan and gestured toward his office, hoping he'd take the hint. He responded, but not the way I had expected. "Great idea, Larry. We'll use my office. I think we have chairs for all of us."

Larry looked stunned. I almost laughed. Dan might have been shut out of one interrogation room, but he was about to create another, and for the first time, I was going to get to sit in.

Chapter Twenty-three

"Everybody comfortable?"

Dan sat behind his desk, watching all of us juggle white Styrofoam cups of what passed for coffee while trying to get situated on the folding chairs crammed into his tiny office. It had always reminded me of an overgrown broom closet, but never more so than today. His desk, file cabinets, and bookcase normally left room for only one small padded chair, the one Aunt Mary was sitting in. Now the folding chairs took up every inch of floor space. If anyone had to excuse themselves, well, they'd better just hold it because there was no way out. There was, however, one window, and it opened. It was the only thing that saved us from oxygen deprivation.

"You can't charge Sabrina with murder," Mark stated. He held his cup so tightly I thought it was going to crush. If it went, none of us would escape a hot coffee bath.

Dan sighed. "Nothing would make me happier, but she was found standing over the body, the murder weapon in her hand. Seems to warrant a few questions."

Even Mark couldn't argue with that statement.

"Larry had a great idea, all of us getting together for coffee." Dan nodded at Larry, who looked confused. Not surprising. This little conclave wasn't at all what he'd had in mind. "This is just an informal meeting; you're not in here for official statements. Yet. But it's a good time to get a few things cleared up."

"What things?" Mark asked, belligerence building again.

The muscle in Dan's right cheek twitched. I'd seen that before. He was holding onto his patience. "Let's start with—why was Sabrina at Carlton's office?"

"She was delivering a case of wine he'd asked for," Mark stated. He didn't look at Dan; instead, he stared into his coffee as if, somehow, salvation would appear out of the steam. "There's no law against that, is there? Can you keep questioning her without a lawyer?"

"I've called one," Frank said. "Good friend of mine. Specializes in criminal law. He's on his way up here from Santa Barbara right now."

Criminal law. The thought made my stomach churn. Or maybe it was the coffee. I set my cup on the floor.

There was a yellow legal pad on Dan's desk, and he started to make notes on it. "Why didn't Carlton pick it up himself?"

"Ask Larry. He's the one who called the winery, asked to speak to Sabrina, and said Carlton wanted a case, wanted it today, and would she please drop it off at his office before noon."

Dan turned to Larry. "Is that true?"

"Yes." He didn't meet Dan's eyes. He took a large swallow of the coffee, turned red, looked around wildly, then swallowed. He fanned his mouth for a second, then his cup also went on the floor.

Dan waited until it looked like he could breathe again and said, "Why did Carlton have you call the winery? Why didn't he call himself?"

Larry sighed. "I called Carlton early this morning. About the house. I needed to talk to him and wanted to make an appointment. I don't think he really wanted to see me, but he finally agreed. He said to come around noon; he'd be gone until then, and asked if I'd give that message to Sabrina. I said I would, and the rest you know."

"Did he expressly ask for Sabrina to bring the wine?"

"Yes." Larry stretched his legs out, hit the back of Frank's chair, and pulled them back and sat up straighter.

"Did he say why Sabrina?"

"No, and I didn't ask," Larry replied before Dan could take that one further.

"Unhuh." Dan leaned back in his chair, a black leather one that swiveled, and took a sip of his own coffee. He made a face and put his cup down on the desk. "So what happened when you got there?"

"I already told the other policemen everything."

"Humor me."

"Well," Larry said, drawing it out. "The front door was unlocked, and I went in, but no one was in the front office. I called out, but no one answered. Carlton's door was open a little, and I walked in. He was sitting in his chair, all bloody, and Sabrina was standing over him, holding a knife."

"Then what happened?"

"I said, "Oh my God,' or something like that."

"Keep going," Dan said.

"She looked up at me and said, 'He's dead.'"

"That's all?"

"Yes. I took the knife away from her and put it on the desk, made her sit down in the chair across the room, and called nine one one. I thought I should."

Dan blinked. I almost laughed. He thought he should call the police when he found a dead body with someone standing over it with what was probably the murder weapon. Right.

Dan finally said, "Okay. That's all?"

Larry nodded.

Dan sighed a little before he asked Mark, "Did Sabrina tell you she was going to deliver wine to Carlton?"

"Yeah. I didn't want her to, but she seemed to feel that because he was a partner, she should. I said he was a common thief and had one hell of a nerve even asking, but she insisted she had to."

"Why?" Dan asked. "Was she angry because she had to do it?"

"No. More nervous than anything. Didn't want to see or talk to him, but felt she had some kind of duty. Probably more to the winery than to Carlton. Look, Dan. Sabrina didn't have any motive of any kind to kill Carlton."

Dan's face said, oh yeah? And suddenly it hit me. There was really only one motive for anyone to kill Carlton, now, today. He'd seen someone last Saturday night, someone where they were not supposed to be, at a time they were supposed to be somewhere else. That someone had to be the one who killed Otto. Carlton, supposedly broke, had been trying a little blackmail.

Dan must have read my thoughts. Our eyes connected, and he shook his head at me, but too late. "But that doesn't mean it has to be Sabrina," I blurted out. "He could have seen anyone."

"What are you talking about?" Aunt Mary asked.

"She's talking about Carlton and why he was killed," Frank answered. "It has occurred to her that our upstanding partner, Carlton, saw someone or something last Saturday night and was trying a little blackmail. Only his payoff wasn't what he expected. Isn't that what you think also, Chief Dunham?"

"It had occurred to me."

"Then any of us could have killed him," Mark said. "Them."

"Anyone who was at the dinner could have killed Otto," Dan said cautiously, "but you all weren't in Carlton's office this morning."

Another silence. "Where is Jolene?" Aunt Mary asked. "And where was she this morning?"

"Why?" Frank turned to her, surprise in his eyes. "Jolene is a piece of work, but I don't think she could be implicated in any of this. She's leaving right after the grand opening dinner to go back to Texas, pictures and notes ready for her article."

"There won't be an article," I said.

This time all eyes were on me. "What?" Frank asked.

"Why?" Dan asked. "How do you know?" He looked downright suspicious. "Have you been detecting again?"

"Of course not, but I just happened to call *Dining Delights* this morning and—well—Jolene was fired. A couple of weeks ago, and she won't be returning."

This time the silence was shattered by Frank. "That lying bitch." The tone was low but thick with fury.

Mark's explosion was more impressive. He was on his feet, his face red, hands clenched, ready to take a swing at something, or someone. "She was fired? No article? Does that mean no article for our dinner either?"

"I don't know," I said, "but the woman on the phone said she'd been gone for a few weeks."

"I wonder if Otto knew," Aunt Mary said softly.

"Oh my God." Frank whirled around to stare at her. "I'll bet that was what their fight was all about that night. That's why he ordered her out of his house."

Watching this crowd was interesting, but watching Dan was more. Nothing showed in those blue eyes. He listened, made notes, while he watched everyone else's emotions overflow. I wondered if they taught that at the police academy, or if he was distancing himself from my family. I hoped it was the police academy. Finally he said, "Interesting point, and we'll follow through, but so far, no one has placed Jolene anywhere near Carlton's office. Larry, did you see her this morning?"

Larry jumped as if someone had hit him with a cattle prod. Finally he said, "No—no. Maybe she wasn't up yet."

"How about you, Frank. Did you see Jolene?"

"I wasn't at the house this morning," Frank replied, a little defensively, I thought.

Dan returned to Larry. "Had Otto found out that Jolene was fired?"

I didn't think Larry was going to answer. His eye had started to twitch again, and he was tearing little bits of Styrofoam off the lip of his cup and dropping them into the dregs of his now cool coffee. Finally he said, "I think so."

"You think so, or you know so?" Dan pressed.

"I know so." Larry looked at Dan directly. "Otto needed a good review and was counting on Jolene."

Frank snorted. "That was his first mistake. Jolene Bixby has been blackmailing chefs for years. Free dinners, free lodging, a little something under the table or the review will be—not so good. Otto should have known better. And sweet Jolene will be out of my house on her cute little Texas"—he looked at Aunt Mary—"as soon as I get out of here."

"This is all very interesting," Dan said, pushing back his chair and getting to his feet, "but it doesn't change anything. Mark, you will have to sign a statement. Larry, I think you have already, and I'll probably have to talk to you both again. Now, I'll go see…"

Before he could finish, the door opened, and a young woman in a sheriff's uniform poked her head in. "Mrs. Tortelli's attorney is here."

Frank and Mark almost collided getting to the door, Aunt Mary right behind them. Dan came around the desk and took my by the arm.

"What made you think to call that magazine?" he asked. "I hate to say it, but you were ahead of us on that one."

I smiled up at him. "Tell you later. Tonight?"

"Probably not," he sighed. "But, we'll see." He stood next to me for a second, close enough to give me a quick hug, but he didn't. Instead, he followed the rest out of the room. Damn! I turned to leave, but Larry was in the doorway.

"I probably should have told earlier about Jolene."

I stopped him from going on. "You probably should have."

"You sound upset. I hope not. I thought we could go get something to eat. Or maybe just coffee? Or a drink?"

I had had enough. "Larry, I am not going anywhere with you. I am going out there to see what is going to happen to Sabrina, then I'm going back to my office to take care of anything that can't wait for tomorrow, then I'm going home. I'm considering getting a raging headache and am going to take three Tylenol, a large glass of wine, and sit down and forget all about today, and I plan on doing it all alone."

I pushed past him but he followed me into the main office, continuing to murmur places we could go, he could buy aspirin for me, and I needed company at a time like this. The only reason I didn't attack him was the scene in front of me. Sabrina was standing tight beside Mark, Frank on her other side. She looked pale and teary-eyed, but smiled slightly when she saw me.

"Oh, Ellen," she said. "You'll never guess. They're letting me go."

Chapter Twenty-four

I didn't make it home until six o'clock. I stumbled into the house, exhausted and grumpy. Jake was equally grumpy, telling me loudly that dinner was late, and he didn't deserve to be treated that way. No message from Dan; although my darling daughter, Susannah, had left one, suggesting gently that college was expensive, and could I possibly make a deposit into her account. I sighed, made a note to do so, reached for the wine bottle, poured a glass, and started rummaging through the papers I throw into the drawer under the phone. I had Mark and Sabrina's new number somewhere, and chances were better than good that it was floating loose, mixed up with the old grocery receipts. I hadn't heard from anyone since we all split up at the police station. Mark, Frank, and Aunt Mary, with Sabrina in tow, her attorney right behind them, left for their house; I headed to the office. Larry took off for destinations unknown, and I was anxious to know what was happening. The number refused to be found, so I dialed Aunt Mary. I was in luck. She was home and alone.

"How's Sabrina?"

"Asleep, finally," she answered. She sounded exhausted as well. "Frank called Dr. Sadler, who got a sedative down her. The poor girl was ready to fall apart."

"Yeah." Sabrina didn't seem to fall apart very easily, unless it had something to do with Mark. This time, however, she had a great excuse. "Tell me what happened. Everything you know." I had confidence it would be a lot.

"You know Carlton wanted a case of wine."

"Yes. We covered all that. What happened after she got there?" I pulled a chair from the kitchen table and sat, but immediately got back up. I'd been sitting all day and was way too distraught to do any more of it. Besides, cordless phones were meant for pacing.

"The door was closed when she got there, and she had a hard time getting in. I guess those boxes are heavy."

I could personally attest to that. "So, she managed to get in the door. Then what happened?"

"She called out, but no one answered. She says she started to get mad and almost left the box on that table in Carlton's little front office but decided to go into his personal office in case he was on the phone or something. The door was slightly open, and his chair was turned away toward the window. She called out to him, but he didn't answer. She put the case down on his desk and walked around to look at him, ready to ask what kind of sick game, her words, he thought he was playing, and that was when she saw the knife."

"It was still in him?" I asked. "Yuck."

"My sentiments exactly. She said she pulled it out."

"No!" This time I was really stunned. Didn't she watch TV? Read mysteries? Besides, how could she? "Why would she do such a thing?"

Aunt Mary sighed, long and hard. There might have been a few tears hovering in the back of that sigh. "She says at first she didn't realize he was dead. Her only thought was to get that thing out of him and get him some help. Only, he didn't move. She says the shock was so great she just froze, and then Larry came in."

"Anything else?" I asked.

"No. I think that covers it. Oh, one more thing."

"What?"

"Frank got her a lawyer."

"I know. I saw him. That man in the silver suit who looks like he belongs on 'The Sopranos.'"

"Light gray," she said.

"What?"

"His suit, light gray. Yes. Jim De Marco, I think his name is. Anyway, he says there must be a big hole in Dan's case somewhere, or he would never have let her go without booking her."

That I had to think about. "What kind of hole?"

"Mr. De Marco had no idea, nor do I," she answered. "I'm just so grateful she's not in jail, I'm not even thinking about why."

I was. "So, if Sabrina didn't do it, who did?" I picked up the wine bottle while I waited for her to say something. Should I? After the day I'd had? Absolutely.

"I don't know," she finally said. "I can't even imagine."

"Of course you can. There's only one real motive for killing Carlton. He had to have seen something the night of the dinner. He was up by the kitchen; he went up the back stairs; he was roaming all over the place looking for someone to bore. Also, Carlton was a bit short of money. Put that together and it says blackmail to me. Someone didn't want to play."

"And you're going to try to find out who that someone is," she stated, rather grimly. "Ellen Page McKenzie, I forbid it. Two people have gotten killed already. Three is not a good round number."

"All I'm going to do is make a few phone calls," I told her, trying to be as matter-of-fact as possible, "get a little background. Help Dan move this whole mess along. It can't be Sabrina, it just can't. Besides, if I don't do something, I'm going to have to call Catherine, and you know what that means."

"Dan doesn't want your help. He wants you alive and well, not laid out on a mortuary slab."

"He doesn't want Catherine storming into the police station either, yelling and screaming and generally creating havoc."

"No, I suppose he doesn't. Well, all right. If you limit it to phone calls and give any information you get to Dan immediately. But I don't know what you expect to find out that he can't, faster and better."

Me either, but I was going to try. After all, I'd found out about Jolene. With another promise to limit my investigations to phone calls, I hung up. I had only one problem. Who was I going to call, and how was I going to get them to talk to me?

Chapter Twenty-five

The next morning Jake and I sat at the kitchen table, me sipping coffee and making a list, him curled up in a chair, reveling in the fact that we were dogless.

First, Mark and Sabrina. I had to be certain Sabrina hadn't killed either Otto or Carlton. I was pretty sure the answer to that was somehow connected to Mark's old job. So, I picked up the phone, called Information, and was soon talking to a sweet-voiced girl at Lighthouse Winery.

"This is Ellen McKenzie, and I'm representing the *Santa Louisa Gazette*." I hate to lie, but sometimes, well, what are you gonna do. "We're doing a story on Mark Tortelli, the new winemaker at Silver Springs Winery, and something's come up about why he left Lighthouse. I wanted to verify my facts."

There was a pause. "Do you mean the fight?"

Fight? Maybe that was exactly what I meant. Crossing my fingers, I said, "Yes, our facts are a little—mixed, and I wanted to make sure I got it right."

"Well," she drew this out, "the lawsuit isn't settled, but I guess it's all right for me to say that none of us here think Mark was at fault. The mistake about the missing wine turned out to be Giorgio's fault, and he provoked Mark into hitting him."

Oh boy. "So, the lawsuit? When will that be settled?" And who was suing whom?

"Soon, we hope. Now that Giorgio's been fired, we're hoping he'll drop it, and then the assault and battery charge will also be dropped. Those charges are plain ridiculous."

Assault and battery. No wonder Mark and Sabrina were nervous wrecks. "Is it true that Lighthouse fired Mark?" Talk about fishing, but some things were starting to make sense.

"Yes," she said, reluctance in her voice. "But I think the owners are real sorry now they understand what happened. Of course, nothing is settled yet." There was a pause. "You're not going to quote me, are you?"

I could hear her shut down, and there were still tons of questions I needed answered, but I had just run out of time.

"I'm sorry, Miss Mc—what did you say your name was?"

"McKnight," I answered hurriedly, "and thanks for the information."

I hung up and stared at the phone. Jake rubbed against me and purred. I picked him up, put him on the floor, and filled his dish, not really noticing what I was doing. Mark had been fired from Lighthouse because he was accused of stealing wine and getting into a fight with someone named Giorgio, who had to be someone important. The head winemaker? Perhaps. That was easy to find out. But what about this lawsuit? Was Giorgio suing Mark for battery? If so, I could well understand why the Tortellis would want to keep that quiet. No one would want a winemaker who beat up on other members of the staff; especially since I was pretty sure a conviction on such a charge meant jail time. Add the charge of theft, and Mark was a cinch to lose his job. Maybe Sabrina was right. It could cost him his career. But how did that connect with Otto? Easily. Otto hated all things Tortelli. The wine and food world, like so many specialty worlds, was small. Otto had contacts up north; it was more than likely he'd heard every detail, and would have been delighted to share them. Had Sabrina killed him because he threatened to tell Mr. Applby, and had Carlton seen, or heard, something that could prove her guilty? Damn. Sabrina had just landed right back on the chief suspect list, with Mark a close second. Now what did I do? Go to work. I had clients waiting.

Chapter Twenty-six

The morning started out pretty well. My new listing was going to be a winner; a young couple I had given up on resurfaced, down payment in hand, and wanted to start looking again. All the twists and tangles in my existing escrows seemed to be straightened out, for the moment anyway, and around eleven, I sat back and took a deep breath. Dan had finally left me a message on my voice mail suggesting dinner that night, his treat, and I was feeling a guarded relief, mixed with anxiety. I had to decide if I were going to tell him what I'd found out about Mark and his problems at Lighthouse Winery. I knew I should, but it felt a little like pushing Sabrina through the jail cell door. I wanted badly to get past this wall building between us. I'd put down the first course of bricks, but I wanted them torn down, not built higher. Only I didn't know how to convince Dan of that, and not telling him what I knew wasn't going to help. This evening was going to be tricky. I was contemplating all this when our secretary buzzed me.

"You have a client waiting for you."

"I do?" I stammered. "I don't have anything scheduled. Who is it?"

"He didn't give a name. Shall I send him back?" It was obvious she wasn't taking any blame for my ineptness.

"Sure." I thumbed through my book quickly, wondering how I had missed an appointment. I hadn't. I walked out of my cubicle, smile firmly fixed, hand ready, excuses forming, to find Larry.

"I hope you don't mind my barging in like this." He didn't look any too sure of his reception. "I had to talk to you, so I took a chance. But if you're busy…"

"I'm very busy. I'm really sorry, but I have clients in—ah—pretty soon and…"

"Oh. Well, could I talk to you until they come? It's really important. It's about the house."

The house. The bed and breakfast house? He'd said that was why he went to Carlton's office, to talk to him about the house. Maybe… "Okay. But it has to be short."

"Can we go somewhere else?" he asked. "It's sort of…not very…"

"Private?" I finished. "We are sort of crammed together. Let's see if the conference room…no. Les is in there."

"How about the Yum Yum?" Larry asked. His blond hair fell over his eyes, and he grinned, just like he had in high school. Very appealing. But not enough to get me to the Yum Yum with him. Dan and I had lunch there almost every day, or we used to, and I wasn't about to feed the local gossip mill.

"How about the doughnut shop?" I gathered my purse, flung my jacket over my arm, and led the way to the door, not giving Larry any choice but to follow.

It took a few minutes to convince Larry I didn't want a lemon doughnut, a maple stick, or a whipped cream-laden cappuccino, that plain coffee would be fine.

"What's this about the house?" I finally asked, pointedly looking at my watch.

"I gave Otto the money to buy it. We were supposed to be partners. Only now everyone talks as if it belongs to Otto's brother. My name should be on the papers somewhere, but I don't know how to find out. You're in real estate. Can you help me?"

I set my coffee mug down very carefully. I'm sure my jaw had dropped about a foot before I closed it and said, "You what?"

"I was a partner." His hand rested quietly on his coffee mug. His eye didn't twitch, and his smile was pure satisfaction. "It's what I always wanted. We were going to be famous. Otto said so. Only he had to go and get himself killed." He shook his head slightly at the folly of such an act. "Frank acts as if he owns the place, or he did until he lost interest. I don't have any papers. I don't know what to do. I thought Carlton could tell me, but he up and got himself murdered also."

I didn't really think either of them died to inconvenience Larry, but this didn't seem like a good time to get into that. Instead, I tried to sort out the house thing. One step at a time. "Did you ever sign an offer?"

"You mean where everybody gets together and agrees on the price? No. Otto did all that. He'd come back and tell me what everyone said, and, if I thought it was all right, then he'd tell Carlton, and we'd go ahead. It all worked fine until Otto found out about the parking. But that worked out, too."

I was beginning to feel a little light-headed. This was starting to smell like major fraud. "Larry, did you ever go into escrow, sign any paperwork there? Anywhere?"

"I signed something that said I was giving Otto the money. It's called a gift letter. Otto said he needed it for the bank. That my name would be on the deed after the bank loaned the rest of the money."

I was afraid to ask the next question, but I had to know. "How much money did you give Otto?"

"Five hundred thousand for the down payment on the house and another two hundred fifty thousand for the kitchen and other things. That wouldn't be enough, but it got us started so we could open." He stopped and grinned, as if at some private joke. "You know, my father left lots of money, and it all went to me. He'd have pitched a fit if he knew I was spending it on a restaurant and bed and breakfast. Too bad."

If there had been any love between Larry and his father, I sure wasn't feeling it. But that wasn't my problem. However, the fact remained that Larry may have been—probably had been—royally swindled. I had only been a real estate agent a little over a year and nothing like this had come up. What had they said in real estate school? Had anything like this even been discussed? I couldn't remember. I had to help him, but how? This was one problem Aunt Mary wasn't going to solve. But Bo Chutsky, my all-knowing broker, could. I'd dump this in his more than capable, and more than ample, lap. However, Larry seemed to be off on another tangent.

"I don't know what to do about Frank, either."

"Frank?" I asked. "What about Frank?"

"He's been strange, and I don't know what to do."

"Frank's been acting strange. In what way?" I hadn't seen any evidence of strange behavior from Frank. He looked tired, strained, and seemed to cover it up with effusiveness. He was also, in my opinion, genuinely worried about Mark and Sabrina and way too attentive to Aunt Mary. But none of that added up to strange.

"He came in like a tornado, started ordering new equipment for the kitchen, changed the menu I had set for our grand opening dinner, told me our breakfast ideas were all wrong and re-did all that, completely scratched all the wines I had chosen, and hired a new decorator to work on the bedrooms. You would have thought the place was really his. He even wanted to change the name."

"I didn't know it had a name," I said. It was the only thing I could think to say.

"Oh, yes. Otto was going to call it Ottohaus."

I almost strangled on my coffee trying not to laugh. When I was able, I asked, "What did Frank want to name it?"

"I don't think he had decided. But that's the point. He's lost interest. He hasn't even come in since Sunday, and when I ask him about Saturday's dinner, he won't answer me. I don't understand it, and I don't know what to do."

Did Larry expect me to do something? I wondered. If so, I couldn't imagine what. But it did seem strange; not at all like the Frank I thought I knew.

"I think he's got bill collectors after him," Larry said, his tone as black as a Halloween cat.

"What?" I asked, putting my coffee cup down too quickly and ignoring the resulting splash. "Frank?"

Larry nodded. He looked like one of those dolls with the loose necks you see in the back windows of cars. "I've overheard him on the phone. I think that's why he sold his restaurant."

"Are you sure? That's a pretty damning thing to say about someone if it's not true."

"I've heard him talking to people about Tortelli's, saying something about payments. Then another time I heard him talking about Otto. He hangs up or waits for me to leave the room if he thinks I'm listening."

"I'm not surprised. Why is he talking about Otto?"

"I think he owed Otto money, maybe because of that recipe Otto was always screaming about. I think Frank sold the restaurant to pay Otto off and now that he's dead, Frank's getting his revenge by taking over the bed and breakfast. Only he's going to ruin the dinner if he won't pay attention."

"If he had money from the sale of the restaurant, why would bill collectors be after him?" I asked, completely bewildered.

"Maybe he had to give all his money to Otto and didn't have enough left to pay the bills." He set his mug down and took a big mouthful of doughnut. Chocolate cream doughnut. The one I'd declined. Oh, well. "I don't know exactly, maybe its something else," he said when he could swallow again, "but something's going on."

Could any of this be true? If so, oh wow. Maybe Frank killed Otto to—what? Keep from paying him off? And Carlton had seen him, or something, and Frank knifed him to keep him quiet? He was a chef; knives were second nature to him. No wonder he looked so stressed and worried in the police station. Sabrina was about to be arrested for something he did. Mark wouldn't like that one bit. Wait. I was jumping to conclusions. I didn't know if any of this was true, from the sale of the restaurant to owing Otto money to murdering two people. I had to go slow, get more information. But it sure would be nice if we could move Sabrina down the suspect list a notch.

"What do you think?" Larry went on. "Should I go ahead, use my own judgment? That dinner has to be wonderful. We have people from half a dozen magazines coming; all of them scheduled to stay in our rooms. These people can make our reputation, or ruin it. It's very important to make a good first impression."

Probably true, but that didn't interest me. Frank did. But I'd bled Larry dry. He didn't know any more, and he really didn't know much to begin with. As to Frank's sudden indifference, I had nothing to offer. "You'll work it out just fine. Remember, this is your big chance."

"Yes, it is, isn't it. I can do it. Thanks."

Pleading my mythical client's imminent arrival and telling him I'd consult with my broker about his real estate problem, I pushed back my chair and left. He was still sitting there, staring into his mug, as I stepped out into the street. Probably making up a new menu or something. I walked back to the office, my mind trying to sort out all of these new facts, and passed the Yum Yum. Who should be sitting in the window, heads close together, talking earnestly, but Frank and Jolene. They didn't look up, and I was sure they hadn't seen me, but I scurried by nonetheless. What were they doing together? His description of her had been less than flattering, and he'd make it plain that he meant to get rid of her. However, they didn't look like mortal enemies just now. They looked like a couple of old friends, sharing a cup of coffee. I walked across the street and doubled back so I could take a second look. Yep. Heads together, talking intently, but it didn't look as if Jolene's claws were out, and Frank wasn't showing any signs of giving her the old heave ho. What did that mean? I had no idea, and my slow walk back to the office didn't produce one.

Sally, our receptionist, asked, "You all right?"

I forced a smile and said, "Pain in the butt client," and headed for my desk. I sat down, stared at the blinking red light on the phone, and wondered what to do next.

Chapter Twenty-seven

Dan turned up around six thirty. I hadn't expected him that early, hadn't been too sure he'd show up at all. I was staring at soup cans, trying to decide, in case he didn't, if I wanted chicken with noodles, minestrone, or neither.

The back screen door slammed, and he announced, "We're going for spaghetti. Or maybe pizza." He took a good look at my paint-stained sweatpants, frayed-around-the-bottom sweatshirt, hair pulled back with a rubber band, and said, "You were expecting us to do home projects? Not tonight. Go change."

We had spaghetti. Probably nothing like the kind Frank served at Tortelli's, if indeed it was on the menu, but the plates were overflowing. Dan polished his off. I barely made a dent in mine.

We talked about all kinds of things, polite, casual friends kinds of things, but not about our future life. Dan's plate was almost empty before I brought up murder.

Finally, I said, "Why didn't you arrest Sabrina?"

"Did you want me to?" he asked, amusement in his eyes.

"Of course not, but you must have some serious doubts, or you wouldn't have let her go. It's blood, isn't it?"

The last piece of bread that he had been buttering went back on his plate. "Blood?"

"I looked at her before everyone left. She had maybe a few stains on her top, but that's all. Carlton must have been dead when she pulled that knife out of him, or she would have gotten spurted."

He just stared at me for a minute then started to howl with laughter. "I'm not letting you watch any more of those CSI programs."

"Well, isn't that right? His heart had stopped pumping, so the only blood she got on her was from the wound and the knife."

"He may have been dead when she pulled it out, but he was alive when she—" he held up his hand as I started to interrupt—"or whoever, stuck it into him. There was only one stab wound, and it found just the right mark. Most of the bleeding was internal. Poor old Carlton died by drowning in his own blood."

I looked down at what was left on my plate and pushed it away. So much for my appetite. "There are a few other things I think you should know." I told him about Larry's claim to the house, about Frank's mysterious phone calls, about Frank and Jolene sitting together in the Yum Yum, but I didn't tell him about my conversation with the girl at Lighthouse Winery. I knew I should; I really wanted to, but I couldn't. There seemed to be a few things I couldn't say to Dan.

"Is that all?" He was looking at me intently, as if he knew I was holding something back, waiting for me to confide in him. I could feel my mouth open, feel words ready to come out, words about Sabrina and Mark, but also words about us. I love you, I was going to say, and I trust you to do the right thing about Sabrina and Mark, about Frank, and about us. But the specter of Brian stood at my shoulder, laughing. Whispering in my ear what a little idiot I was, first to think I could play detective, but mostly that I was fool enough to think I could keep a man like Dan Dunham. "Yes," I heard myself say, "that's all."

Dan paid the check, and we left. Not much more was said about anything. He pulled up in front of my house and waited for me to open the door.

"Aren't you coming in?"

"Not tonight. Another time."

Another time. Depression shrouded me like a Victorian widow's veil. Why couldn't I say what I so desperately wanted to? Because that specter kept hanging there, laughing at me, taunting me. Assuring me that the only way I'd be safe was to keep building up those barriers around me, building them so high I'd never be able to tear them down. Damn the man. Why was I letting him win? I was a different person than I was a year ago, when he'd literally kicked me out to move in his practically teen-age nurse. I didn't need to let him win anymore. I'd built a life. I had a home of my own. Never mind that I rented it from my parents; it felt like mine. I had a great new career that was growing by the day, and I'd fallen in love with a wonderful man. I wasn't going to let that die. But more than my insecurities stood in the way of my repairing Dan's and my relationship. There was a little thing called murder. My niece still seemed to be the chief suspect. Dan had almost arrested her and probably would do so in the next couple of days, and that wasn't going to help get our relationship back on track. I hadn't told him about my conversation with the Lighthouse Winery this morning. Maybe he already knew, maybe not. But I knew this whole thing couldn't be dragged out any longer. If Sabrina was guilty, there was nothing I could do about it. But, if she wasn't, and I really couldn't believe she was, then I needed to start collecting facts. Now. I walked into the house with renewed resolve, looked at the copy of *Mature Bride* on the coffee table, the one with the dress on the front cover I had planned on ordering, and burst into tears.

Chapter Twenty-eight

Wednesdays can be pretty quiet, but this one hadn't started out that way.

"Finally," I said to no one in particular. I hung up the phone and shoved the stack of files back in my desk drawer. I leaned back in my chair and thought about a fresh cup of coffee. It hadn't been a very good night, and maybe the headache hovering around the back of my skull would give way to a little more caffeine.

"Is this chair taken? Because if it's not, I'm sitting in it. My feet are killing me."

It was Aunt Mary. "Where've you been?" I took a look at her outfit. Dark gray polyester skirt that needed to be shortened, a white polyester blouse that was too small, and a multicolored jacket that was too big. All in all, an improvement over the way she usually dressed.

"Christmas Bazaar planning breakfast, then bank, the sale at Michael's for Christmas ornaments and Thanksgiving stuff, and then the grocery. I'm beat."

"Sounds like quite a morning." I laughed, but immediately sobered. "Have you seen Sabrina?"

"She's back at the winery. I was against it at first, but she insisted, and maybe it's best. No sense sitting around brooding. Want to see what I got?" She started pulling autumn colored dried leaves out of the huge shopping bag she had put down beside her. "These will look great on the table for Thanksgiving, and I got these things, also." She pulled out a package of dried red and orange gourds. "I'm not sure what they are, but they're pretty. And they were on sale."

Of course they were. She stuffed everything back in the bag, leaned back in her chair, and studied me. "How are you?"

"Me?" I answered, surprised. "I'm fine. Why?"

"I heard you and Dan went out for dinner last night."

She waited, but I didn't say anything. "Okay. Anything else new?"

"Actually, yes." I didn't want to talk about Dan and me, but she was one person I was willing to tell about what I'd learned from Lighthouse Winery.

"Could Mark actually go to jail for assault and battery?" she asked when I finished.

"Sure," I said with great confidence. I'd looked it up on the Internet. "It's a felony. Not to mention what it would do to his career. And even if he's found innocent of that, suspicion of wine theft could be enough to ruin him. Rumors are harder to kill than anything."

"I hope you didn't intend that as a pun," she said, trying not to laugh. Then she sighed. "And ruining Mark is the one thing Sabrina wouldn't be able to stand." There were lines around her eyes and mouth I had never seen before. "Do you really think she would be stupid enough to murder those two men?"

"I don't know about stupid," I replied, "but maybe frantic enough. She's fixated on Mark, and anything that threatens him…" I let this last thought trail off while we both sat and thought.

"Let's suppose that Sabrina really didn't do any of this," Aunt Mary said finally. "Where does that leave us?"

"With Frank and Jolene. Speaking of whom…" I told her about seeing them in the Yum Yum. I watched her face go from anger to pain, all in the space of a few seconds.

"Not Frank," she finally said.

"Why?" I asked, as calmly as I could. "What's going on with you two?"

"Nothing," she said, much too quickly.

"Not true. I watched you. There's a lot more than nothing. So, give."

Her eyes took in everything. The computer on my desk with the picture of a Halloween haunted house for a screen saver, the phone with all of the extension buttons, the In and Out boxes, the pile of open files. Finally, she leaned back and looked directly at me. "I don't know. I've gotten very fond of Frank in the last few days, but things have moved so quickly. He's funny, great company, and a good man. He's also a royal pain, egotistical, and sad."

"Sad!" I exclaimed. "Sad?"

She nodded. "Underneath all that bombastic exterior, he's very upset and sad about something."

"His restaurant?" I guessed.

"I don't know. It's a subject he won't talk about."

I thought about what Larry had told me, how he had over-heard Frank's conversations about money. Could Frank have been talking to Jolene about—no. Why would he tell her about his problems? But I sure wanted to know why they had been talking so intently. I didn't say anything more to Aunt Mary about that, I'd said enough, but I'd explore Jolene a little more, the one person we both agreed made a perfect suspect. I didn't get a chance. The phone rang, and the number calling was the winery.

"Oh, Ellen." Sabrina's voice sounded one notch below hysterical. "Something's happened, and you have to come over here right away."

"What? What's happened?"

"The missing bottle is back. The Boy Scouts found it. Dan's men think I put it there. They're going to arrest me right now. I need you."

"Boy Scouts?"

"Yes. Come now."

"Where?"

"Here. At the winery." She hung up.

"What's happened?" Aunt Mary asked. "What's wrong?" Her worry lines were deeper.

"That was Sabrina."

"I know that. What's the matter, and where are we going?" She was already on her feet, picking up her shopping bag, looking around for her purse.

"The Boy Scouts found the missing wine bottle, and Sabrina's going to be arrested."

"The Boy Scouts? Found the bottle that killed Otto? What Boy Scouts?"

"I don't know." I was on my feet as well, fishing through my purse for my car keys, "But I think we'd better get over there right away and find out before Dan's cops drag Sabrina off to jail. Again."

Chapter Twenty-nine

An unmarked police car drove away from the front of the tasting room as Aunt Mary and I pulled up. Sabrina wasn't in it. We rushed into the winery to find her sitting behind Mark's desk, looking like someone whose sentence on death row had just been converted to life. A mixed blessing.

Aunt Mary pushed Paris out of an armchair and sat down. "What on earth is going on? What is all this about the missing bottle and Boy Scouts?"

Sabrina looked from me to Aunt Mary and actually smiled. "The scouts found it because it was full."

"What?" we said together.

"A full one weighs more," Sabrina said.

Aunt Mary's lips pursed, and her eyes narrowed. "Sabrina, you'd better start at the beginning, and this time don't stop until you get to the end." When Aunt Mary uses that tone of voice, people do as directed.

"We donate all of our empty bottles to the Boy Scouts. They come every couple of weeks and take them to a recycling place in town. It's one way they raise money. They came this morning and started loading the cases of empties in their truck. One of the fathers noticed that one of the bottles was still corked. He pulled it out, and sure enough, it was full. He called me, thinking it was a mistake. Only I don't think it was. We did an inventory of opened cases after the Harvest Festival Dinner.

We counted empty bottles and put them all back in the open cartons, then we counted all of the unopened bottles. There was one bottle missing. I put the case it should have been in aside. I know, because I'd marked it. Today, there was a full bottle in a slot in one of the cartons with empties, and no bottle had been put back into the carton with the full bottles. So, that has to be the bottle that killed Otto."

"Where did you put that case, the one with the missing bottle?"

"Downstairs, in the kitchen."

"Not with the other cases?"

"No. It was all by itself, and I'd taped it shut again. The ones with the empty bottles are kept by the big roll-up doors."

"Someone was trying to get rid of that bottle and slipped it into the first open case they saw?" Aunt Mary asked.

Sabrina nodded. "That's what it looks like."

"So," I said slowly, feeling my way, "if that father hadn't noticed that one of the bottles was corked, it would have gone to the recycle place."

"That's right." Sabrina actually smiled. "The police have taken it away to do whatever they do. Forensic stuff, like looking for traces of Otto's hair and blood, and of course, fingerprints. And, since I had no reason to touch that bottle, mine won't be on it."

"I assume you called the police?" I asked.

"Just as fast as I could get to the phone. And that bottle and that wonderful man are going to clear me. I didn't kill Otto. I didn't kill Carlton. I didn't do any of it, and this will prove it. Mr. De Marco said so."

"I hope he's right," I said. "Oh, how I hope he's right. But how could someone, besides you, know you put the empties out by the back door for the Boy Scouts?"

I watched her face fall. "I never thought of that."

"Has Frank been over here the last few days?" I asked.

Aunt Mary glared at me, but Sabrina didn't seem to notice. She said, "Yes, he's stopped by a couple of times. He and Mark were tasting different wines he might serve at some of his dinners."

"Was he ever alone?" I went on, ignoring Aunt Mary's pursed lips.

"I have no idea. Why? Do you think Frank…"

"Of course not," Aunt Mary said, with vinegar in her voice. "How about Jolene? Was she here at all?"

"Yes, she came yesterday, and I think another time. She wanted to take pictures for her article."

"Her mythical article. Was she alone?" Aunt Mary asked, shooting me a triumphant look.

"Most of the time," Sabrina answered. "She came in the morning, right before I left for Carlton's office. With all that happened afterwards, I forgot about her."

Aunt Mary and I looked at each other, both thinking the same thing. It all fit, even the times. She had a great motive to kill Otto. Carlton must have seen her doing something and threatened to tell. I could see her, batting her eyes, leaning over him a little, maybe pleading with him while he preened, feeling his power. Until she stuck that knife in his throat. "The knife."

"What?" asked Sabrina.

"The knife you pulled out of Carlton. What kind was it?"

"Oh, ugg. I don't want to think about it." Sabrina started to get white, and her hand flew up to her mouth.

"This is no time to get sick," Aunt Mary said. She was following my train of thought, I could tell, and was determined we were going to get an answer whether Sabrina liked it or not. "Think about it. Was it a specific kind of knife?"

"A long French boning knife."

"Where would you find a knife like that?"

Aunt Mary looked at me pityingly. "Every well-equipped kitchen has one," she said, which told me what she thought of the state of mine, "and certainly every commercial kitchen."

"We have one here," Sabrina put in. "Oh."

"Oh, indeed." Aunt Mary was already on her feet. "Where do you keep your knives?"

It wasn't there, of course. The same person who had returned the wine bottle must have "borrowed" the boning knife and then deposited it in Carlton. Jolene again seemed the perfect candidate. She had been all over the winery yesterday. She could easily have returned the bottle, but when had she taken the knife? Sabrina said Jolene had been here earlier in the week as well. She could have taken it then. Jolene had time yesterday to stop by Carlton's office for a little visit, leave him dead, arrive at the winery, find the bottle where she had left it, and plant it in the carton. None of this meant she did, but she sure could have.

Sabrina was starting to leak tears. I couldn't blame her. The missing knife could put her back at the top of the suspect list, especially if Mark's troubles came out of hiding. Aunt Mary had her arm around her and started to lead her back toward Mark's office. She looked at me, one eyebrow raised. I mouthed that I was going to look around. She nodded and closed the door. I stood in the kitchen for a moment, examining it. The knives were in a shallow drawer in a stainless steel prep table equipped with a deep sink and a large cutting board. If you knew where they were, taking one would be easy.

Who would know? Frank would, Mark would, Sabrina would, but Jolene? Maybe. She'd been in here, arguing with Otto. She could easily have seen where they were kept. All right. Where would she have hidden the bottle?

In here? No. Too visible. And why not put the bottle back in a case with unopened ones? It would never have been noticed. So, Jolene, or whoever, hadn't had time to get it back into the building and had to hide it quickly. That meant, bushes? I went out the front door and slowly walked along the path, examining the shrubbery as I went. It looked as though the gardener had been here. All of the leaves had been raked, all of the bushes freshly trimmed. If the bottle had been hidden out here, I was pretty sure the gardener would have found it. So, where else?

I was on the crush pad, looking up at the platform that held the wooden fermenting tank. A ladder ran up the side from the concrete floor, and a door, almost not visible, opened into it from the winery building. The deck was reachable from the platform by another short ladder that led up to the wide gate. I walked into the building, struck as always by the abrupt temperature change. High above me, the catwalk ended on one side of the roll-up doors directly into the small platform door. The walk on the other side ended at a long, steep flight of stairs that descended onto the cellar floor. I started down the aisle between the stainless steel tanks, looking at each one, trying to find a place where one could hide a wine bottle, when a voice shattered the silence.

"Hey, Ellen, are you looking for something?" It was Mark, high above me on the catwalk. "Hold on. I'm coming down." He walked along it, disappearing momentarily behind each tank, and ran down the steep stairs with ease.

"Did you lose something?" His tone was guarded, and his body language clearly shouted "defensive."

"No," I said, trying to project helpfulness, support, friendliness, all the things that wouldn't alienate an already stressed out Mark. "But, I am looking for something. A hiding place."

"For the no-longer-missing wine bottle." He didn't look any less defensive. "The cops have been all over this place, looking for the same thing."

"Mark, I don't think Sabrina killed anybody, and I'm trying to help prove that, so back off a little, okay?" I was getting tired of tears, evasiveness, and other people's stress. I had some of my own to deal with, and right now the only way I could see to solve my own problem was to help solve his and Sabrina's, and a little cooperation would be nice.

"Sorry," he muttered, "but all this murder stuff Sabrina's going through is making me crazy."

Among other things. "Did the police look down here, on the floor?"

"All over. Behind the tanks, in the middle of the stacks of barrels, through the hoses, everywhere. They did all that before the damn bottle turned back up. I guess now we'll never know where it was hidden."

"Maybe not." I looked around at the shining tanks, the wooden barrels stacked in large rows, the filled boxes stacked on pallets waiting to be delivered to wine shops around the country, and wondered. "Mark, why couldn't the killer have stashed the bottle in one of those cases?"

"They're all sealed. The only open ones are in the tasting room."

I thought about it. The killer coming back into the tasting room, filled with guests, calmly using the sink to wash Otto's blood from the bottle, then slipping it back onto a shelf or back into a wine box. Hardly. So, the bottle had to have been hidden somewhere else. But where? I had no idea, and standing on the cellar floor, chilled to the bone, wasn't helping me to figure it out.

"I think I'll run up and see how Sabrina's doing," I told Mark.

"She's doing fine, now that the police have that wine bottle. She's convinced that they'll find someone else's fingerprints on it and that will be the end of all her troubles."

I started, but didn't have the heart, to tell him about the missing knife. Of course, it still didn't mean Sabrina—oh, to hell with it. I tromped up the stairs into the tasting room, wondering what to do next. There were two couples at the tasting room bar, sipping, making notes, and comparing nose, fruitiness, and other winely things. I watched for a moment, then walked over to the big window and looked down. I had never really taken in the view before and was impressed. The whole floor was visible. Mark was doing something with what looked like an overgrown chemistry kit while Hector dragged a hose across the already wet floor. I watched for a moment, then looked up, trying to find the catwalk. It was almost invisible. I had to stoop a little and look up to see anything. Anyone seated at a table, having dinner, looking casually out, would never see anyone on the catwalk. But then, Otto had walked along the cellar floor. I turned and went to find Aunt Mary.

"What are we going to do now?" she asked when we were finally in the car.

"Have lunch," I replied.

Chapter Thirty

"You want to do what?"

We were sitting in the bowling alley eating BLTs and drinking iced tea. The hollow sound of rolling balls followed by the crashing of pins was getting on my nerves, but no one was there except the lunch hour league and none of them was interested in our murder.

"I want to go over everything that happened that Saturday night," I said, wiping mayonnaise off my face. "As close as we can remember. Carlton saw something, or someone, so let's start with him."

Aunt Mary doused her french fries with ketchup, ate one, and nodded her satisfaction. "Don't you think you should leave the detective work up to Dan?"

"That's not what we're doing. We're just helping. So think."

"All right," she said around a mouthful of sandwich. "Wait a minute." She chewed, swallowed, and went on. "We know where he was until the break. That had to be when Otto was killed, so let's concentrate on that."

"Okay. He came up to Dan and me when Mark was doing that tasting thing. After he left, I never saw him again. But you did."

"Yes, going up the back stairs."

"When was that?"

"Oh, I don't know. I was talking and noticed Carlton mainly because he wasn't following someone around trying to impress them."

"We know he put his head into the kitchen, looking for Otto," I said.

"How do we know that?"

"Larry told me. Wait. Larry said something else. What was it? Yes! He said Carlton wanted to know where Otto was, and Larry told him he was out on the deck."

"Oh my." Aunt Mary put her sandwich back on her plate, right in the middle of the ketchup. "So we can—at least we are going to—assume Carlton went out on the deck to talk to Otto and instead saw someone bash him over the head with a wine bottle and push him into the fermenting tank."

"We are indeed." I was feeling pretty good, so I indulged myself with a couple of french fries. Not that I wouldn't have anyway. "Now we just have to figure out who he saw."

"That's a bit more difficult," she said. "It could have been anyone. We weren't exactly keeping tabs on where people were."

"Yeah." I kept nibbling on the fries. They were almost gone. I eyed Aunt Mary's plate but thought better of it. Not only would my waistline suffer, but I was very likely to get my hand slapped. "You, Dan, and I got back to the table about the time the waiters were coming out with the main course. Everyone else slid into place after us."

"Giving them all time, in theory, to have finished off poor Otto," she said. I noticed she had pulled her french fry plate closer to her.

"Waiters! Of course. Why didn't I think of it earlier?"

"Think of what?" Aunt Mary paused with a fry halfway to her mouth and stared at me. "What are you talking about?"

"Who was on the floor all night? Who took plates of hors d'oeuvres around, who poured wine into every glass that was empty, waiters! I need to ask them who they saw and when. Then, maybe, we'll have something. Or, better yet, someone."

"Waiters," Aunt Mary said thoughtfully. "Sure. They're like postmen. You don't notice them, but they see things. And I know just who you need to talk to."

What a surprise. Of course she did. "Who?"

"Mary Alice Wilson's son. He goes to Cal Poly and moonlights as a waiter. He was there on Saturday night."

Aunt Mary had once more saved the day. I'd find this waiter, and through him the others if I needed them, and we'd know, once and for all, who'd been on that deck.

Chapter Thirty-one

It wasn't until the next morning that I was able to reach Mary Alice Wilson. Aunt Mary had given me her number and said to call her as she had no idea where her son lived. I'd tried that evening until after nine and most of the morning. The line rang busy every time. Finally around two-thirty, I got through.

"You're Mary McGill's niece, aren't you," she said. I'd just told her that, but maybe she hadn't been listening. "You're one of the Page girls. Are you the younger or the older one?" There was a trace of caution in her voice as she asked that question. Catherine had a long reach, across continents and across years.

"The younger one."

"Good," she said. I almost laughed. "You want to do—what now?"

"Talk to your son for a few minutes."

"Which one?"

How many did she have? "The one who was working at the winery the night of the murder."

She sniffed. "I couldn't believe it. Thomas may be in college, but he's still young, and to have a thing like that happen where there are young people, it's a disgrace, that's what I think."

I wasn't sure that was the way I would describe a murder but didn't want to get into an argument with her. I only wanted to talk to her son. Besides, I'd be willing to bet Thomas didn't agree with his mother. "Can you tell me where I can find him?"

"Upstairs in his bedroom, studying," she said, with some reluctance. "I'll see if he wants to talk to you."

He did, and an hour later, Thomas and I were having a cup of coffee at Krispy Kreme. Thirty minutes, one chocolate dough-nut, and one cup of black coffee later, I was sitting in my car, staring out the window, trying to absorb what I had just heard. If what Thomas told me was correct, I was pretty sure I had my murderer.

Facts were taking their places with a certainty that was absolutely terrifying. I closed my eyes and pictured the winery. Entryway, bathrooms off to the right, tasting room straight ahead, with the large picture window beside the fireplace. The walkway in front of the building led around the side of the building to the deck. Inside, the offices and the kitchen were down a hall to the left, ending at the stairs that led to the cellar floor. And running around the top of the tanks was the catwalk. The murderer had made sure Otto would be on the deck, and, bottle in hand, had crept along the catwalk, waited on the deck, hit Otto over the head and dumped him in the tank, and returned the same way. No one would have seen a shadowy figure on the dim catwalk. The wine bottle had to have been hidden behind one of the tanks and retrieved later. I hoped I wasn't right, but I knew I was. I sighed heavily. This was not turning out the way I had thought. I turned on the engine and headed for Aunt Mary's house.

She was waiting for me. "Did you learn anything?"

When I was finished, she said simply, "Oh dear."

We sat looking at each other, trying to come to terms with what we had learned.

After a while, I said, "We have to go to the bed and break-fast."

"You have to call Dan."

"I can't."

"Why?" she asked, incredulously. "You just proved who killed both Otto and Carlton."

"No, I haven't. I have a theory that seems to make sense, but what if Thomas is wrong? He's pretty vague on times and things, and this whole thing hinges on times. We—I—have to verify what he said before I can go to Dan. And we have to do it now, before someone else gets hurt."

"I still think you should call Dan." When she gets an idea in her head, it's hard to dislodge.

"Dan will simply tell me it's a good theory, but I have no proof. We have to go. If you don't want to, I understand, but I'm going."

"Damn," she said, and pushed her chair back. "You always were a willful child."

I pushed mine back also and reached for my purse. But the sight of her, standing in front of me, made me pause. "Ah," I said.

"What's the matter?"

"Ah," I repeated. "We have a few minutes. You might want to change your top." In my agitation, I hadn't noticed this one. Bright red, with little ball tassels all over it, and, given Aunt Mary's ample chest, gently swaying in all the wrong places.

"You don't like it?" she asked, with a trace of a smile. "Ellen McKenzie, you're a wimp." But she changed.

Chapter Thirty-two

I'd pulled up in front of the old Adams house, now Frank's as-yet-unnamed restaurant and B&B. Aunt Mary and I sat in the car and looked up the long brick walkway toward the front door.

"Where is everybody?" asked Aunt Mary.

"I've no idea," I said. "Yesterday this place was crawling with people. I see they got the deck finished."

Aunt Mary made no effort to climb out of the car. "I've always loved this old house, and the new paint job fits. White house, green shutters. It's nice Frank left the original door, that beveled glass is wonderful. I wonder where he found those wicker rockers. They're even older than mine. Or yours. But that deck, it looks kind of raw."

"It's new, that's the trouble. Once it weathers a little, it'll be great. Wait until you see the back. It's huge, goes right down to the pool. Are you going to get out, or are we going to sit here all day, admiring the house?"

"I don't know. Something doesn't feel right." Aunt Mary reached for the door handle, but not very fast.

"That's why we're here, because none of this feels right," I said. I climbed out of the car, walked around to the passenger's side, and opened her door.

"I don't see Frank's car, do you? I don't see any cars. Don't you think that's odd?"

"There're all in the back," I replied, feigning a confidence I didn't feel. Yesterday there had been cars and trucks everywhere.

Today, nobody on the street; nothing in the freshly paved next-door parking lot.

Aunt Mary was finally out of the car, still staring at the house. "Isn't that Larry?"

"Where?" I joined her on the brick pathway.

"There. Right behind that curtain. See? It moved."

"I didn't see anything move. You're spooked. Come on, let's go find someone."

I marched up to the front door, Aunt Mary trailing behind. The planters on each side of the door had roses, still in cans, sitting on top of them, pony packs of unplanted pansies beside them.

"This looks a little messy," commented Aunt Mary.

"They got the shutters painted." I turned the handle on the old-fashioned doorbell, but I had to agree. If the front porch needed to make a good first impression, it was about to fail. The major work was probably going on inside, preparations started for the dinner and all that, but someone needed to get to this as well.

I rang the bell again, but was answered by silence.

"I know I saw someone at the window," Aunt Mary said. She reached over and turned the bell hard. "Why doesn't someone answer the door?"

"Maybe they're all in the kitchen. Come on. We'll walk around back." I was beginning to get a little uneasy. The place was much too quiet for a bed and breakfast expecting eight over-night guests in a short forty-eight hours, and triple that amount for an elaborate, grand opening, formal dinner.

"This place looks as gloomy as a funeral parlor." Aunt Mary stopped to stare at the heavily draped French doors that yesterday had stood open invitingly to the front porch. "Why do they have it all closed up?"

"I've no idea. That's the dining room, and it was all open when I was here before. Larry had the china unpacked, the serving pieces out. It looked pretty impressive. And expensive. Haviland—old Haviland—sterling silver, all kinds of stuff. Why he let Otto, and now Frank, borrow such valuable things is beyond me."

She turned back toward me, surprised. "What? Frank picked out dishes, silverware, crystal. Nice things, but all from a restaurant catalog. Are you sure it was Haviland?"

"Positive," I told her. "The house is full of those kinds of things. It would worry me to death, wondering if someone were going to drop it."

"Or walk off with it. I wonder where it all came from?"

"It came from Larry."

"Larry?" She stopped. "Of course, Larry."

"This way." I headed for the kitchen door. "Hey," I called out. The door was ajar. I pushed it open further. The kitchen was no longer full of packing boxes, and the open shelves were stacked with dishes.

"That's what Frank ordered," Aunt Mary told me, looking around. "Creamy white, with that little embossed pattern around the rim. I don't see any Haviland."

"It was in the dining room," I said. "Probably still is. The important question is, why isn't anybody here?"

"Someone must be around somewhere. Look at all this food!"

I couldn't miss it. There were crates of vegetables, bottles of wine, bags of flour and sugar, and a multitude of pots, pans, ladles, and knives everywhere. But no people.

"I don't understand this. Shouldn't someone be here, doing something with all this?"

I had no answer.

"What's that?" Aunt Mary pointed at the freezer door.

"A walk-in freezer. Larry showed it to me the first time I came here. It's wonderful, holds all kinds of stuff. Here. I'll show you."

"Don't go in there." The voice came from the breakfast room and was so unexpected my hand flew off the door handle.

"Larry. Good grief. You scared me to death," I protested.

"I'm sorry, Ellen. Mrs. McGill, how are you. I didn't hear you come in."

"I brought Aunt Mary over to see the house." I wondered why I felt so nervous. "I've been telling her what wonderful things you've done. And I had a couple of questions…" I let my voice fade away. Larry didn't look as if he heard me. He kept looking around the room, letting his gaze rest on the crates of food, then on the stacks of dishes, all the while alternating between pushing his hair back away from his eyes and pulling the sleeves of his yellow polo shirt over his hands.

"Maybe this is a bad time," I said, backing up. "We don't want to bother you. We'll just look around, you must be frantically busy."

"There is a lot to do." He looked around the kitchen as if he was seeing it for the first time. "Yes, a lot to do." He made no move toward the towering mountain of unprepared food.

"Don't you have any help?" asked Aunt Mary, also looking around. "It's going to take hours to get this together."

"I had help. Lots of help. I sent them all home."

"Home!" exclaimed Aunt Mary. "Larry, you can't get all this done by yourself. And the rest of the house, are the rooms ready? When are the first guests due? Where on earth is Frank?"

"Frank?" repeated Larry.

"Yes, Frank. Where is he? Why isn't he here, doing something? Larry, what on earth is the matter with you?"

Aunt Mary's voice clearly said she was losing patience, and I had a horrible feeling she was going to grab an apron and start making that kitchen hum. Larry must have had the same feeling, because he began to seem more alive. Only it wasn't the threat of Aunt Mary putting away lettuce that had gotten through.

"Frank." He made it sound like a dirty word. "He couldn't wait to take over after Otto died. That lasted a couple of days, then he turned everything over to me, and now he's back. This is wrong, that isn't good enough, why did I put out all of my own things? I hate him."

Larry's face was getting blotched, his hands waved in the air, and his eye had started to twitch. Frank was not good for Larry's nervous system. What I was about to ask him wasn't going to make it better.

"Larry," I said, standing directly in front of him so he would have to look at me, "Thomas, one of the waiters last Saturday night, tells me you delivered a message to Otto from Frank. Is that true?"

"What?" Larry seemed to have a hard time leaving his hatred of Frank for a moment and concentrating on the question. "Message?"

"Yes." I moved toward the breakfast room, letting him follow. I hoped movement would calm him down, make him think about what I wanted to know. "Thomas says you sent Otto out to the deck to meet Frank." I looked back at him. He looked confused. "Is that true, did Frank ask you to send Otto out to the deck?"

He stopped in the middle of the room and looked around. He reached out and picked up a hand-hemmed napkin, shook it out, smoothed it in his hand, refolded it, and placed it back on the table. The sterling silver fruit bowl, filled with red and green apples lying on autumn leaves, got moved a quarter inch or so, then he started toward the sideboard, his back to me.

"Larry?" I said, following him. "Did Frank ask you to do that?"

"Yes," he said, still not looking at me. "Yes, he did. But I told you that. I felt bad afterward." He finally turned to face me, the vague look gone. "Do you think Frank killed him? He must have, you know. I hope it wasn't my fault."

"When did Frank ask you to do that?" Larry was still wandering around the room, picking things up, admiring them, putting them down, and I was following him. It was beginning to get exasperating.

"When?"

"Yes, Larry. When. You said you never left the kitchen, so when did Frank come in and where was Otto then?"

Larry's eyes were shifting back and forth. "I don't remember," he told me.

"Was it after you told Carlton Otto was on the deck?"

"Did I tell Carlton that?" He was beginning to look like a cornered rabbit.

"You said you did. When did Otto go onto the deck, and who came in after he'd left?"

His eye was starting to twitch again. He put down the silver bowl and picked up a small marble egg. "Isn't this beautiful? It's Chinese. Or maybe French."

"Larry, when did you leave the kitchen?"

I had his attention now. "Oh, I never left. Otto was gone, and I had to direct the waiters. Someone had to take charge. Someone had to make sure everything was going to go the way I—we'd—planned it."

"Where's Jolene?" I asked him. "Isn't that her car out back?"

The shift of subject seem to really unnerve him. "Jolene?"

"Yes, Jolene. I moved right in front of him, trying to get his attention directly on what I was asking. "Is she with Frank?"

"No, no. I don't think so." He made a vague gesture and looked around as if expecting her to materialize out of a corner. "She was here a while ago. Maybe she went into town."

Her car was there, and she wasn't with Frank. How had she gotten into town? Should I try and find her? Or leave? I'd learned what I needed from Larry. It was time to spill all this on Dan, but I was worried about Jolene. Where was she?

The scream was low, gurgling, and horrified. Aunt Mary. I whirled around, bumped Larry out of my way and ran toward the kitchen. The freezer door was wide open and staggering out of it were Aunt Mary and a very blue, very frosty Jolene.

"My God!" I exclaimed. "What happened?"

"I was putting some of that food away," Aunt Mary puffed, dropping Jolene down on a chair, "and when I opened the door, there was Jolene. I'm afraid I screamed."

"Yes," I agreed. "And it was a good one. Scared me to death. How did Jolene get in the freezer? Is she all right? Shouldn't we do something?"

"A blanket would be good for starters. Larry, go get one. Ellen, you call nine one one." Aunt Mary rubbed Jolene's hands, then took off her sweater and wrapped it around her shoulders. Jolene was shaking uncontrollably, little icicles hanging from her extravagant eyelashes, her hair a mass of white. Her fingers were blue, and she couldn't close them, but she was still trying to talk.

"What's she saying?" Aunt Mary leaned down to try to hear. "I can't make it out. Where's that blanket?"

"No blanket," Larry said, "and no nine one one. I'm real sorry you and Mrs. McGill got involved in this, but now that you're here, well, you haven't given me much choice. Have you?"

I turned to face him, the full impact of Jolene's plight, and now ours, sinking in. He stood by the chopping block, a long French boning knife in his hand, calmly contemplating us.

"Larry!" Aunt Mary looked up from rubbing Jolene's arms, indignation giving way to shock as she saw the knife, "What are you doing? We have to get a doctor, right away. How she could have gotten locked in a freezer, I can't imagine. Oh. Oh my."

I would have put it a little stronger. Realization that I had gotten my answers sank in, along with the fact that Larry had understood the questions. Worst of all, for the first time ever, I saw Aunt Mary at a loss. She glanced quickly at me, but I wasn't much help. My eyes were glued to that knife.

"I'm going to have to think," Larry said. "I could put you all in the freezer. No, that wouldn't work."

That, at least, was a relief, but the list of Larry's options didn't look promising. Neither did ours. I let my eyes drift around the kitchen, frantically wondering if there were something I could use in our defense. I spied a large wooden tray. Could I? Too far away. My hand touched the edge of the chopping block, and I moved it along, watching Larry's face, hoping I would come on something.

"Are you going to try and stop me with that bunch of carrots?" There was amusement in Larry's voice and a confidence that was new. And terrifying.

"What's the matter with Jolene?"

None of us had heard Frank come in, but there he was, all six wonderful feet of him, slamming the kitchen door behind him, striding toward us.

"She looks blue, and she's shaking." He examined her critically before turning his attention to the rest of the kitchen. "Where's the help? Nothing is started. For God's sake, Larry. What is the matter with you? Do something about this woman, and then get going! Mary, Ellen. What are you doing here? It is wonderful to see you, but…"

It finally dawned on Frank that all was not right. He stopped, took a good look at Larry, who held the knife as if he was ready to carve, took a better look at Jolene, then back to us.

"What's going on here?"

"It seems that Jolene found out who killed Otto and Carlton, and got shoved into your freezer so she wouldn't talk," I said.

The expressions that passed over Frank's face would have been laughable any other time. I watched him go from astonishment to incredulity to full realization.

"No. Surely not. Larry? You? But why?"

"Never mind why." Larry was beginning to lose his confidence again, and his eye started to twitch. That didn't seem like a good sign.

"I have to think what to do with all of you. Frank, you should have stayed away a little longer. I hate you, but you are a great chef, and it will be a shame to kill you."

"Kill me! What are you talking about!"

There is, after all, something to be said for arrogance.

"Give me that knife," Frank demanded. "This is utter nonsense. Mary, you and Ellen take Jolene out to the car. Get her to a doctor. Larry and I will talk about this after you're gone."

I'd misjudged him. Frank had started circling around, slowly edging himself between Larry and the chair where Jolene still shivered. Larry backed up slightly, away from the kitchen door. Frank didn't look at us. He kept moving, never taking his eyes off Larry, but waved one hand behind his back, motioning to us. Aunt Mary looked at me; I nodded. She grabbed one of Jolene's arms, I grabbed the other and she was on her feet. A low moan escaped her, but we had her moving.

"Hey!" Larry shouted.

"Go!" yelled Frank.

We did. I don't know how I got the kitchen door opened so fast, but the next thing I knew, we were on the deck, half dragging, half pushing a stiff Jolene toward the front of the house and my car.

We got her into the front seat, I turned the heater on full blast and handed Aunt Mary my cell phone.

"Lock the doors," I said. "Call nine one one. Call Dan."

"Where are you going?" she asked, clutching the phone.

"Back there."

"No. You can't." She reached out to grab me, but I shoved her into the driver's seat.

"I have to. Frank is no match for Larry and that knife."

"And you are?" Tension had tinged her voice with hysteria.

"Two is better than one. And I can't leave Frank alone. Lock the door."

I wasn't being heroic. I was reacting to worry and adrenaline. Otherwise, I would never have gone back into that kitchen. But I did. And there was Frank, face down on the floor, a thin trail of blood escaping from under his left arm.

Larry stood a little off to one side, his back to the door, his right hand hanging down by his side, the knife barely held between slack fingers. Small drops of blood dripped from it, making a tiny crimson pool on the black and white tiled floor.

I stopped just inside the door, paralyzed, unable to speak. Unfortunately, that didn't last.

"Oh my God, what have you done?" Bad mistake. I knew it the minute the words were out, but it was too late.

Larry turned toward me, his eyes glassy, but it didn't take long for him to focus. "You came back."

"Ah," I said, backing toward the door. If I could get through it, I could slam it in his face. He was too fast, and too close.

"Where are you going?" He lunged, grabbed me with his left hand, and pulled me off my feet, into the kitchen, and almost onto Frank.

"You can't go anyplace. Not now."

He dragged me into the formal dining room, dim behind drawn drapes. The knife was clutched more firmly in his other hand. I wanted desperately to struggle, to scream, to signal for help in some way, but was afraid to. That damn knife was way too close.

"It's a beautiful room, isn't it?" He wasn't listening for a response. "Otto said I couldn't use my things, that I couldn't be part of all this. He said this place wasn't mine." This time he seemed to want me to say something. But what? I sort of mewed. That seemed to be enough because he went on. "Not mine?" He shook his head. "It was my money that bought it. But he said it was only a loan. Only it wasn't. It was so I could be a partner."

Larry seemed to be in some world occupied only by him. Surely he couldn't have forgotten Jolene fresh from the freezer, Aunt Mary locked in the car, hopefully calling the cops, and Frank. Poor Frank, lying bleeding, probably dead, on the kitchen floor. But he acted like the only thing that mattered was the tour of the dining room we were taking, him clutching me and the knife, me stumbling along after him, agreeing with whatever he said.

"It was mean of Otto not to let you be a partner," I said, a little breathlessly. It was hard to get the words out with my left shoulder practically in Larry's face.

He stopped. "Yes, it was. He promised, you know. Otto. He said if I'd give him the money to buy this place, I would be a full partner. He lied." He loosened his grip on my arm. I started to straighten up a little. Maybe I could—no. He tightened down.

"He laughed at me, you know." Larry said this in a conversational voice, much like he'd say, "warm for March." That was more scary than anything. But it brought up something I didn't quite understand. Now wasn't an especially good time to ask him, but on the other hand, it might be the only time. "Why Carlton?"

"He laughed at me, too," he said, in that same conversational tone. "He and Otto together. He said I was stupid because I trusted Otto, didn't have him sign something when I gave him the money. The whole world will laugh at you, he said. So I killed him." He stopped in front of the cherrywood server and stared at the Waterford sherry glasses sitting on it, next to what looked like a very old bottle of Spanish sherry. "That was a great vintage," he said. "Don't you think so?"

Larry was gone again, in that world I couldn't inhabit, and as long as he was there, I thought I had a chance of staying alive and uncarved. It was when he came back to earth that I was in real trouble. My best chance seemed to be humor him, admire the plates, the tablecloths, the sherry, anything, until help came. Help in the shape of Dan and the troops. I glanced at the dining room French doors, but the curtains were still drawn, and I couldn't think of any way to get to them. Damn! Aunt Mary couldn't see me; she couldn't know I was still alive but a captive. I sent up a silent prayer she knew how to work a cell phone.

Larry let go of my arm. Maybe I could get to the drapes and somehow fling them open. I gave that idea up instantly. Instead of holding me, Larry held up the knife.

"How long have you known? All about Otto and Carlton. I didn't want you to know."

He was like a man waking up from a dream, the vacant expression fading into an alert, hard stare. I may have been scared before, but now I was terrified.

"You kept trying to find out things, didn't you? Asking people questions that were none of your business. The police—your boyfriend, Dan—think Sabrina killed them both. That's what they were supposed to think. Why did you have to spoil things? I thought you loved me. You were supposed to love me."

"Sabrina's my niece," I said, trying to keep the quiver out of my voice. "She's family. I had to do something."

"I don't have any family." No quiver in Larry's voice. "Only the restaurant and this bed and breakfast. Otto tried to take that away from me, but I stopped him. Then Carlton, and Frank tried. I stopped them, too. Now you. I can't let you do that, now can I?" The chilling logic of that statement, at least to Larry, grew my goose bumps to the size of pigeon eggs. "You know, I had a mother once. But she died and left me." This was getting worse. Not only was there no quiver, but his voice had hardened and deepened. "My father hated me, and I hated him. When he had a heart attack and died, I laughed. I was finally free to do what I wanted. But people keep getting in the way. Why, Ellen? Why?"

"I don't know. But they won't anymore. Everyone will forgive you. They all know Otto was an evil man, you'll be fine." I was babbling. I couldn't help it. But Larry somehow seemed to be reassured.

"Yes, that's right. I'm going to make the dinner. I'm going to do it all. For Saturday night. Frank isn't going to do it, and neither is Otto. Finally, I'm going to do it. All by myself. I can do it. You believe I can do it, don't you?"

He was gone again. "Of course you can do it. You're going to, and it will be wonderful." I tried not to let anything show in my voice but reassurance. I wasn't at all sure I succeeded. Please, please let Dan hurry up, was running through my head like a litany.

Larry frowned, then rubbed his head with his free hand. The one that wasn't holding me anymore. I experimentally took one step backward. The dining room door that opened into the entry hall was right behind me. If I could ease my way out, maybe, just maybe, I could open that front door and run for my car. Maybe.

"We'll have to do something about Frank," Larry said. "I can't cook with him on the floor. The cellar. We'll put him in the wine cellar. You'll have to help."

I almost gagged. Frank in the cellar? Me helping? The man was stark raving mad. I took another step backward. Larry didn't seem to notice, and I bolted. I almost made it.

Larry exploded across the room after me, catching me with my hand on the latch. He swung me around, and I landed, hard, against the wall at the bottom of the stairs. The knife was in front of me, the sharp blade coming toward my throat. We were face to face, so close I could feel his breath, so close he had to hear my heart pound. He leaned into me, bringing the knife slowly closer. He whispered, "I'm sorry. Things could have been so nice. I know how you've always felt about me, but…"

That did it. Rage and terror lent me strength. I shoved. He let go of my arm and staggered backward. Only a step or two, but it was enough to send me up the stairs.

I didn't pause until I reached the landing, where I risked a glance back. Larry climbed slowly after me, a small smile on his face, no twitch in his eye, and the knife firmly held in his hand.

"Where do you think you're going, Ellen? There's no way out, you know. No way but down these stairs." He kept coming up, stair by stair, his voice soft and sounding oh so reasonable. "Did Mrs. McGill call the police? Did she call your friend, Dan? You know, I never liked him when we were in school. I haven't changed. But he likes you. And he won't want you hurt. But you don't much care for him, do you, my dear. You won't marry him. It's me you like. So come on, Ellen. Give me your hand. After I explain that to Dan, after I make him go away, we can get rid of Frank and start the dinner. You can help. You'd like that, wouldn't you?"

I started to back down the hall. Larry's words were echoing off the closed doors, bringing up pictures I didn't want to see. Me with Larry's knife at my throat, standing at the kitchen door while Larry bargained with Dan, the Dan I cared about a whole lot, the Dan I might never see again. Me helping Larry throw Frank's body down to the cellar, me thrown down to the cellar. There had to be a way, some way. A window. I'd jump out a window. I opened the closest bedroom door and looked in. There was a window all right, shut tight, latched, and clear across the room. Larry was getting closer, and I suddenly thought, if I go in there, I'm trapped.

Larry laughed. "Trying for a window? You'll never make it. I'm a lot faster than you." His expression changed again, and his tone was no longer reasonable. "You're making me angry, Ellen," he hissed. "Very angry. Stop right there and give me your hand."

"Like hell," I said, startling myself even more than Larry. My hand was on another door handle, and I turned it, expecting nothing, but there were the back stairs, the blessed servant stairs. Steep, treacherous, but they looked to me like the stairs to salvation. I leapt around the door and slammed it shut. Another piece of luck. There was a latch. My fingers had a hard time obeying me, but the lock clicked shut as the door started to rattle.

"Ellen." Larry's voice was muffled, but every word came through. "You won't get away. And now I won't wait for Dan. I'm coming. I'm coming."

There was no place to go but down, and I went as fast as trembling legs would take me. The stairs came out in the pantry beside the kitchen, and I knew I had to make that kitchen door before Larry did.

I stood behind the pantry door, listening. He must have run back down the main staircase, but where was he now? I eased out a little and dared a look around the kitchen. Frank was still on the floor, but no one else was in sight. Again I listened. Not a sound. He had to be somewhere, waiting. Why couldn't I hear him? See him? Where was he hiding? The kitchen offered few hiding places, so he must be in the breakfast room or the dining room. In either case, he would have to make a huge lunge to catch me. I had a slim chance of making the back door, and I knew I had to do it now, before whatever nerve I had left disappeared. My best chance was to get to that door before Larry realized where I was, and that meant silence. Off came my shoes. I started across the kitchen floor in my stocking feet, edging past Frank, desperately wanting to stop, to do something for him, knowing that the only thing I could do was escape.

My hand was on the door handle when I heard the groan. Frank? Was he alive? I hesitated, turned the handle, pulled the door open a little, then paused again to look back at Frank. Was he moving?

"Got you."

A strong hand grabbed my wrist; my feet slipped, and I screamed. Larry's face loomed over me, contorted in fury, while his other hand waved that awful knife.

"You can't get away from me. Why did you try? You were probably laughing, too. Just like all the others. Just like my father, like Otto. You don't think I can do this dinner, do you? Well, you'll see. No. You won't. For I have to kill you, don't I?"

The knife was getting closer, but somehow I had managed to hold onto the door handle. If I could only—I did. I lunged backward, ripped my arm from Larry's grasp, and propelled myself in a half circle and out the door. It partly closed behind me, but not enough to stop Larry. I heard him yell and knew he was right behind me.

Stockings are not good for running on decks. I slid over it toward the stairs and bolted down them, much too fast. I could hear him behind me, not yelling now, but breathing hard, and I didn't have to look to know that the knife was slicing through the air. I wanted to scream, but was concentrating too hard on where to run, and how to keep my feet under me. I didn't dare head for the side of the house that would take me back to my car, not without knowing if Larry could cut me off, so I sprinted toward the pool. If I could make it to the far side, I could at least see where I had to go next. Only it didn't work out that way. My stockings refused to grip the deck and I found myself sliding into one of the lounges set beside the pool. Sudden pain swept up my leg, and I could feel myself falling, could see the pool deck rising to meet my face. I flung myself a little more to the left, and hit the water with a huge splash.

"Omph," I think I said as I sank.

I must have swallowed half the pool before I managed to make it back to the surface. Coughing and gagging, trying to see through soggy hair, I started to tread water.

"Oh, Ellen. What a silly thing to do."

I finally focused, and there was Larry, standing by the pool steps, smiling down at me. The knife was still there, as though it had grown into his hand, both hanging relaxed by his side.

"What are you going to do now? You can't get out, you know. Not unless I let you. Shall I let you? I might. If you promise to be good. You can help me with Frank, and with the dinner, and you can wear that dress you had on at the winery. I liked that dress. But you mustn't laugh at me. You won't, will you?"

I had no idea what to do. I had never felt less like laughing, so that would be an easy promise, but the rest? Somehow I didn't think Larry had any intention of letting me out of that pool, at least alive. But I couldn't keep treading water forever, I was already getting tired, and I didn't know when, or if, someone would get around to attempting a rescue.

"I'm not coming out. The water's fine. Why don't you come in?" If he did, maybe I'd have a chance to make the ladder by the diving board.

"You don't want me to do that. I'm an excellent swimmer. I'm an excellent chef, too. And I have superb taste. I like really fine things. Don't you think so? So why do people laugh at me?"

An excellent swimmer. Just my luck. I let myself drift toward the diving board anyway. If I could keep him talking, maybe I could get up those stairs before Larry could reach that side of the pool. "Nobody laughs at you. I've heard Frank say many times how talented you are."

"He did?" His expression was eager, like a little kid getting praise for a good report card. "I didn't know that. He should have told me." Another lightning change of expression, but now his face was thundercloud dark. "No one ever tells me."

"Sure they do." I was getting closer. Another couple of feet and I would be able to grab the ladder. "Everyone knows how talented you are."

"Otto didn't. Neither did Carlton. They lied. Both of them. And they laughed at me."

Keep him talking. Almost there. "How did Carlton lie?"

"He knew Otto never planned on making me a partner. He told me by lending Otto the money I would be half owner of this place. But they never put my name on any of the papers. I told you that. You said you'd help me, but you didn't. I thought I could trust you."

"I tried." My legs were starting to feel like logs, dragging me down, and my arms were protesting the constant movement. I'd better get to that ladder pretty soon, or I'd end up on the bottom of the pool. "I talked to my broker, and he gave me the name of an attorney who specializes in these kinds of things. I'll give it to you just as soon as I get out of here." If I get out.

Larry didn't act as if he'd heard me. He was moving slowly around the pool, following me as I drifted. He was almost at the diving board, now past it, almost to the ladder. "Otto said I was no chef, that I couldn't cook my way out of a paper bag." He stood on the side of the pool, watching me struggle. I had to get to the side, and soon, but Larry was waiting. My choices were not looking good.

"He said I was a danger in the kitchen, always knocking the pots over. He laughed at me, and said I had to get out with Jolene. But I had the last laugh. I—no, Ellen. You can't do that."

Damn. I was almost there, but as my hand reached out Larry dove in. He hadn't lied. He was an excellent swimmer. He had me before I could grab the ladder and pushed me down, down. I swallowed more water, felt the chlorine burn my eyes, then managed to get to the surface, but not to get away. The knife was coming closer, and this time there would be no escape.

"You're a traitor You tried to leave me; you laughed at me. I know you did. You—"

Kerplunk. A loud, hollow kerplunk. Larry stopped talking. His eyes rolled back, his jaw went slack, and he started to sink. His fingers opened, and the knife floated by me. I stared at it, unable to believe what was happening.

"Grab him before he goes under. For God's sake, Ellen. Hurry up."

I looked up, and there, kneeling on the diving board, a large cast iron frying pan held in both hands, was Aunt Mary!

"Grab him!" She pointed down at the rapidly sinking Larry and I finally came to. I reached for his hair, which was all I could see, and started to tug him toward the side.

"Help me. He's heavy."

"Keep his face up until I get off this blasted board. If I fall in, you'll have two of us to rescue."

I watched, fascinated, as she crawled backward, dragging her frying pan. What a shame I didn't have a camera, I thought. I felt Larry struggle, and all thoughts of Aunt Mary's behind, inching its way toward a safe haven, fled.

"Hurry up. He's coming to, and I'll never hold him."

"Shove him a little higher," she said. "There, I've got his collar. Once more, nope. Lost him. Shove harder."

"I'm trying. He's heavier than he looks." Or waterlogged. I shoved again.

"Got him," Aunt Mary said. "He's on the deck. Oh, oh. He's coming around."

"Bang him on the head with that thing again."

"Ellen McKenzie! I couldn't."

"You did once."

"That was under extreme duress." She watched Larry stir, then sputter and start to cough.

"There'll be more duress if he gets that knife back. Watch him. I'm going after it."

The last thing I wanted to do was get back in that pool. No! The last thing was to let Larry get his hands on the knife. So, I went back down the ladder, swam over to the knife, and got back out in time to see Larry on his hands and knees, Aunt Mary standing over him, the frying pan held over her head, ready for another frontal attack.

"You can put it down now. We'd kind of like to take him in alive."

Dan. Finally! The deck was alive with police, with a couple of paramedics mixed in. Dan instructed them to look at Larry while he looked at me.

"Seems you two had yourself quite a time."

"Why are you letting them treat Larry?" I got out between water-spewing coughs. "Frank's lying in the kitchen, stabbed. He needs someone—something—he might be dead."

"He's on his way to an ambulance right now, and so is Jolene," Dan said. "Let me have that knife."

I hadn't realized I was holding the damn thing, and gratefully handed it over to Dan, who immediately handed it off to someone else.

"This is evidence, so bag it," he told the uniformed officer. "Not that it will do us much good. Ellie, are you all right?"

I had started to shake. Like Jolene. I couldn't seem to stop. My teeth were chattering, I could see my hands turning blue, my clothes hung on me, wet and clammy, and I could feel my hair dripping down my collar. I felt like crying.

"Get me a blanket," Dan said to someone, and the next thing I knew, I was wrapped in something warm, there was a towel around my head, and strong arms were holding them both in place. A soft kiss glanced across my cheek, so quickly I almost didn't recognize it.

"Come on. Let's get you in the car, and home to a hot bath."

I was in the passenger seat, Aunt Mary behind the wheel. I felt the blanket being tucked more securely around me before someone closed the door. The heater was on, and blessed warmth blew on my soggy toes.

Dan was at Aunt Mary's window, still giving instructions, but I tuned them out. The only words I wanted to remember were "hot bath," maybe accompanied with "hot tea."

"I'll be over later," he said. "I've got a lot of questions I need to ask both of you. Like how you two thought you were going to flush out a murderer without getting killed yourselves. Of all the dumb stunts."

"We saved Jolene," Aunt Mary told him tartly. My chilled lips cracked a little. We had indeed. And we'd solved the murder, vindicated Sabrina, and we were still alive. Well, sort of.

"You did save Jolene. And, Mary, you did a little more than that. But then, I always knew you were handy with a frying pan."

Chapter Thirty-three

The claw-foot bathtub had been a refuge and a solace many times during my growing-up years, but never as great as now. Hot water gradually warmed my body, and numbed my mind. I let the steam evaporate everything that had happened. I would soon have to face it all, but right now, it was time out. Finally, I could avoid it no longer. My skin was as wrinkled as an elephant's, it had turned from blue to red, my tea mug was empty, and my living room was filling up.

Voices, lots of voices, rose up the staircase. One in particular got me out of the tub and into my best-fitting L.L. Bean chinos and my sky blue tee shirt. I ran a comb through my steam-curled hair, added lipstick, and descended the staircase.

"Oh, Ellen." Sabrina threw herself at me, burying her face in my shoulder, letting tears stain the sleeve of my shirt. "Oh my God. He almost killed you, and it was all my fault. Can you ever forgive me?"

"How do you figure it was your fault?" I managed to say, trying vainly to push her away. Mark pulled at her arm, but she stayed stuck.

"I can't believe it was Larry," she said between sobs. "Poor Larry, I never dreamed it was him. And to think I let him—"

"Let him do what?" Aunt Mary said. "Sabrina, let Ellen go. She survived Larry's knife, but she might not your guilt. Here, go sit down beside Mark. Have some wine."

Free of Sabrina's embrace, I looked around the room. Mark sat on one of my matching sofas; Aunt Mary was in the large reading chair. Sabrina perched on the arm of the sofa, as close to Mark as she could get. She wiped her eyes with a tissue, then picked up a full wineglass off the coffee table and took a sip. Mark reached over and patted her leg. She wiped away another tear and smiled down at him. Dan stood in the doorway of the living room, leaning against the jamb, also sipping, much to my surprise, a glass of white wine.

"Hi," he said to me. "You look a little better than you did a while ago."

"Thanks." I looked at him, at the expression on his face, but couldn't read it. Aunt Mary handed me a glass of wine, and I took it, then went to the other sofa and sat on one side. Lots of room for someone else, but no one sat beside me.

"Dan wanted to know why we went over to the bed and breakfast this afternoon," Aunt Mary said. She sounded a little hesitant and kept giving Dan small glances.

"What did you tell him?" I asked, trying not to do the same.

"Nothing yet."

"Maybe you'd like to tell me." He didn't sound mad, he sounded…how? Unhappy. That made two of us. I deliberately didn't look at him, choosing instead to twirl the wine in my glass.

"Well, everything seemed to point to Sabrina, but we knew she was innocent, and we—I—thought we had to do something. So I started talking to people. I started with Lighthouse Winery." I glanced over at Mark and Sabrina to see how they were taking this breach of family trust, but they seemed just fine with it. "Someone there told me about some kind of fight and lawsuit. I was afraid that made Sabrina seem even more guilty. So…"

"You found all that out and didn't think to tell me?" Dan asked. He sounded weary.

"I—well—Oh, damn it. I wanted to, but was trying to think of some way to make it seem less like a motive." I sounded weary, also.

"That's a material fact." His face was expressionless, but his grasp on his wineglass was a little too tight. "Not telling me could be construed as obstruction of justice. That, in case you didn't think about it, is a crime."

"Really, Dan," Aunt Mary said. "She would have told you. Eventually. Besides, you already knew."

Dan didn't look at either of us. He shifted his weight and leaned his other shoulder against the wall. I knew that move. His back hurt. "Okay, I'll let that go. For now. But what's all this about the waiters?"

"I kept thinking someone besides Carlton had to have seen whoever went out on that deck. The most logical person would be one of the waiters. They were everywhere. It was Thomas, Mary Ellen Wilson's son, who told me what I needed. It wasn't who he saw, but who he didn't."

"What?" Dan pushed away from the doorjamb to stare at me. "Who didn't Thomas see?"

"Larry. He was gone, out of the kitchen, for quite a little time. That's why the main course was late getting out. The waiters were furious because he was supposed to be overseeing everything. Larry had already sent Otto away, telling him Frank wanted to see him on the deck. Not long after that, he left. Only he told me, over and over, that he had not left the kitchen at all.

"I remembered the catwalk and figured out how he did it. He sent Otto out on the deck, walked around the cellar on the catwalk, and went through the little door onto the platform the tank sits on. From there it was easy to go up the ladder onto the deck. I think they argued. Larry said Otto laughed at him, and we know the rest. He went back to the kitchen the same way. No one on the cellar floor would have seen him. He probably hid the bottle in the kitchen somewhere, retrieved it when he came back for his pots, and that's when he took the other knife. I was right, wasn't I?"

"As it turns out," Dan said. "But why didn't you come to me?"

That was the hard one. "I didn't think I had enough evidence. It still could have been Jolene. So, I thought I'd ask Larry if Frank had indeed sent a message to Otto, and if so, when. That way, I'd get his side of the story, and he wouldn't know I suspected him. Then I was going to come to you." My sentence sort of faded away at the end. It had made so much sense when I had made Aunt Mary come with me. It made none now I was retelling it.

Dan sighed and walked over to the bookcase where Jake was lying on his regular perch, the third bookshelf up, draped nonchalantly over the works of Charles Dickens. Dan scratched him behind the ears. The cat purred.

"Jake," he said. "You're the only one in this bunch with a lick of sense. Including, for the first time in recorded history, Mrs. Mary McGill."

He turned to face all of us. "First, I was pretty sure Sabrina hadn't killed either Otto or Carlton. However, when you find someone standing over a corpse with a knife, you do usually have to ask a few questions."

Sabrina gasped and her hands flew to her mouth. "Then why…?"

"Why what?" Dan asked. "I asked you questions, but I didn't arrest you. That should have told you something. And when Catherine called me—oh yes, she called me—I told her, when I finally could get in a sentence, that I didn't think you had done it." He looked thoughtful. "That was an interesting conversation. Where was I? Oh yes. Sabrina, how tall are you?"

Sabrina and Mark looked at him as if he'd suddenly gone crazy. Aunt Mary and I looked at each other.

"Stab wounds," she said. She either watched CSI or had been reading up on pathology.

"She's about five foot two," I said. "Wrong angle?"

"She'd have needed about another foot to be Carlton's killer. Of course, Mark could have done it and let us suspect Sabrina. But somehow, I didn't think so." He said this rather hurriedly. Mark's face had started to get stormy. "And then, we had another small lead."

"What?" I asked, wondering what I had missed that Dan had found.

"Larry's car was parked in back of Carlton's office for at least a half hour before Sabrina arrived. We do ask about things like that, and it took almost no time to find someone who noticed it."

It wasn't something I'd missed. "Why didn't you talk to the waiters?" I asked. "Thomas and those other kids had the missing piece all along."

"We did, we did. We talked to them Saturday night, and the next day, and then several days later when we were putting everything together. No one mentioned the fact that Larry had left the kitchen. Unfortunately, I don't know if that was asked. But I plan to find out." His face looked grim. I felt sorry for whoever had failed to include that question. "However, we were beginning to take a good look at Larry. The car thing clinched it."

"Then why didn't you arrest him?"

"We were getting the warrant while you were swimming in the pool." His voice and face were still expressionless.

"So, all my detective work was for nothing?" I felt cheated somehow. After all, I had discovered that Larry was our murderer and why.

"Except for the fact you almost got yourself killed, you helped a lot," Dan said. He didn't sound as if he were happy about his admission. But it made me feel better.

"How?" I asked.

"The bottle and the knife." This was costing Dan something. I hoped I didn't end up paying for it as well. "After Sabrina called us about the bottle, we started asking her about who had access to the cartons. You were way ahead of us there. You and the Boy Scouts. And I hadn't connected the knife to the winery, but you pointed us in the right direction there, too. By that time, we were pretty sure Larry was our boy, but we weren't sure why. Motive does matter, especially to a jury. We were digging away at his relationship with Otto when we got that nine one one call from Mary. Between what she told us and what Larry is spilling, we have more than enough to go for murder one. Only, he'll probably spend the rest of his life in a mental hospital." He looked around at all of us. "So, Mary, next time you and Ellen think you've solved a murder, how about coming to me first. And, Sabrina, next time you find a corpse, if the cops don't arrest you right away, believe that they have other possibilities they're considering."

"She does have a tendency to get carried away," Mark started. He let the last of his sentence fade as the full blast of Sabrina's gaze rested on him. She wasn't her mother's daughter for nothing.

"As for you," Dan went on, looking for the first time directly at me, "you knew someone was a murderer. Didn't it occur to you that one murder could lead to another? That the next victim could be you? Why didn't you talk to me before you went off tilting at windmills?"

"Talking isn't something we've done a lot of lately." I wondered if those words sounded as mournful to Dan as they did to me.

The front door opened with a bang. There stood Frank, his left arm in a sling, his face pale. He stood for a moment, leaning his right arm against the doorjamb, beaming at all of us.

"I'm here and I'm alive," he announced.

And milking the moment for all it's worth, I thought uncharitably. The man's timing was uncanny. Why did he arrive now? Just when Dan was going to say something? Maybe something I wanted to hear? A vision of Frank getting us out of the kitchen, of Frank lying on the floor, bleeding, immediately came to mind and smote me with guilt.

"Frank," I exclaimed with the others. We all scrambled to our feet, but Mark got to his father first.

"Here, Dad, sit here." He guided Frank to the sofa where he and Sabrina had been sitting, grabbed a clean wineglass, filled it, and handed it to his father.

"My goodness, Frank," Aunt Mary said, starting to bustle around. That didn't last long. Frank reached out his good hand and pulled her down beside him. He winced and let out a little gasp.

"Oh my God, Frank," Aunt Mary exclaimed. "Why did they let you out of the hospital?"

"I'm sore but fine, Mary, just fine. I didn't even need a transfusion."

"That's good news," said Sabrina. She looked at her father-in-law with her usual distaste, but it seemed mixed with compassion. Or something. "How about Jolene? Where is she?"

"Jolene has moved to the Santa Louisa Inn. They have hot tubs, and last I heard Jolene was planning on climbing in one." He readjusted himself and let his good arm slide behind Aunt Mary. She didn't move away.

"I'll bet she takes a full glass of wine with her," laughed Mark.

"How about the whole bottle," Sabrina said. This time, the look of distaste wasn't tempered with anything.

Frank looked at her with extreme sadness. "I wish I didn't think you were right. You know, Jolene and I used to be—friends. Years ago. She's—gone downhill. I gave her the name of a place she could go where she could get some help, but she laughed." He squeezed Aunt Mary again and smiled down at her. "Well, I tried."

So that was what was going on at the Yum Yum. My, my. Frank did indeed have hidden depths.

Dan had left the bookcases, and Jake and I had settled into the big chair that Aunt Mary had forsaken for her place beside Frank. I looked directly at him and asked, "What happens to Larry now?"

I hoped he'd realize I wanted to know because Larry had almost killed me, because I knew Larry was sick. Only this wasn't about Larry and what I had done right or what I had done wrong in connection with him, and Dan and I both knew it.

"Larry's been transported to the county jail. They have lockdown facilities for violent prisoners and our Larry qualifies, big time." I might not have been in the room. He addressed his remarks to everyone else.

"Poor Larry," I said.

"Poor Larry!" Sabrina exclaimed. "He killed two people and was going to let me take the blame!"

"I know, but Otto and Carlton not only cheated him, they laughed at him. He'd had too much of that in his life, and they were his straw."

"Straw?" Frank asked.

"As in camel," Aunt Mary explained. "How do you know about all that?" she asked me.

"He said so. Right before he started chasing me up the stairs."

"Why did he push Jolene in the freezer?" Sabrina asked. "She didn't know anything, did she?"

"Actually, she did," Dan said. "Only, she didn't realize it until this morning."

"Oh," I said. "I'll bet…" I stopped.

"Go on," Dan said. "You've been right so far. What do you think happened?"

I wasn't fond of the look on his face, it was a bit grim, but what the hell. I'd come this far, and I couldn't do our relationship any more damage by a lucky guess. I hoped. "She was at the winery the day he stopped by for his pots, and she either saw him put back the bottle or take the knife. Probably the bottle."

Dan nodded. "She saw him put back the bottle. It didn't mean a thing to her at first. But she somehow heard that the wine bottle used to kill Otto had been found. Probably when she came back to take more pictures. She was there, a couple of times, taking pictures, wasn't she?" This was addressed to Sabrina, who nodded. "So, she asked Larry about it, and he answered her by pushing her in the freezer."

"That seems incredibly stupid," Aunt Mary exclaimed. "He'd already murdered two people. What made her think he wouldn't kill her, too?"

"Greed," I said. Everyone turned to look at me. Almost everyone.

"Blackmail," stated Sabrina. "I'll bet she was trying to blackmail Larry. He had plenty of money. She probably thought he'd pay her to keep quiet."

Frank snorted. "Blackmail has been a guiding principle of Jolene's life."

"Didn't work too well this time," Mark said. He laid his hand lightly on his father's shoulder and looked down on him almost fondly. "Now it's your turn, Dad."

"I don't know what you mean," Frank said, trying hard to sound innocent. The smirk under his pencil-thin mustache gave him away. "It's time for what?"

"To tell the truth," Aunt Mary said. "Frank Tortelli, you've been skulking around here for days. You had us all thinking terrible things, and I think you enjoyed every minute of it. But that's over and we want to know what's going on." She sat up straight and turned toward him. Frank's arm dropped back into his lap. He took a good look at her face, with it' stern, "I'll brook no more nonsense" look and laughed.

"All right. I'll tell all."

"Start with selling your restaurant," Mark demanded. "Why did you do that? You loved that place."

"I used to." Frank started to make one of his expansive hand gestures, glanced over at Aunt Mary, and let it drop. "The La Costa family has been trying to buy my place for years and I'd always said no. Then, a couple of months ago, they came in with a huge offer, all cash." He sighed, and this time the hand went up. If a gesture could register regret, that one did. "It was one of those days. I'd caught one of the busboys stealing, my best waiter had quit, and my meat supplier brought all the wrong cuts. I looked at the sauce that was not coming out right, thought about the cash and what I could do if I retired, and said okay."

"Oh my," said Aunt Mary. "And you were immediately sorry."

Frank beamed at her. "My dearest Mary, how do you know me so well?"

"It's not hard," she said. She leaned over and squeezed his hand.

"How about the rest of it?" Sabrina demanded. "All that stuff about taking over Otto's restaurant, then not caring and leaving it all to Larry, then coming back. What was that all about?"

"Actually, that's a little surprise I've been saving." No cat who'd swallowed the canary had ever looked more pleased with itself. "Remember, I told you about Otto's brother?" He addressed all of us, but it was Aunt Mary he was looking at. "We traded."

"You—what?" exclaimed Mark. "What do you have to trade? You don't own Otto's place."

"Technically that's true," conceded Frank, "but Otto's brother is sick of New York and I love cities. New York sounds like fun. So, Gunther is coming out to run this place and I'm buying his New York restaurant."

"What about Larry?" I couldn't believe poor Larry could be dismissed so cavalierly. He might be crazy, he was crazy, but the money and all the furnishings that went into making the old Adams mansion so beautiful had been his.

"Larry's name isn't on anything," Frank started. Both Aunt Mary and I began sputtering, and he held up his hand. "Now, now wait a minute. We'll make sure he's properly taken care of. How you go about doing that for someone who's about to be convicted of murder, I don't know. But, wait, wait," he stopped us again. "Our attorneys are already working on it. Now, the two most important parts."

Frank looked over at Mark and smiled. Mark must have known what was coming for he leaned forward, his face creased by the biggest smile I'd seen in a month. "The wines. Are you going to—?"

"I am. Silver Springs wines will be our house wine. A bottle on every table, along with a complete wine list and a picture of my son, the winemaker. I will make you famous. And, now that the idiot you flattened has dropped all of the charges, as well as the lawsuit, I guess it's safe to make you famous."

"How did you know about that?" Mark asked, his mouth dropping. "I just found out this morning."

"I haven't been in this business for years for nothing," Frank told him with no small amount of complacency.

"So you knew about the lawsuit and the assault charges all the time?" Mark said. His expression was a mixture of surprise and defensiveness.

"Of course. It's the main reason I came down here. I thought maybe I could help."

"Help?" Sabrina asked, suspicion etched in her voice, only to fade away under the realization of what Frank had said. "The charges have been dropped? And the lawsuit? Are you sure?"

"Positive," Frank said, grinning broadly. "You'll hear officially later this afternoon."

Sabrina's smile started out small but quickly grew to gigantic. "Dropped. That means, oh Mark, that means…"

I thought Mark was going to break her arms, he hugged her so tightly. "It sure does," he told her. When he let her up for air, he turned to his father. "Thanks, Dad. I really appreciate that." He let his arm slide around his wife's shoulders and gave her a huge squeeze. Sabrina leaned up against Mark and actually smiled at Frank.

"Thank you," she said.

"What's the second part?" I asked. I wasn't sure I cared, but the tenderness between Mark and Sabrina was smothering me in sadness. Dan still hadn't looked at me, hadn't come near me, had said nothing to me except that first brief remark. It was really over, I realized, our romance, and evidently our friendship also. I needed something else to think about, at least until everyone was gone. I got it.

"I'm going to take Mary with me to New York," Frank stated.

There was a pause while we all looked from Frank to a stunned Aunt Mary.

Dan spoke for the first time in a long while. "That should be fun for you, Mary," he began cautiously. "You haven't visited New York in—how long?"

"Not for a visit," Frank boomed. "To live. I have to go right away. Sunday in fact. But Mary can pack and come out later. There's a wonderful little apartment over the restaurant, so we'll be there all the time."

I almost burst into tears. First Dan, then Aunt Mary. This new life I'd been building was suddenly crumbling. Career, liberation, they were wonderful, but the foundation was people you loved, and I was about to lose the two most important bricks in my foundation.

"I'm not going to New York," Aunt Mary said. She scrambled to her feet and looked around wildly. "What ever gave you the idea I'd do something like that?"

Frank was on his feet, also. "Why, Mary," he said, reaching for her hands. "Think of the adventure."

Aunt Mary grabbed her hands back, put one under each arm, and hugged them to herself. "Adventure. Running a restaurant in the middle of a smelly, noisy city isn't my idea of adventure." Then she softened. "Oh Frank, this is my home. This is where my family is. I don't belong in New York. I belong here." She reached out and touched him lightly on the arm. "I'm immensely flattered you want me, and I'll come and visit, but move? No."

He looked down on her for a moment, then enveloped her in a one-armed hug. "I didn't really think you would, but it was worth a try." He looked around at all of us. "Well, I'd better get busy. I still have to give that dinner. Saturday is almost here, and Sunday morning I'm off."

"Tell you what," Aunt Mary said. "I'll help you. Just this one time, mind you, but with everything else that's gone on, it's the least I can do."

"I knew I could count on you," Frank chortled. "I don't suppose you'd like to help also?" He looked at Mark and Sabrina hopefully and turned so that his injured arm, hanging useless in its sling, was blatantly obvious.

Mark gave Sabrina a look that appeared mixed with inquiry and appeal. She gave him a long one back, groaned, and got to her feet. "I know I'm going to hate myself for this in the morning." Mark pushed himself up from the sofa and smiled at his father. "Okay, Dad, you've got your work force."

"We'd better get going," Aunt Mary said. "There's tons to do and not much time." She was already headed for the door. "Ellen, are you going to be all right?"

"Fine," I said. "I'll be fine. Go, have fun. But don't have so much you change your mind about New York."

"Not a chance." She paused, looked from Dan to me, shook her head slightly, and went out the door.

The room seemed very large and very quiet. Dan sat in the big chair. He looked down at his feet, encased, as always, in cowboy boots, then out the window. He seemed captivated by the leaves quietly leaving the elm tree to form a carpet on the grass. I sat, not moving, maybe not breathing, staring down at the untouched wine in my glass. The only sound was Jake purring on the bookshelf.

After what seemed like an eternity, Dan pushed himself out of the chair. "Guess I'd better go."

"Oh," I said, "well." I had no idea what to do. I knew what I wanted to say but didn't know what Dan was thinking. If I said, don't go, I love you, I want you to stay forever, how would he react? Was it too late for that? There was only one way to find out. I took a deep breath and said, "Don't go."

He stood very still before moving over to the bookshelves again. He reached out to stroke Jake and, with his back still turned to me, asked, "Why?"

"Oh," I said. Why was it so damnably hard to get the words out? "I thought I might make sandwiches, or something?"

"Ellie," he started. "I don't want sandwiches." He turned toward me, and for the first time that afternoon, looked me full in the face. He looked so sad, so lost, so like what I was feeling, I burst into tears, and with the tears came all the stopped up feelings, all the unsaid words.

"I love you, Dan Dunham," I said between sobs. "I didn't want to. I didn't want to love anybody after what Brian put me through, but I can't seem to help myself."

He took a step closer. "You love me—how? Like a brother?"

I sniffled, looked around for a tissue, couldn't find one, and settled for one of the paper napkins Aunt Mary must have set out. "Hardly like a brother." I blew my nose.

"Then how?" he pressed. But he took another step closer.

"Like a friend, like a lover," I said. I wiped my eyes, dropped the napkin on the coffee table and took another deep breath. "Like a husband."

Dan didn't say a word, but he was close enough now to reach out and hold me. If he wanted to.

It was his turn to take a deep breath. "Do you know what you just said?"

I nodded, sniffed a little, blinked back a few more tears, and nodded again. "I've been thinking. A lot. It took Brian twenty years to erode my self-confidence and ability to trust. It took you exactly a year to help me build all that back. Probably counts for something."

Dan laughed softly. He reached out and touched my face, letting his finger trace a line down my cheekbone and under my chin. He lifted it just a little so that I had to look directly into his eyes. "I think that does count for something. But how about next year, and the year after? How about twenty years from now? Because, if you take me on, it's for the duration."

"I know," I said. "I know."

"It means every morning for breakfast; it means having to watch Monday night football and letting me do the driving when we go somewhere. I'll be overprotective sometimes and order you around, but…"

I put my finger on his lips. "It means sometimes no dinner because I have late clients. It means I often have to work weekends, and if someone wants to write an offer, I'm out of here. But now I'll have someone to take out the trash and weed the backyard. And don't forget. I'm a liberated woman. We'll order each other around."

This time Dan laughed out loud. "Deal." Then the laugh faded and the most wonderful expression came over his face. Sweet, tender, and so very loving. I don't know who stepped toward whom, but Dan's arms were around me, one hand gently stroking the back of my neck. His lips sought mine, and there was nothing tentative in that kiss. It was hard, passionate, wonderful. His tongue probed. Mine probed back, his mouth moved down my neck, to my shoulder, I felt buttons give, and about there I moaned. Dan's buttons were a little more stubborn but were coming undone nicely when the phone rang.

We pulled apart and stared at it.

"Are you going to answer it?" he asked. There were a lot of emotions mixed up in his tone.

"It could be Susannah," I said slowly.

"It could," he answered. I could feel him waiting, waiting to see what I would do.

I reached over and lifted the phone off the hook, gave Dan the smallest of smiles, and pushed down the disconnect button, eliminating some man on the other end who was shouting hello. Then I picked the receiver up again and laid it on the table.

"My, my," Dan said. He chuckled and reached out for my hand. I gave it to him willingly. Together, we went up the stairs.

C023803320

NO LONGER PROPERTY OF
TACOMA PUBLIC LIBRARY